PLOT TWIST

BREEA KEENAN has been writing professionally for eighteen years. She has a first-class honours degree in English Literature, Journalism and Creative Writing from Strathclyde University, and worked as a journalist for various media titles before moving into communications and marketing. Her poetry was selected for inclusion in *Blether* (Scottish Book Trust) and *Living During the Coronavirus Pandemic* (Legend Times). Breea lives near Glasgow with her husband and three children. *Plot Twist* is her debut novel.

PLOT TWIST

Breea Keenan

ACCENT

First published in Great Britain in 2024 by Headline Accent
An imprint of HEADLINE PUBLISHING GROUP

1

Cataloguing in Publication Data is available from the British Library

ISBN 978 1 0354 1208 2

Typeset in Bembo Std by CC Book Production
Printed and bound in Great Britain by Clays Ltd, Elcograf S.p.A.

Headline's policy is to use papers that are natural, renewable and
recyclable products and made from wood grown in sustainable forests.
The logging and manufacturing processes are expected to conform to
the environmental regulations of the country of origin.

HEADLINE PUBLISHING GROUP
An Hachette UK Company
Carmelite House
50 Victoria Embankment
London EC4Y 0DZ

www.headline.co.uk
www.hachette.co.uk

1

Nothing quite like a smear test to start the weekend in style.

Said no one, ever.

'Appointment time?'

'Well, it was five minutes ago, actually. I'm so sorry I'm late, I couldn't get a space and—'

'Which doctor is your appointment with?'

'The nurse,' I said.

She sighed heavily and tapped on her keyboard for a moment. The phone started ringing but she ignored it. I noted her name badge. Moira.

You definitely wouldn't fuck with Moira.

The silence hung between us.

'Look, I was allocated a ten-minute slot so technically I still have five minutes left. I could just nip in really quickly. Whip my pants off. I won't even have any small talk about how I've not shaved my legs. I promise.'

'I find that hard to believe.' She arched her eyebrow. 'If you want to take a seat, I'll see whether the nurse can still carry out the procedure. You may have to come back another day though.'

'OK. Sorry, Moira.'

She didn't even flinch at the mention of her name.

Why didn't I listen to my own instincts? You clearly weren't supposed to fuck with Moira.

I wondered where this little game of cat and mouse would take us as I moved over to the waiting area and took my seat amongst the row of people staring intently at their phones. Glancing at my watch, I stretched my legs out, hoping my punishment wasn't going to last too long. Thankfully, I had another teacher lined up to cover my class in case I was late back. All arranged behind the Demon Headmistress's back, of course. You don't fuck with her, either.

I tapped a quick message out to Riley.

Me: Late for appointment. Fate now in the hands of Moira, the grumpy receptionist. What's a girl got to do around here to get someone to collect cells from her cervix?

Riley: Slip her some bank notes over and see if it helps to 'move the situation along'?

Me: I get the strong sense that won't work in my favour. Clearly NTBFW.

Riley: NTBFW??

Me: Not To Be Fucked With. Thanks for your comments on my chapter, by the way. I'll read through tonight. If all else fails, I could write a steamy romance featuring Moira the doctor's receptionist?

Riley: Yes! Eyes meet over the huge plastic shield at the reception desk as Tom comes in to see the doctor about his piles.

Me: Not sure that would make the wedding speech but, y'know, it's better than her ex, Eric with erectile dysfunction.

Riley: Poor old Eric. A stand-up guy, in all ways but one.

Me: Lol. How's the writing coming along today?

Riley: Aaaargh, don't ask. Going to try more yoga. Speak later. Happy smear test, by the way. If you get it.

Me: Thank you. Hope your writer's dysfunction passes soon . . .

'Becca Taylor?'

My name echoed through the hallway and I scrambled to stand up. Moira obviously hadn't wanted to admit that the nurse was still free, so she'd got her to collect me rather than letting me off the hook herself.

Well played, Moira. Well played. I followed the nurse down the corridor.

'God, you know, I just hate these things. My hands are sweating and everything,' I said, trying to build a rapport with the nurse so she didn't take Moira's side when they inevitably talked about me later.

'I know, no one likes it, I'm afraid,' she sympathised. 'A necessary evil. Now, if you don't mind, we actually have a student with us today. It helps with training and development if students can be involved and observe the procedure. If you'd prefer not to, please just let us know. You're the only appointment this afternoon and it really would help with her practical experience . . .'

Ach, shite. I couldn't say no now. Not after I'd kept them all waiting.

'That's fine, I guess. The more the merrier!' My high-pitched laugh echoed as we entered the room.

'We'll be as quick as we can, if you just want to get yourself ready.' The nurse smiled.

I always thought they should give more explicit instructions about these things: what exactly to take off and leave on.

My best friend, Rae, had seen it all. She'd trained as a beauty therapist while studying for her psychology degree. She figured she'd spend most of her wages on beauty treatments when she graduated anyway, so might as well learn how to do it all herself. Always planning ahead. Plus, she said it was the best insight into the female mind.

Rae giggled over the wax appointments gone wrong, like once when the customer got completely starkers, boobs out and everything, when she turned her back to get set up. The lady had only come in for an eyebrow wax. She quickly learned that the customer wasn't always right.

I lay back on the thin sheets of paper covering the long, faux-leather bed, trying to think about something nice. Meeting Rae at the weekend. Focus on that. I was so desperate to see her, I'd managed to convince her to come home a week earlier than she'd originally planned. We'd spent the previous day planning where to meet and had exchanged several voice notes.

'*I'm going to find you a man this weekend,*' she'd vowed.

I'd rolled my eyes and reciprocated with a voice note: '*Like I need any more hassle in my life. Thanks but no thanks.*'

A response came back in record time. '*You do realise you are "hesidating". It's a thing, you know. Google it.*'

4

I snorted. *'Also known as common fucking sense. With a side serving of "I can't be arsed". And anyway, since when were you Little Miss Relationship? You got something you want to tell me?'*

Rae sighed on her next voice note. *'Come on, Becca. You need to get out a bit more! What about that new dating app I sent you a link for?'*

'I am getting out. With you, this weekend, remember? All I want to do is sit in the sunshine with our gins in the air like we just don't care and LAUGH. I haven't seen you in forever.'

'Me too! But I am on a mission. I'll find you a Mr Right, or even just Mr Right Now, this weekend, if it kills me.'

I didn't reply to her last voice note. When Rae got something in her mind, it was best not to argue.

It still amazed me how much we could chat and yet always have more to tell each other. And, for once, the Scottish summer was showing signs of actual beer garden weather. It was like all the stars were aligning for us reuniting.

I could hear the nurse explaining everything to the student as she went along. The words cervix and speculum floated around in the air. I curled my toes.

'At least once it's done, it's over for a while.' The student smiled at me. The Sadist.

Jesus, she must have been about twelve.

'Yes. Great,' I said. I wished I hadn't agreed to the student thing. It was taking forever and a day, plus I really hadn't shaved my legs properly, never mind anything else. I wondered if they'd talk about me when I left the room.

'Now, that's you all done,' the nurse said eventually. 'I'll leave you to get dressed again. You should get a letter through in a few weeks.'

I wobbled, slipping my tights back on, before straightening my skirt and pulling back the curtain.

'Brilliant, thanks. That's the most action I've had in a while,' I said. 'See you later.'

The student opened the door to let me out without even so much as a smirk. Twelve year olds really were professional these days.

I checked my phone on the way to the exit, as my flat shoes squelched against the floor through reception. Seventeen missed calls from an unknown number. What the . . . *squelch*.

There were no voicemails, no messages. If it was one of those scam calls about being in an accident, I planned to give them intimate details about my smear test. That would definitely have me promptly struck off their marketing list for future calls.

My phone vibrated again, and this time I answered. 'Becca? Is that you?'

'Sorry, who's this?'

'It's Adam. Rae's brother.'

A flashback popped into my head of the Halloween he'd dressed up as Big Bird from *Sesame Street* for a fancy dress party he was heading to in Glasgow's West End (i.e. 'the posh end'). I was horrified; Rae was mortified. We tried to convince him to change but he just kept flapping his wings at us.

'It's about Rae . . .' he said.

Next thing I knew, I'd dropped the phone at my feet.

2

'The wee chapel up the hill, aye?' the taxi driver asked.

'Aye.'

I always felt the need to exaggerate my accent when I was in the company of someone who seemed more Glaswegian than me. Prove I belonged there too. Rae used to call people 'hen' when we were at school. I'd never been able to pull 'hen' off. I can't remember when she stopped but I hadn't heard her use the phrase for years.

The driver pulled over and I tapped my card on the machine. He was in the middle of a monologue about the Tories and bloody Brexit as I leapt out of the car, closing the door firmly behind me. If there was one thing I knew about taxi drivers, it was how much they hated slack-door-closers. I wasn't about to be caught out. Not a chance, hen.

I smoothed my blond hair down and buttoned up my mint-green coat. My trusty black heels moulded around my feet. I hadn't worn them in months but they'd welcomed me back like I'd never left them. The heels were slightly too high, perhaps, for a funeral, but I'd had so many good nights wearing these shoes.

With Rae, of course.

All the best nights out had been with Rae.

The church sat at the top of a hill, beside the school where I'd met Rae in primary three, when she'd started as the new girl. She'd marched straight up to me and introduced herself, demanding that I assume the role of her best friend. I was impressed with her ballsy attitude. If we hadn't declared each other best friends that day, we would probably have become arch enemies. Instead, we'd admired each other's balls.

I felt my cheeks flush and my skin prickle as I strode up the hill towards the church. We'd made our First Communion in the same chapel. I'd gazed enviously at Rae's dazzling full-length dress, while my plain number grazed apologetically at my ankles. Rae's whole family turned up en masse, eclipsing all other families. Dad and I didn't have that problem of course. Party for two, as usual.

The whole Mass thing always freaked me out. Rae had always been on hand to whisper instructions in my ear about the whole 'sign of the peace be with you' bits during school Mass. Everyone would be too caught up in their own thoughts today to care about whether I was doing it all properly. I knew that. But I couldn't shake the uneasy feeling that they'd all be looking at me.

It was my fault, after all. Rae was driving to Glasgow to meet me. We planned to put our gins in the air like we just didn't care. She was meant to come the following weekend, but I'd begged her to make it earlier. I felt like I hadn't seen her in forever.

She didn't stand a chance when the lorry smashed into the side of her black Mini as they both turned into a dual carriageway. Apparently she would have died instantly. The police said that as though it made the whole thing better somehow.

And now I'd never see her again.

I smoothed down my coat. Breathe, Becca.

I picked up pace and eyed the crowds outside as I made my way inside.

A blur of faces, black clothing and big hankies passed by as I entered the church. Rae's family loved the whole Scottish vibe, from traditional attire to necking a good whisky, so I wasn't surprised to see many had donned their kilts, despite the warm weather. Rae always said she was a sucker for a guy in Scottish uniform.

I gasped as I caught sight of the coffin. Should that thing even be in here? I'd thought they'd be carrying it in. Surely they hadn't just left her by herself here overnight? The flurry feeling intensified. I reminded myself to breathe as I sat down.

A tall figure in a short, black jacket and deep green kilt stood at the end of the row in front of me. I frowned, trying to work out who he was. Unless Rae had a hot cousin she hadn't told me about, I was lost. I drew my eyes away; now was hardly the time to be eyeing up the talent.

Rae wouldn't mind. She was going to find me a man if it killed her, after all.

The service started with a low hum of the organ. I glanced around at the church's ornate decor, the candles in the corner and then up at the altar, avoiding the coffin at all costs. I remembered Rae telling me that the funny smoky smell at Mass was called incense. I'd thought she'd said incest. We'd giggled about that for ages.

The priest's low voice rolled off the words he'd no doubt said a million times. I studied the back of the head in front again. His very presence and somehow familiar head were annoying. I clocked a tiny bit of dandruff on his shoulders. Just as I spotted it, he flipped his hand up to brush it away. I looked down, worried he'd somehow heard my thoughts. Or worse still, I'd said something out loud.

Everyone sat down for the first reading. He turned his head to the side, as if he was looking for someone. Then he turned right around.

We locked eyes. He managed to deliver a carefully executed nod of acknowledgement that conveyed his recognition but also sadness at the situation.

My mouth fell open. What the actual fuck was he doing here?

3

TEN YEARS AGO

'Gawd, Bec, if we want to get to Tenerife this summer, we really need to get these jobs. I hope I don't fuck it up. I'm useless when they ask me things like where I'd like to be in five years. Eh, hello? Rich husband, obviously,' Rae said, gazing over her sunglasses at me.

'Well, that's truly aspirational.' I rolled my eyes at her. 'We will totally get these jobs. They'll be begging us to come and work for them. We're free for the summer and we're sober most days. What more could they want? Plus, it's a theme park so I'm not sure they'll care where you'd like to be in five years.'

I was right.

'Uniforms are hanging up inside. Shift finishes at six,' the boss said, barely giving us a second look.

'What, we're starting today?' Rae asked.

'Yup. Smile and don't steal, you keep it.'

He opened the portacabin and showed us to the staff toilet to get changed.

'Eeeek!' Rae exclaimed, as she flipped open her lipstick and adjusted her hair in the mirror. 'You go first, I'll fix my face. Tenerife here we come! If you like piña coladas . . .'

She sang as I wrestled the small top over my head in the single loo.

I buttoned up the shirt and opened the door.

'Weeet, woo!' Rae said, applying her bright red lipstick. 'Give me a twirl.'

I laughed and twirled around in my new khaki trousers and light blue top, shaking my bum.

'I see you baby, shaking that ass,' she sang on the way into the loo.

'I'll wait for you outside,' I called as I opened the door to leave.

'Hey,' a voice said.

A tall twenty-something man wearing the same light blue shirt stood with one hand tucked into his shorts pocket.

'Hey,' I replied. 'You working here too?'

'What gave it away?'

'Wild guess,' I replied, raising an eyebrow at our matching uniforms.

'You're new?'

'I am. Starting in the ice cream truck apparently.'

'No shit,' he said. 'Well, you must be the girl I've been told to train. Don't worry, you're in the best possible hands. So, who did I end up with? The boss said it would be Becca or Rae?'

'You've ended up with Becca.' I smiled.

PLOT TWIST

He grinned. 'Nice one. I'm Drew. I work in the ice cream truck. They call me Mr Whippy.'

I looked up at his mischievous brown eyes and grinned.

I knew then and there that I was a goner.

4

I could almost hear Rae's voice whispering in my ear: 'All family and no fucking fun. Let's get out of here.'

They all greeted one other with warm hugs and muttered words of disbelief and condolences at the reception. The hordes of family members narrowed their eyes when they saw me, trying to place whether I was on Jim's or Linda's side of the family. I wanted to shout at the top of my lungs that I was Becca, the one who'd been a firm fixture by Rae's side practically all her life. The friend that held her when she was sobbing after Lee Kilburn broke her heart in second year. The pal that held her hair back when she was sick after one too many cocktails.

The one whose fault it was.

'Becca?'

I would know the voice anywhere. A warm, familiar feeling flooded my stomach until my head caught up and reminded me: Drew should not be here. Or anywhere near me for that matter.

I swung around and came face to face with him. He looked into my eyes, bold as brass, and offered me a small, almost smile.

'What the hell?' I sneered up at him. 'Why are you *here*?'

I'd promised myself I wouldn't cause a scene. But the sight of his short dark hair, perfectly shaven face and smug smile in his stupid kilt, blending in with the rest of the family, was just too much. Worse still, he was still hot. Damn him. Although he looked exhausted. Shattered.

'Rae and I were always close, Becca, you know that.' He shifted his balance from one foot to the other.

He set his glass down beside mine. The prick.

'I don't think gatecrashing the funeral is appropriate. I hope it wasn't because of me.'

He threw his head back and laughed. The bloody nerve of him and his stupid loud laugh. How inappropriate to practically guffaw at a funeral. Rae's funeral. My face flushed in anger. I blinked as I realised my expression mirrored his. He had the cheek to look angry, too. What the fuck did he have to be angry about?

'God, Becca, you're so full of shit. I came to say goodbye to Rae. Nothing to do with you. Not everything in life is about you, believe it or not. Let's not do this . . . not here.'

I gulped as his furious gaze fixed firmly on my eyes. My big baggy eyes that needed to rest so badly.

What did he mean with all this cloak-and-dagger 'not here, not now' anyway? God, he was always so over the top.

He let out a huge, dramatic puff into the air and turned to leave. I stood still for a moment before deciding to follow him.

15

I wasn't bloody well finished telling him all the reasons why he shouldn't be here.

I walked out towards the bar area but there was no sign of him.

'Becca?'

I spun around.

Rae's brother, otherwise known in my mind as his child-hood nickname 'Adam-the-Absolute-Worst', towered over me.

He must have missed the family kilt memo, but he did look sharp in a black suit, white shirt and black tie, along with his trademark wide-framed, black-rimmed glasses. Imagine if he'd worn his Big Bird costume to the funeral. Rae would have killed herself laughing.

Oh.

'I'm sorry, Adam, I'm just looking for someone . . .' I mumbled.

'Drew,' he stated.

'How did you know?' I frowned. 'What the fuck is he even doing here? I thought Linda said it was family only. And me, obviously.'

He cleared his throat.

'Rae never wanted this . . .' Adam started, looking down at his feet and then back up to meet my gaze.

'What, a funeral? Pretty sure I knew that, Adam, but thanks for the memo,' I said, looking over his shoulder for Drew. The bastard.

'No,' he said, lightly placing his hands near my shoulders. 'I mean, she would have hated you finding out from someone else. She was determined to be the one to tell you.'

I narrowed my eyes, feeling my stomach clench. What was he talking about?

'Tell me what?'

'They were together, Becca.' He spoke so quietly I had to strain to hear him. 'They had been for ages. They moved in together in Edinburgh. She was going to tell you, the day she was coming home. The day that . . . well, you know. She was so worried about it, but I told her that you'd be fine. I mean, you and Drew were up and down, weren't you? Plus, it was ages ago now. I mean, years have passed, haven't they, and—'

I staggered slightly in my black heels.

'Rae and Drew?'

He must have been mixed up. Rae and I literally told each other everything. Every little detail of life. We were in contact every single day. It wasn't possible. This wasn't possible.

'I don't think so,' I stammered, my voice barely recognisable as it adopted some sort of high-pitched squeak. 'She would have told me.'

'She was going to tell you. She needed to be sure it was right.' His eyes narrowed, as though he was trying to play some sort of mind game with me, convincing me that this was all normal.

I was silent for a moment as my brain struggled to process the new information.

'So, if she was going to tell me that day −' I frowned − 'that meant it was. It was right?'

'Yeah,' he said, relieved that I finally understood. 'He wanted to propose to her, but she told him to hold off.'

I briefly wondered if my heart had actually stopped beating.

'Hold off, why? Until she told me?' I managed to whisper, like I was passing on the secret.

'Yeah,' he replied. 'She wanted you to be a bridesmaid, like you always planned.'

'A bridesmaid. For Rae and Drew,' I repeated.

We had it all planned. I'd be her bridesmaid when she married, she'd be mine. I planned a big wedding in the Bahamas, while she wanted to stick to the church, to make Linda happy. The grooms hadn't been worked out yet, or so I thought.

My face started doing that weird wobbly thing that happens when you yawn and try to hide it.

'And you knew about it?' I almost laughed, my voice rising. 'She didn't even like you, Adam. Like, no offence. She would send me pictures of her lunch. I knew when she had her period, yet she couldn't tell me that she was planning to *marry* my ex?'

Adam looked weirded out by the whole period mention, as though it had only just occurred to him that Rae would have had one.

'Look, I'm sorry to be the one to tell you, Becca. But you and Rae had a whole lifetime of friendship. Don't let this overshadow it.'

'Thanks for the advice, Dr Phil, but I really have to get going. There's a bottle of gin at home with my name on it.'

He sighed, as though this was all rather inconvenient to him. Although I knew he was only trying to help. I wished I could stop being so mean to him. He'd lost his sister, after all. His only sister.

His only sister who was screwing my ex-boyfriend.

18

I frowned.

God, Drew's smug smile was burning in the back of my brain. Telling me not to cause a scene. Who the fuck did he think he was, anyway?

I swallowed the salty taste in my mouth as my eyes began swimming with tears.

'Becca.' Adam pulled me towards him. 'Don't get upset. We can talk about it.'

His brown eyes shone earnestly. Of course, he was hurting, too. He'd just lost his sister.

'God, Becca, everything is falling apart,' he sighed. 'Mum and Dad are devastated. And Drew – I mean, I know you don't want to hear this, but Drew is just crushed.'

I snorted.

'It's not that I don't want to hear about him. It's just that I don't believe it. The Drew that I knew . . . Well, let's just say he can put on a good act. And I wouldn't say too much has changed in that department.'

He frowned, deep in thought.

'People do change. I don't know what Drew did in the past, but I do know one thing.'

'What's that?'

'I wouldn't exactly dress up as Big Bird these days.'

A loud noise that sounded like some sort of strangled laugh escaped my mouth.

'Did she really hate me, Becca?' he whispered softly.

I didn't tell him that we'd cut a picture of Adam's face out of the family album and put it on the dart board in his room when he'd left for university. Rae had cut holes out of his eyes and drawn a large penis on his head, with balls and everything.

'Of course she didn't hate you, Adam. You were her brother; you're meant to want to punch your brother. I'm sure she loved you, deep down. Like, way deep sometimes.'

He smiled sadly.

'Look, I know you're upset but can you do me a favour? Whenever you think about her or have a funny memory or whatever, will you tell me about it? Even if it's just something small. I'd just like to get to know her a bit better. Even if it is too late.'

The words hung between us. Adam was right; it was too late. Rae had kept a huge secret from me and now she was dead and it was all my fault. The heavy guilt tumbled around my gut.

Then the liquid started flowing. And not just tears either, the snot was coming out in full force as I gulped and hiccuped.

'I've got to go,' I said, the door slamming behind me.

5

I resisted the urge to get totally shifted and sing 'All by Myself' in my living room. Instead, I did what any self-respecting person would do. I spent hours scrolling on my phone to see if Rae had dropped any hints about the whole ultimate betrayal thing with he-who-shall-not-be-named. I checked all of her social sites, our WhatsApp feed, our private messages on social, everywhere. Right back to when Drew and I broke up.

My finger was sore from all the scrolling. Rae had said worse things about him than I ever did. She'd hated him, back then. How had it all changed?

Rae's more recent messages mentioned going out for dinner here and meeting up for lunch there and staying over somewhere. The more I read, the more I realised she was the Master of Changing the Subject when it came to what (or who) she was actually doing. A couple of times I'd probed further and she'd shut me down fairly quickly with a funny memory, meme or update on some meaningless celebrity gossip.

Little Miss Relationship. She'd dodged that line of accusation too.

And I'd fallen for it every time – hook, line and sinker. Little did I know, they were both holed up in some boudoir drinking Champagne together, wondering how to break the news to me about their forbidden romance.

A message popped up on my screen.

How did it go today?

I'd never really felt the need to have any other friends, apart from Rae. I'd always had my leggy blonde cousin, Paula. I liked my colleagues, but they were very 'teacher-y'. They seemed to have a habit of going on a few wild nights out, promising me a good time, but then swiftly finding the loves of their lives, getting married, having babies and never coming out again. I'd given up on the whole idea. New friends weren't worth the hassle.

Then there was Riley O'Connell. She wasn't a best friend, school friend or a colleague, but she was the closest thing I'd had to a rival best friend recently. Ever, actually. Rae had joked just last month that she was going to 'bring that book bitch down'. I'd laughed because, of course, no one could compete with Rae. Plus, I'd never actually met Riley in person. She lived in Ireland and was a beta reader for my aspiring writing career. I'd quickly formed a huge professional crush on her after we met on a social media group for writers.

We'd first connected when a woman called Kate posted the opening paragraph of her book and asked for feedback. The comments flooded through. People had clearly never heard the term 'if you can't say something nice, don't say anything at all'.

One grumpy-looking man in particular was trying to bedazzle everyone with his linguistic jargon. He pointed out that her book sounded 'far too much like a mindless chick lit'. Then Riley jumped in.

Riley: I'm a mindless romance writer with a pretty decent advance for my debut novel. Just here to back up all the 'mindless chick lit writers', as you called it. Your concept sounds great, Kate. Keep working on it. I'd be happy to read it, if you'd like some feedback in a private setting rather than all this public bashing. Good luck.

Then the tide started to turn. I cheered out loud. Riley's comment received thirty-six likes, including mine. Everyone chimed in with their support. In the end, the man apologised for being so blunt, reasoning that romance wasn't really his thing anyway.

I couldn't let it pass without firing over a quick private message:

Well done and thanks for intervening. You're like a literary Robin Hood, robbing from the highfalutin snobs and supporting us dreamers.

I wasn't really expecting a response, but a message popped up straight away:

Can't stand all that up-your-own-arse shit. We're all trying our best. These groups are meant to be supportive. Thought I'd get a barrage of abuse in response but luckily everyone seemed to get on the same page pretty quickly.

That's when I knew Riley was a good egg. The kind of

person you wanted in your corner. And to my surprise, she was now in my corner.

Riley had an actual publishing deal for two books. The first one had been a piece of cake, she said. When I read it to give her feedback just before her final edits, I was captivated. The words were beautiful, her characters so believable and the steamy scenes left me more than a little flustered. Before I knew it, I was turning the pages of her manuscript in my hands at three o'clock in the morning.

She was also my biggest cheerleader. Riley said the early chapters of my book for children were 'hilarious'. I'd danced a little bit when she'd said that. Of course, some of the credit had to go to Rae. My story, *Queen Bee*, was based around two girls who were at drama camp together, battling it out for the lead role. They kept getting annoyed with one another for being so similar. I guess it was a take on what could have happened if Rae and I hadn't teamed up at the start. I knew my characters, Anna and Rosie, would become firm friends for life by the end.

I wasn't sure if I could write their happily ever after now.

Riley was also struggling. Her second story wasn't flowing nearly as well as she'd hoped. I'd read every single word of her latest false start and tried to offer constructive criticism. But the truth was, it just didn't have the same flow. She had lost her mojo.

Me: Funeral was awful. I cried, finally. Yay. Go me. I have a heart, after all.

Riley: Sorry to hear it . . . Worse than you thought?

Me: Long story but my ex-boyf was at the funeral.

Riley: Whaaat?

Me: Turns out he was The One.

Riley: Eh?

Me: What kind of romance writer are you? Do I need to spell it out?

Riley: Your ex-boyfriend was going out with your best friend?

Me: Yup. Put that in your Mills and Boon and smoke it.

Riley: And you didn't know?

Me: Nope ☹ But everyone else did, apparently. They were planning to get
married. Wtf.

Riley: Ach, shite. That's really balls, Becca. Bet he was a tool, anyway.

Me: SUCH a tool. You should have seen him, parading around in his
Scottish skirt like he owned the bloody funeral.

Riley: Sure they're all tools, aren't they? Exes are ex for a reason and all
that. Bet he was the biggest tool of them all.

I smiled a little and poured myself a small red wine. Then
topped it up because, well, now I had company.

Me: Just wish I could pack up my bags and fly off somewhere fabulous.
That's what they usually do in novels when they need to escape from a
shitty ex-boyfriend, isn't it?

Riley: Me too. I'd go on a yoga retreat. Or writers' retreat.

Me: More like rehab for me. Although, I have always wanted to go on a
writers' retreat. Just spend the whole day frolicking around with my novel.

Riley: Me too. Writing all day. It's all rose-tinted glasses at the start of a
novel. You can't get enough of each other, then you spend so much
time together that you can't even look at each other any more.

Me: Oh you're totally right! I loved my first few chapters but then I hit the middle of the story and I'm just like . . . meh.

Riley: Exactly! The saggy bloody middle. Now I can't even get the start of mine done.

Me: The saggy bloody middle . . . sounds exactly like my relationship with he-who-shall-not-be-named.

Riley: Your ex is . . . Voldermort?

Me: No. Voldermort would be an upgrade, believe me.

Riley: I hear ya. Maybe that's why I wanted to write romance books, so I could pen my own happily ever after.

Me: Spoiler alert! Not all stories end with happily ever after. Far more realistic when they don't.

Riley: Bah, humbug. I'm a sucker for a happy ending.

The conversation continued to flow – along with the wine – and I even laughed, a tiny bit, feeling a little less like the whole world was against me.

Another message flashed up from Joanna, my closest teacher colleague, asking how the funeral had gone. Joanna had been one of the culprits of the wild-nights-before-marriage-only and had recently come to the end of maternity leave with her adorable baby boy, Tate. She had been asked to cover my class while I was at the funeral today and my leave of absence tomorrow.

I typed back: **Thanks for taking my class. Hope they behaved for you. Awful day. Don't know how I'm going to deal with going back to the classroom.**

J: I know, kids are high as kites with the summer hols just round the corner. So hard to match their energy levels, especially when you feel like shit! I can take your class for the next couple of weeks, if you're taking time off?

I stopped typing for a moment. I had never been absent from teaching outside school holidays. It was more than frowned upon, especially by the Demon Headmistress, Mrs Pender. How she ever managed to become a headteacher in the first place was beyond me, especially with her very apparent dislike of children. She barked at them in the corridors, complained about the noise in the playground and physically recoiled if a pupil happened to come too close to her. In fact, she treated teachers pretty much the same. She snapped if we dared to speak to her, never mind raising any issues (most of which stemmed from her).

Asking for time off for Rae's funeral had been brutal. She'd asked if it was a family member who had passed, staring at me sternly over her desk. Obviously, I'd had to say no, but explained that Rae was my best friend. She'd sniffed and folded her arms, as though having a best friend was such a childish notion. I'd practically had to beg, promising I would arrange my own cover for the class.

Mrs Pender would have died herself if she'd had to stand in front of a classroom of children. So, she would have a fit at the very idea of me taking extended leave.

Me: Mrs P will have a hissy fit if I don't go back. Can you imagine?

27

Joanna typed back: **Screw her. You'd be doing me a huge favour too. I need the extra cash coming back part time after mat leave but I can cover the next two weeks.**

I paused.

The pit of guilt in the bottom of my stomach took on an extra layer as I pictured their innocent faces dropping at the news I wasn't coming back to finish their final days in primary three with them. Olivia would almost certainly wail in protest, while Jordan would quietly tug on the new teacher's sleeve to ask for me every single day. I'd been helping Jamie learn to tie his shoelaces, too. Plus, Joanna would never be able to tell the difference between the identical twins, Faye and Lila. Faye needed more support than her chatty sister, but she had made huge progress over the year. I wanted to tell her how well she'd done. In fact, I wanted to tell them all that I was so proud of what they'd achieved.

But my energy was completely gone. I was drained. I could hardly tell them I was too sad to sing our numbers song at the start of the day or that sports day on the last day of term was cancelled. The thought of trying to scramble my way through was painful but even worse was the thought of letting them down. They deserved a teacher who could give them a lovely end of term celebration, the way I usually did.

Joanna would give them a good summer send-off. Plus, she said herself that she would be glad of the cash. I would be doing them all a favour by staying away and keeping my sadness all to myself.

I found myself typing back to say I would, indeed, take

some time off. I took another gulp of wine and sat back, relief flooding through me. I would email Mrs Pender in the morning. I could do that. Joanna was right, screw her. She brought nothing but misery every day, just with her presence.

Now I'd made the executive decision, I could concentrate my efforts elsewhere. I sat back and opened social media.

I clicked on Drew's social channels. We weren't online friends, or real-life ones for that matter, so I couldn't see much of his content. Someone had, however, tagged him in a post in January. Upon further inspection, I realised that Rae was there, in the background wearing a short black sparkly number, with a glass of bubbly in her hand.

Rae had told me she was probably staying in on New Year's Eve. Instead, she was having what the post described as 'the happiest of new years'.

'Best times spent with the best of friends.'

I sighed.

I couldn't spend the next two months torturing myself by scrolling through social media. I refilled my glass, opening Riley's latest email with the first few chapters of her new novel to distract myself.

I willed myself to read the words and be swept away, the way it was with Riley's first book. But the first few paragraphs just fell flat. The main character was meant to swear off men for life after a series of bad relationships to concentrate on her work, but she was coming across as smug and a little bit desperate.

Poor Riley. She knew it wasn't working. I could feel the tension and the worry about her deadlines coming off the pages.

My mind started to wander as I tripped over her typos. I wondered if Rae and Drew had a big dramatic build-up to their romance. Maybe Rae pushed him away at first because she knew how much it would hurt me. I knew Drew wouldn't give a shit. In fact, he probably loved the idea of screwing me over. Again.

I picked up my phone and shook the thoughts of them away.

Me: Finished your chapter.

Riley: Don't even say it. You hate Jessica.

Me: I don't hate her. But I don't love her either.

Riley: Sigh. I hate her. Why is she coming across as such a bitch?

Me: Maybe lose the rich parents? You could even change her career? But, on a positive note, your story did distract me from all the ex-boyfriend / dead best friend drama.

I felt a lump in my throat. Dead best friend. It sounded so cold. How could my beautiful, full-of-life best friend be gone? I instantly regretted making light of the situation in any way, shape or form. A wave of grief consumed me. I breathed in deeply and back out again.

In.

Out.

I hoped Riley wouldn't jump on my stupid bandwagon and chime in with her thoughts on Rae keeping such a huge secret from me. I couldn't handle that right now.

Riley: I'm sorry, Becca. I shouldn't be asking you to read this stuff when I know how much you're going through right now.

PLOT TWIST

I breathed a sigh of relief.

Me: No, it's what I need just now. I can't think of anything better than burying my head in the sand and being distracted by your sexy Greek waiter waiting to sweep the lawyer lady, or whatever she ends up being, off her feet.

Riley: But why is she such a bitch?

Me: Riley, it'll come together. Try not to panic. Try and forget all that pressure and just write from the heart. You're a fabulous writer.

Riley: Thanks, Becca. I don't feel it right now.

Me: If it's any consolation, I am feeling pretty shitty right now too. I'm not going back to work before the summer. Can't face it. So I need to distract myself. Try and keep my mind off everything.

Riley: I wondered if you'd take some time off. Good for you.

Yes. Good for me. In the last decade of teaching, I'd never taken one sick day. I was often first to arrive and last to leave the school. I could take time off for bereavement. I should. I mentally awarded myself a gold star for decision-making.

Riley: Well, since you've said you'll be off work . . . I actually wanted to ask you something.

I took a large slug of wine.

Me: Go for it.

Riley: I don't know if this is the right thing to say just now so feel free to tell me to f*** off.

She put little stars in when she swore. My heart stung. Rae would have just said it all outright, unapologetically. But Riley wasn't Rae.

Me: Now I'm intrigued?!

Riley: You know you said you are DREADING the summer holidays on your own?

Me: Yes, and in capital letters too. Thanks for reminding me how pathetic I am.

Riley: You're not pathetic. I do hate capitalising in the middle of sentences, but anyway, here we are. I was wondering, and feel free to say no if you're not sold on the idea, but I was wondering . . .

Me: Spit it out, ffs.

Riley: I have a book deadline, a very full-on four year old and an even more impatient agent asking me whether I'm going to meet said deadline. My writing is just not working. My character is meant to be likeable but even I want to stab her in the face with a fork. You want to write more over the summer and you have extra time on your hands, plus you're a teacher so I presume you like kids?!

Me: Yes, this is all true. Apart from the fork part. I can't comment on your murder weapon of choice.

Riley: Feel free to say no. I won't be offended or block you online or start stalking you like that creepy character in You. But . . .

Me: Riley?!

Riley: Come spend the summer here? We'll work on our books?

I stopped typing. It had been the longest week in history and my head spun. I wasn't sure that I'd read it correctly but yes,

PLOT TWIST

Riley O'Connell the romance writer with an actual publishing deal was offering me some sort of pity lifeline.

Imagine. She actually wanted to spend time with me in real life.

I wasn't even sure where exactly she lived. In fact, I realised I wasn't even sure what Riley looked like, given her profile picture was a snap of her cute four-year-old little girl, sporting the most adorable little bunches.

It might have been the thought of getting the hell out of the country that I still shared with my sneaky ex-boyfriend who was dating my Rae. Or, sure, it might have been the accumulation of all the wine, but the offer was the most appealing I'd had to date.

Spending time writing with Riley the actual romance writer working towards my dream of becoming a writer, versus moping around at home feeling sorry for myself, was a bit of a no-brainer.

I took another large glug of wine, a deep breath, and fired the message back.

Me: Count me in.

6

I woke with a dull headache and the thoughts immediately started swirling around my mind. The aching realisation that Rae was dead brought on a lingering feeling of panic that quickly slid into shock. At least I'd managed to sleep a little. It must have only been for a couple of hours. And yes, it had taken me several glasses of wine, but I'd bloody well done it.

Thoughts of the day before flooded back. Drew and Rae. Rae and Drew. Fleeing the funeral after the revelation. Then I remembered. I sat bolt upright in bed. My credit card sat on my dresser beside a large glass of water. My phone was charging beside my bed, minding its own business. I grabbed it and scrolled through my emails.

I'd emailed Mrs Pender at 2.05 a.m. to say I wasn't able to come back before the summer holidays. It sounded quite professional until I reached the 'Best wishes' at the end, which read 'Best kisses'. I groaned and put my face in my hands, my heart thudding in my chest. I peered through my hands to see what other damage I'd done.

Ah, double shite.

I frowned reading the next email. A boat booking? A memory of the evening before quickly came flooding back, as I remembered all the wine and something about a writers' retreat with Riley. It sounded like a perfectly lovely *idea* at the time, but it was now actually reality. I was booked on the three p.m. ferry to Ireland that afternoon.

I did a double-take. Was I crazy? I hadn't told a soul. I was going to stay with a stranger for the summer – a woman no one had met before, least of all me.

Gawd, I'd even packed a suitcase. I remembered feeling so smug, so *sure* of myself, as I'd piled my jeans and T-shirts into my suitcase the night before. I leapt out of bed and rushed over.

On closer inspection, I realised that despite heaping clothes on top of one another along with several miniature Scotch whisky bottles my dad had left at my flat, I hadn't actually packed any pants. I groaned. Things had to be evened up a little bit, plus I'm pretty sure they sell alcohol in Ireland so I didn't really need the whisky.

I washed away the shame of my solo drinking in the shower. How could I have made so many life decisions in one evening? It was one thing to decide to take a leave of absence from work but to actually book to leave the country? That was verging on crazy, wasn't it?

As I played out scenarios in my mind, I decided maybe I wasn't going mad after all. Going to Ireland to stay with Riley was still the best offer on the table right now. And something deep down seemed to be agreeing with my decision. It had been the best night's sleep I'd had since Before Rae, after all. Bring that book bitch down, that's what Rae had said. But what if that book bitch was my next shot at an actual friend? I needed one right about now. Plus, I had no job to go to now anyway. I could hardly email Mrs Pender back and say I'd been pissed and had changed my mind now, thank you very much.

But . . . oh, the shame. The guilt. My stomach lurched as the water cascaded down my face and I wiped the previous day's mascara from my eyes.

Rae and Drew. Drew and Rae. I couldn't get them out of my thumping head. I switched the shower off and wrapped a towel around myself.

After I got dressed, I picked up my phone to check in with Riley.

Me: Did I really agree to come and stay with you last night? Gawd, my head is sore. Too much wine.

She texted back straight away. She was good like that.

Riley: Ah, shit. Are you regretting it now? I wondered if it was the wrong time to ask. Didn't know how much wine you'd had. Listen, if you want to cancel then don't worry about it. We'll totally understand.

Me: We?

Riley: Yes, well, I happened to mention it to Ivy this morning and she got a little bit excited about having you over . . .

Me: What did she say?

The most adorable drawing of a lady holding a wee girl's hand flashed up on my phone. She had written my name, kind of. B–E–K–A.

Me: That's so sweet. OK, tell her I'm coming.
Riley: You are?
Me: Riley, it's so kind of you to have offered. You have a deadline. I need a break. We both want to work on our books. It's the perfect solution really, isn't it?
Riley: Well, I think so. But I don't want you feeling pressured. Maybe having a friend will help? I did think maybe you'd like to do some yoga with me too? I've been at some outdoor sessions recently . . .
Me: Now you're taking it too far ;). I'm booked on the ferry later but I've still got a lot to do. I forgot to pack any pants, for a start. I guess . . . I'll see you later?
Riley: This is going to be so great!

It was on.

I repacked my suitcase (replacing the miniature whiskies with practical things, like a toothbrush) and ignored the nagging doubts in my mind. Yes, I'd made an irrational move, but in the sober light of day, it was still a good decision.

I was going. I could do this.

7

22 minutes to Rathcliffe.

'I know what I'm doing, Dad.'

I realised Google Maps was upside down on the phone, which was positioned on my dashboard. I'd taken the wrong turn down a one-way street.

Bollocks.

'Is that right, Becca? You don't even know this woman. She might be a serial killer. Or, even worse, a Man United supporter,' he joked.

'Dad, she's not. I do know a lot about her. Well, enough anyway. She has a daughter called Ivy and she's a real author. A romance writer. Published and everything. And she likes yoga.'

He exhaled loudly in disgust.

'Authors can be psychopaths, Becca. Where do you think they get all the ideas for their murder books? And just because she does a bit of deep breathing doesn't mean she's not a crackpot.'

'Thanks for that insight, Dad. I think I'm going to take my chances. Plus, I knew Rae most of my life and she was keeping a huge secret from me. I guess you never really know anybody. I can't believe that Rae and Drew were a couple.'

'Couple of fannies, by the sounds of it.'

He'd been so relieved when Rae and I became best buddies when I was younger. It meant I wasn't begging him to play dolls or paint nails. He let her stay over and treated her like his own daughter. Dad never really said no when it came to Rae. A bit like me. The whole idea of her being dead was far too much for him to bear, too.

'Well, let me know when you arrive and what this Riley is like. She better not leave you babysitting while she goes off gallivanting around the pubs.'

'Dad, I know how to handle myself as an actual adult human being, you know. I am in charge of a class of children. I manage to count out my pennies to pay a mortgage every month. I am a grown-up,' I declared.

I wondered whether this was strictly accurate, given that I'd called him to scoop a spider out of my bathtub recently. But that's what dads were supposed to do. I was pretty sure he'd forgotten about it, anyway.

'I know, I know. Listen, drive carefully over there.'

I'd been to Belfast a few times with my dad, as a child. My great-grandparents were Irish and Dad had spent his summers there growing up. He'd booked a boat for us whenever he wanted to take a trip down memory lane. The journey always seemed to last forever. I remembered the pangs of jealousy as

I watched siblings playing games on board, squabbling over cards or laughing over lunch. Instead, I'd kept my head down and leafed through whatever book I was reading while Dad concentrated on completing the crossword.

'I will. And stop worrying. It's better for me, being with real human beings than being alone in my flat. Or worse, haunting you at your house.'

He paused.

'You can come and stay with me anytime, Becca Bear, you know that,' he said, eventually.

'I do, Dad. Thank you. I'll call you soon, OK?'

17 minutes.

The views were incredible. Rolling fields of all different shades of green whizzed by, with the majestic mountains sitting proudly in the distance. Despite the dismal weather, which would be described in Scotland as 'dreich', it was still beautiful, and for the first time since I'd learned about Rae's death, I felt like I could breathe. Or, at least, like I was going to be able to breathe soon. Breathing was in my reach.

But as I continued to follow the directions to Rathcliffe, the doubts crept back into my mind.

I'd texted Adam the Absolute Worst to apologise for freaking out so much at the funeral. It wasn't his fault that he'd been the one to tell me about Rae and Drew, after all. He was just caught in the crossfire. We'd exchanged some messages before I told him about my trip to Ireland. He was aghast when I confessed I'd never met my 'friend' in real life. I watched the black dots appear, typing back furiously, and then disappear. He seemed to write back several possible responses before coming over all 'big brother' on me.

ARE YOU MENTAL?

He went off on a rant about how crazy I was and how I could be going to stay with anyone. Blah, blah, blah. I'd disabled the notifications on my phone for his messages. Just for a few hours.

14 minutes.

I stopped at the lights and quickly checked my phone. Riley had sent me a video. Checking the lights, I hit play to see Ivy jumping up and down with a huge grin on her face.

Is she here yet? Is she here yet? (actual footage of Ivy anticipating your arrival).

I smiled. No one with a child that cute could possibly be a psychopath, could they?

13 minutes.

I was grateful to Riley for taking me under her wing. Psychopath or not, I didn't know what I'd have done without her messages over the last week. Maybe it was because she was a writer; she always seemed to know the right thing to say at the right time and, somehow, make me smile, even when I felt the lowest I'd ever felt.

Smile. Not belly laugh, the way I used to with Rae.

Rae with her extra-loud and easy contagious chuckle. Whenever something mildly funny happened, you could bet Rae would be clapping along enthusiastically like a seal. It was enough to make anyone laugh along. Even Drew, apparently.

12 minutes.

Then there was Drew, with his carefully pressed suits and

shirts. He even ironed his bloody boxer shorts and tracked his earnings and outgoings with spreadsheets, the last I'd known of him anyway. Before everything changed.

Of course, he hadn't always been like that. Mr Whippy hadn't been like that.

Drew and Rae. Rae and Drew.

3 minutes.

God, I was nearly there. Time to come face to face with this possible psychopath that I'd been conversing with so freely and had agreed, on a whim, to spend the summer with.

What. On. Earth. Was. I. Thinking?

Welcome to Rathcliffe, the sign read.

The green fields turned into rows of shops – the barber's, the newsagent, the baker's, the coffee shop. People stood outside, exchanging pleasantries like a sunny scene out of a Dickens novel. Children played out in the street and queued at the sweet counter.

What was it Riley said? When the satnav says to turn right at the bridge, ignore it and turn left. I spotted the blue gate she'd mentioned and turned right, as instructed, up the bumpy lane.

I approached the end of the lane and caught sight of a single-storey L-shaped white cottage boasting an extraordinary number of brightly coloured plant pots. The garden looked like it stretched for miles, surrounded by green grass with the mountains cushioned proudly in the distance. I couldn't think of anywhere more idyllic to write for the summer. No wonder Riley was knocking it out of the park when it came to writing romantic settings. She was surrounded by the most beautiful scenery I'd ever seen. All my senses tingled as I rolled down the window to breathe it all in, as I spotted the oak sign with the words 'Bellinder Cottage' beside the front door.

My heart was beating wildly in my chest. I'd made it.

The white panelled front door of Bellinder Cottage flew open and Ivy came bursting out into the driveway.

'She's here, she's here!' she squealed.

I grinned at the small child, who already felt so familiar to me from her adorable pictures. I couldn't recall seeing any pictures of Riley herself, but I felt that I knew what she would look like. In my mind, her long, flowing blond hair and baggy skirt were about to emerge from the low white cottage.

So when a man followed out of the front door, walked over to put his arm around Ivy and waved at me, I felt slightly confused. Even though I reciprocated with a smile and wave, my mind was reeling.

Riley hadn't mentioned a partner to me. Not once. She'd talked about her fictional characters' relationships, she'd talked about Ivy, but she'd never, ever mentioned a boyfriend or husband. Especially not *this* man. I mean, I'd have mentioned him if I'd just walked past him in the street. All six foot something of him towered above Ivy, his broad shoulders and bulky arms snug under a blue and white Gaelic football jersey, with his dark shorts showing off his muscular legs. He looked like some sort of mythical Irish God. His deep black wavy hair was longer on top and shaved closely at the sides, leading to his tanned skin and dark facial hair dusted across his chin. He had the widest, most welcoming grin and his bright eyes sparkled like he was sharing some sort of joke with me. His Irish eyes were smiling, indeed, and I seemed to have lost my ability to function.

I turned the engine off, fidgeting with my handbag strap. It seemed odd to tell this drop-dead gorgeous man, whoever he was, that I was coming to stay here. I kept looking at the door behind him, hoping Riley would follow him out.

But there was still no sign of her as I opened the car door and Ivy almost tripped over herself as she dashed towards me.

'Hello! Do you want to come and see my dolls' house?'

He casually strolled towards the car. If this was Riley's partner, she had done well for herself. He was even better close up as I noted he sported the most gorgeous green eyes I'd ever seen.

'Hi.' I smiled, holding out my hand. 'Pleased to meet you, I'm Becca.'

'Great to finally meet you too, Becca.' He shook it with a firm grip, holding my gaze the whole time. I felt myself blush.

'I'm just back from nursery,' Ivy announced as I forced myself to draw my eyes away from him. 'We had a birthday party today. Daddy says every day is like a party at nursery 'cause at least one person always pees themself with excitement.'

He laughed and Ivy beamed up at him. Yup, definitely Ivy's dad.

'I'm so happy you're here.' Ivy grinned at me.

'Me too.' I smiled. 'Where's, er, your mummy?'

The man frowned slightly as Ivy looked down at her shoes.

'She left; a while ago,' she whispered.

'Oh,' I said.

I turned to the man.

'Is Riley . . . has she gone out somewhere?' I asked.

He narrowed his eyes. 'What do you mean?'

'Riley. Will she be back soon?'

His lips turned down at either side as he frowned, confused at my question. Then he looked me straight in the eye and offered me a curt nod.

'I'm Riley,' he stated.

'What?' I stammered. 'I'm here to stay with Riley, the romance writer.'

'Becca, *I'm* Riley, the romance writer.'

'No, sorry, there's obviously been a mix-up,' I said, with a short exhale of breath. 'Riley's a girl. A girl's name.'

'A girl's name? Ah, Jaysus, horrible flashback to my school days,' he laughed, clutching his chest. 'Riley is also a boy's name. A man's name. And clearly is, in my case.'

A man. Riley – the yoga-loving, long-skirted, clean-living, romance writer I'd envisaged – was not a she at all. Riley was a he. A tall, broad-shouldered, messy-dark-haired, green-eyed, athletic, manly-man.

Bollocks. Literally.

'I don't understand. How can you be a man? And how could you not *tell* me you're a man? I told you about my smear test last week,' I stuttered, as if that clarified that he was most definitely in the wrong.

'I didn't know! Well, obviously I know I'm a man. I did wonder about the smear test thing, though,' he said quietly, as though it was all starting to dawn on him, too. 'But I thought *you* knew. I sent you a picture of me with Ivy. Well, that website link anyway. The one about my book. There was a picture of Ivy and me in the link. You couldn't miss it.'

I groaned. Of course, I hadn't clicked on the freaking link. I didn't realise it had been about Riley's book. I thought it was another link to try and entice me into starting yoga instead of drinking wine and I'd been too busy furiously checking my ex-boyfriend's and best friend's social media pages. I certainly hadn't noticed any picture.

'Oh God, I am mortified,' I admitted, my face burning. 'I didn't see the picture. I just assumed. You have Ivy, you write romance books and you do . . . yoga. I'm so sorry. I have spent this whole time talking to you thinking you were a woman. And now I've arrived on your doorstep to stay with you, but I'm going to have to go. I can't stay here—'

'You can't go!' Ivy protested. 'You just got here!'

'What do you mean, you can't stay here now? It's not the nineteen forties, Becca,' Riley said. 'A man and a woman can be friends. This is crazy.'

Friends. I could be friends with a man, of course I could.

But not *this* man. I definitely couldn't stay in a house with him. Definitely not unchaperoned. My whole face flushed. Riley's grin widened, resuming its cheery welcoming role. I wanted to curl up in a hole and die.

'God, I know, you're right, but . . . I just feel . . . this is so stupid.'

'You can't go all the way home now. Come on in, at least, for a while. Don't just rush off.'

I looked up at his green eyes shining earnestly at me. It wasn't like he'd lured me there under false pretences. It was my mistake. And she'd been so kind to me over messages. He, I meant. Riley. The Man.

'Come in. I've got some wine. You've been through a hard time recently, no wonder you weren't taking everything in. I'm sorry this is such a shock.'

He was apologising to me, for my mistake. Although I wished he wasn't there so I could furiously scroll back through our interactions to check how much I'd revealed to him. Words flashed through my mind: smear test, pants, periods, maybe even the odd boob reference. All the good stuff. I was pretty sure I'd inadvertently thrown it all at him.

'Well, OK,' I found myself saying. 'I will come in.'

'You thought my daddy was a lady,' Ivy giggled. 'Auntie Ellie said Daddy was mad, inviting a stranger to stay with us. Said you could be a crazy person and that he would write a book about it called *The Utter Nutter.*'

Riley shushed her, but with a small smile.

Maybe Auntie Ellie was right.

'Right, well, anyway, I'm glad that's all sorted,' Riley said. 'Let's get you settled.'

We walked towards the cottage.

'Do you want the wine, or would you prefer some tea?' Riley asked.

'Definitely wine!'

He laughed and I relaxed slightly, hoping that this was the end of the whole awkward thing.

Just then, Ivy piped up.

'Daddy,' she said. 'What's a smear test?'

I groaned and he laughed.

'I'm sure Becca will tell you all about that. Once she settles in, of course.'

8

Ivy insisted on showing me around their home, as Riley followed a few steps behind. I was completely mesmerised by Bellinder Cottage. Each room had its own individual personality, from the deep blue tones in the living room with its oversized fireplace and mismatched antique furniture, to the bright burnt-orange kitchen with wide windows looking out to the mountains, complete with exposed brick wall beside the rustic oak dining table and corner woodburning stove. The patio doors beside the dining area opened out to the garden, with the grass area seemingly stretching for miles, resting peacefully under the mountains.

'Everyone prefers everything plain and grey or neutral these days,' Riley said. 'We're not exactly on trend here, but it's cosy.'

He led the way along the hall and stopped in front of a door near the back of the house, pushing it open to reveal a narrow room with sloping ceilings. I audibly gasped as I glanced around. It was like some sort of writers' paradise, with a bookcase stacked with novels sitting against one wall and a long, navy desk with wooden worktops, which took up the long space underneath the window, and the most stunning uninterrupted view of the countryside. A tan-coloured leather-look computer chair, with a laptop in front of it, sat at one side, with another black suede computer chair arm's-width apart. A polka-dot gift bag rested on the wooden surface.

'So this is where the magic happens.' He grinned. 'Or is supposed to, anyway.'

'Ah, yes, the old writer's dysfunction,' I said. 'Happens to the best of us.'

'Lucky you're here to help then. Welcome to my favourite room in the house and official home of our writers' retreat. Think you could write in here?'

'Um . . . yes! I could live in here. Just pass me water and bread through every five hours or so. That view is to die for. The mountains are just stunning. And everything just looks so . . . literary. It is literally literary heaven.'

'Try saying that after a few Guinnesses.' He grinned. 'I'm glad you like it. I set up a spot for you so we could, you know, work together here. But no pressure or anything.'

Write here. Together. Riley, the man, and me, within touching distance. I gulped.

'This is for you, Becca,' Ivy said, picking up the black and white polka-dot gift bag. 'I drawed the card, too.'

'Drew,' Riley corrected her.

I flinched at the word.

'That's what I said.' She rolled her eyes, as I opened the bag and peered in, first retrieving a handmade card from Ivy with three stick figures drawn on the front along with the words 'Well come Beka'. Stick Riley and I were both writing at our desks and little stick Ivy was grinning from ear to ear playing with what looked suspiciously like a large pair of breasts.

Riley tried to hide his smirk as I admired the card.

'Oooh, I love your drawing, Ivy,' I gushed. 'Can you tell me about it?'

'That's you and Daddy writing your books and I'm watching you through the window with my binoculars.' She grinned proudly.

'Ah, binoculars!' Riley exclaimed, squinting at the picture. 'Now I see.'

'Well, yes, that's what they help you with, Daddy,' she said, as though he were the silly one.

I smirked as Riley threw me a grin over Ivy's head.

I took out the rest of the gift bag's contents: a brand-new black notebook with the words 'A New Chapter', a 'Wine in Disguise' coffee mug, a huge bar of chocolate and a single key. I smoothed my hand over it and was speechless, for a moment, gazing at all the goodies. I was more than a little embarrassed to suddenly feel my eyes filling with tears.

'If you don't like the chocolate, we can have it,' Riley said, laughing. 'It's just a little welcome present, no big deal. Plus, a key to Bellinder Cottage so you can come and go as you please.'

'I'll eat the chocolate!' Ivy exclaimed.

'Thank you both,' I said in a low voice. 'That was so thoughtful.'

Pleased with herself, Ivy skipped to her bedroom. I turned my attention to the bookshelf behind me, running my fingers along the spines of some books I recognised.

'A male romance writer,' I mused, still getting my head around it all as I checked out the titles and author names. The books were all written by females. 'Who would've thought?'

'Men can write romance too, you know,' he said, gesturing to the framed copy of the front cover of his book, *The Fall Out*, which took pride of place on the wall.

'And clearly can, in your case. Your first novel was amazing. Looks like it's your favourite genre to read, too?'

'Yes ma'am, and proud of it,' he said, giving me a small salute. 'And watch, too. Love a good romcom.'

He leaned against the door frame with a wide, infectious grin. I wondered how Bellinder Cottage was strong enough to contain Riley the romance writer. He looked like he could knock a wall down just by leaning against things. How could he be a romance writer? He wouldn't look out of place on a football pitch. Or a rugby pitch.

'Can Becca come and play now?' Ivy asked, appearing behind him at the door with a well-loved doll under the crook of her arm.

Riley rubbed his daughter's hair. 'Let Becca settle in.'

'It's all right, Riley the romance writer,' I said, smiling at them both. 'Ivy, I'd love to play.'

The truth was, I was glad to escape from all his wide, laid-back grins and all the *testosterone* floating around in the air. That's what it was, I was sure of it. And it was so distracting, I was glad of the excuse to leave. To breathe.

I sat cross-legged on the fluffy carpet in the living room and picked up one of Ivy's dolls. Riley disappeared to do something, with all his testosterone in tow, and I realised I'd secretly been banking on some female company. Some it's-hard-to-be-a-woman chat about sticking together, supporting each other and burning bras. I craved that.

I missed Rae so much, my whole body ached.

But Bellinder Cottage in all its glory, Ivy's adorable chatter and Riley's infectious grin felt like the gift I didn't know I needed. Then there had been the actual gift, which had melted my heart. Plus, he wanted me to work in his office *beside* him.

I blinked. I was sure I'd be able to get over the whole tingling sensation every time Riley looked at me.

'So, you pretend you're asleep and then I come in and tell you to wake up for breakfast.' Ivy interrupted my thoughts as she rearranged the cushions on the living room floor.

My thoughts turned to Ivy as I wondered where her mum was. She said she'd left, but what did that mean? When had she gone? Should Bellinder Cottage, with its magical charm, be credited to her? Had she chosen the vibrant colours, the soft furnishings and the mixture of old and new furniture throughout the house?

I settled back into my games with Ivy. Her sweet, lyrical voice drifted in and out of my thoughts, asking me to help her build a fort.

'Becca?' Riley called out from the kitchen.

I scrambled to my feet and smoothed down my T-shirt, suddenly feeling self-conscious. I'd thrown on a casual blue

T-shirt and black gym leggings for the journey, my hair tied back in a loose, and distinctly messy bun, with a hoodie tied around my waist. If I'd known who I was actually meeting, I'd have made more of an effort.

In fact, if I'd known Riley was a man, I wouldn't have come at all.

But I was here now. I swallowed.

I left Ivy building the fort, totally engrossed in her own thoughts, and walked into the kitchen where Riley's 'famous homemade lasagne' was almost ready. The smell filled the whole kitchen and I breathed it in.

Normally, I was a ready-meal-for-one kinda gal. I was punching above my culinary weight here.

'So,' he said, pulling plates out from the cupboard. 'Cards on the table. Yup, I am a man. I'm sorry, I genuinely thought you knew. But I really would like you to stay. We can bounce ideas around, do writing sprints and read each other's work like we planned. I think it'll really help us both. But it's your call. The ball's in your court.'

Riley's eyes shone earnestly as he spoke. I knew I shouldn't let *his* balls get in the way of the best offer I'd have for the summer, but I wasn't sure I could commit to spending all this time with Riley. I would be actually *living* with him. The phrase 'if you can't stand the heat, get out of the kitchen', sprang to mind. Watching his green eyes shining earnestly, I wondered how long I would last here, writing inches away from him. Sleeping yards away. I folded my arms across my chest at the thought, creating my own little mental and physical barrier.

'OK,' I nodded. 'I'll give it a few days and see how it goes. How does that sound? We both need to see if it's going to work though. I might really do your head in. Cards on the table . . . I'm used to living by myself so I talk to myself sometimes. Plus, I can't really cook and I'm not exactly the tidiest.'

Riley sat against the worktop and folded his arms across his chest.

'I take too long in the shower and my chat is shit. My dad jokes are out of control. Ivy thinks I'm hilarious, but I hear myself talking sometimes and wonder where it all went wrong.'

I let out a long sigh, shaking my head.

'Shit jokes are a major issue for me.'

'Oh really?'

'Oh, Riley.'

'Yours aren't the best, either,' he said, smiling as he arched an eyebrow. 'I guess we both have a lot to work on.'

'I guess we do.' I smiled.

9

Dishes clattered in the sink as Riley whistled to himself in the kitchen. At one point, he broke into a full verse, something about being back in the country, before reducing the tune back to a low whistle and, eventually, just a hum. I vaguely recognised the tune as something my dad played in the car when I was younger.

'Ivy, this is your five-minute warning before bed,' he called out during a lull in his song.

'Don't worry,' she whispered to me conspiratorially. 'He says that but it's never five minutes. He always forgets and lets me play longer.'

I sat back against the sofa and lifted my glass of wine from the coffee table. Riley was right – he described her as 'a dote'. Totally adorable.

He had tentatively shown me to the spare room after dinner. My room, he'd said, for as long as I wanted to stay. It was bright yellow with a gorgeous grey and yellow floral bedspread. I looked out at the view, with the sun setting in the distance. If I hadn't still felt like such an idiot for mistaking him for a her, I'd have been delighted with the whole set-up.

But, yup, I still felt like a dick.

It had all been relaxed as Ivy chattered away, but now her bedtime approached, I was apprehensive all over again. My phone kept beeping with questions from my dad about the trip so far, asking if Riley seemed sane and advising me to keep one eye open at night, just in case. I hadn't worked up the courage to tell Dad about my big mistake. Instead, I assured him everything was fine and promised to call soon. I'd sent the same to Adam to tell him I'd arrived safely. He seemed to have calmed down after his mini rant and I promised him I'd keep in touch.

'Right, munchkin, let's get those teeth brushed.'

'OK, Daddy,' she said. 'Becca, I'm glad you decided to stay with us. Tomorrow my aunts are coming over so you can meet them. They're ladies in love.'

'Oh, that sounds lovely,' I said. 'Do you mean ladies that lunch?'

'No, silly! I mean ladies in love with each other. Do you love ladies too or do you love men?'

'Ivy,' Riley warned. 'It's time for bed.'

'Daddy loves ladies, too,' she said. 'That's why I got born.'

'That's why I *was* born,' Riley corrected her.

'That's what I said,' she replied.

My mouth twitched at Riley's exasperated expression as Ivy came to give me a hug before bed. Her tiny Little Mermaid nightdress smelled like minty toothpaste. Riley scooped her up and carried her into her room. She waved goodbye to me until I couldn't see her any more.

'Night night, Becca!' she shouted from her room.

'Night, Ivy, see you in the morning,' I replied.

I heard her quizzing Riley on when she was allowed to get up, what time I would get up and whether she could come into my room or not. I wanted to call out to assure her that she could come and see me anytime, but I didn't want to undermine Riley. He was the boss, after all.

I tapped some messages back on my phone until he reappeared. Riley. The sight of him took my breath away a little. He was off the freaking scale when it came to looks. Like, hall-of-fame worthy.

I moved forward a little as he sat at the end of the couch, stretching his long, tanned legs out in front of him.

'Gawd, I still can't believe how stupid I was,' I replied, feeling my face getting hotter again.

'Easy mistake to make. I didn't pick up on how uber-feminine I sounded but I scrolled back through the messages and you're right. I bloody well sound like a woman. I think the yoga maybe tipped it over the edge. I am the only man in the class.'

'It's because you use words like "uber",' I pointed out, laughing. 'No, it was totally my mistake. Ivy is just adorable by the way. She's so funny. And very articulate, especially for her age.'

I didn't want to sound like a sycophant or a psychopath. I wanted everything to be normal between us. Easy. The way it had been when we'd messaged before. But it felt like it had all shifted, thanks to my stupid mistake. Ivy was the one saving grace. The safe topic we could stick to, without any tension.

'She's a right cracker, isn't she?' Riley's whole face lit up at the mention of his daughter. 'We've had some interesting conversations since you arrived actually, everything from gender confusion to smear tests and sexuality.'

I blushed. Again.

'Sorry about that,' I cringed.

He grinned. 'I'm only having you on.'

'So, one of her aunts that she mentioned, is that your sister?'

Aha. Another safe topic. I eased myself back into the couch and he lifted his glass of wine to his lips. He preferred beer, he confessed earlier, but had bought the bottle in for me. How could this man, who looked like *that*, be so thoughtful?

'My sister is Bridget and Ellie's her partner. They're the only gays in this very small village, as far as we know. But no one actually seems to give a shit, which is nice,' he said. 'You hear all sorts of stories about Ireland and how backward everything is, but she's not had any of that since she came home with Ellie. They met while they were backpacking around South America years ago and have been together ever since.'

'That's lovely. You should write a story about that.'

'Maybe. One day.'

A huge yawn escaped my mouth.

'You must be knackered after all the travelling,' he said.

'It's not the travelling,' I said. 'I haven't been sleeping well, since, you know.'

He paused.

'Since . . . your friend?'

'Yeah.'

'And that tool? Drew was his name, wasn't it? I'm a good listener, you know. If you wanted to talk about it.'

I paused.

'Not just now. I don't think you need to be part of my impromptu therapy session. Especially when I turned up on your doorstep asking where Ivy's mum is and wondering why you weren't a woman,' I said, my cheeks flushing again. 'I'm sorry about that, too, by the way. Bringing Ivy's mum up.'

I watched Riley closely for his reaction, but he simply smiled and shrugged it off.

Bellinder Cottage, with its wooden floors, thick rugs and cosy corners, displayed countless pictures of Ivy as a baby and as a toddler. There were a few pictures of Ivy with Riley, too. But there were no pictures of Ivy's mum anywhere in the house. I'd kept an eye out for them the whole way around.

'More wine?' Riley asked.

'Yes please,' I agreed, and he topped up my glass. 'Do you want to talk about our books instead? Since it's the start of our writers' retreat? I have to earn my keep after all.'

I was joking, kind of, but there was pressure. Especially now that I'd made such a dramatic, over-the-top entrance, I had to make sure this stayed on track and Riley wrote the second bestselling novel that he'd signed for with his publishers.

Riley leaned back in his chair and put an arm above his head, in a way that showed his muscles off in all their glory.

Who knew yoga could be so good for arms? I blinked the thought away.

'I'm seriously stressing, Becca. I need to get this book drafted over the summer. My agent is breathing down my neck. The publisher's been asking questions. I've written the synopsis and tried a few chapters but that's about it. I keep deleting every attempt. I've tried to plan but you know I'm rubbish with that. I'm a pantser.'

'You're not a pantser,' I said reassuringly, wondering if it was a typical Irish expression that I'd never heard.

'No, I am. It's a writers' term. You're usually either a plotter, mapping everything out, or a pantser where you fly by the seat of your pants. I'm a pantser,' he explained.

'Oh, I thought it meant you thought you were pants,' I laughed. 'I get it now. I've never heard of that. So, wait, you actually don't plot, you just dive in and write? How does that even work? I have pages and pages of notes and chapter outlines. I write notes about notes. I even drew Anna and Rosie's family trees.'

He smiled. 'Ah, yes. You are a plotter.'

'A plotter who's lost the plot,' I replied.

'We'll find the plot, Becca,' he said. 'At least I hope we do. Nothing seems to be working for me. Thank God you're here. Your notes have always really helped me.'

The way he called me 'Becca' so smoothly, it was like spreading butter on really hot toast. I beamed at the thought of supporting Riley, of providing words that helped him hone his craft.

OK, so I had mistaken him for a woman, told him all about my smear test and asked his daughter where her absent mother was. Plus, I hadn't slept in so long that I looked like the walking dead. And that feeling of deep dread and unshakeable grief followed me around like a shadow.

I wasn't exactly a catch. And I knew he just felt sorry for me. The crazed, grieving woman who had nowhere to go but a stranger's house to escape her misery.

But still.

'Your notes always help me, too,' I replied. 'It's great to get someone else's input. Why don't you start off with your one-line elevator pitch and we'll go from there. You could even try and make some background notes. Try and be a bit less pantser and more plotter.'

Riley took a deep breath.

'Right. Well. Ah, Jaysus, I don't know, Becca,' he said. 'I don't think I can plan it. Everything just kind of came to me for my first book, you know? No creative juices flowing here. The writing well has dried up.'

He sighed and put his head in his hands. I worried for a minute that he was going to cry. While I have absolutely no objection to men showing their softer side, I wasn't sure what I would do if Riley lost it. Maybe I should suggest whipping out the yoga mat for a breathing session. He seemed to like that kind of approach.

'You should go for a walk and clear your head,' I said.

'I can't go for a walk. Ivy's in bed.'

'But I'm here,' I said.

'I'm not just going to leave you here while I swan off for a walk,' Riley said. 'Remember what Auntie Ellie said. You could be an Utter Nutter.'

I laughed. 'She's not far wrong.'

'You should be the one going. Get familiar with the area.'

'Plenty of time for all that.'

'Is there? Does that mean that you'll be sticking around?'

His green eyes looked . . . hopeful. Like he actually, truly did want me to stay, whether I was an Utter Nutter or not.

'I don't know what I'm doing. Like, at all. One step at a time, I guess. I feel a bit lighter since I arrived though. I think it's the mountain air or something. It's absolutely beautiful here.'

'It is,' Riley said. 'I guess that's why I never left.'

'Have you lived here since you were a child?'

'Yep. Born and bred. This is the family home, my parents passed away a few years ago so it was left to me and Bridget. She lives down the road now. Rathcliffe is the place where everybody knows my name.'

'I'm sorry about your parents,' I said. 'That's awful.'

He smiled sadly. 'Thanks. My dad died of cancer and my mum followed not long after. I think she died of a broken heart. Bellinder Cottage feels like a part of them are still here, though, you know? Although we had a break-in last year and some bastard stole their wedding rings.'

'That's terrible!' I cried. 'And so sad. My mum died of cancer, too, when I was four. I don't really remember much about her but I have lots of her jewellery, too. I would be devastated to lose it. I'm sorry.'

'Ah, that's awful. So hard to lose a parent when you're so young.'

We paused.

'It was. My mum loved writing,' I said. 'She was a journalist but wanted to be a novelist, too.'

'Like mother, like daughter,' he mused. 'Like pantser, like plotter.'

'Such a way with words, Riley,' I laughed. 'Well, how does it feel to be a famous romance writer? Everyone really does know your name.'

'Not famous enough for you to know I'm a man.'

He laughed and I cringed.

'You're never going to let me live this down, are you?' I laughed. 'I am sorry that I didn't read the link you sent me.'

'Don't worry. You just need to make it up to me by helping me put one word after the other in the next few weeks. I'm pretty sure once I get into the groove, it'll all come together. I'm counting on it.'

'It will.'

I wasn't sure whether I was reassuring him or myself. My phone began vibrating.

'Excuse me,' I said, walking outside to take the call.

I sat on the bench in the garden, which was surrounded by bright potted plants. A watering can with Ivy's name on it sat beside a bright yellow garden spade and a larger green spade. Instead of a traditional wooden garden gate, Bellinder Cottage boasted a fence painted all the colours of the rainbow, which danced under the evening sun.

I never usually answered unknown numbers on my phone, but since missing all the calls the day Rae died, I'd come to learn that they might be important.

'Becca?' a muffled voice said.

'Who's this?' I said.

The phone line was silent for a few seconds.

'It's me.'

Drew.

What the absolute fuck was he doing calling me?

'What do you want?'

'I just wanted to . . . I don't know.'

'Right, well, I'm hanging up now,' I said.

'Becca, please.'

'Don't bloody "Becca, please" me. Do you even know you crossed a line? I mean, you were way over the line before you started seeing her and now you're so far past the line. You're actually so far past the shitting line, Drew.'

'You don't need to tell me about the line. I know exactly where the line is and what I crossed and what I didn't.'

His speech was slurred. I should have known.

'You're shitfaced, Drew. Call me when you're sober.'

'That won't be for at least a year or so,' he slurred.

'Listen, I've managed a whole lot longer than that without hearing from you. I don't need this shit.'

'I miss her, Becca.'

Tears stung in my eyes. I swallowed the lump in my throat.

'If you're looking for sympathy, you've come to the wrong

place. I am the last person you should be calling right now, Drew. Don't you get that?'

I began pacing up and down in the garden.

'You're the only one who understands, Bec. You're the only other person who really knew her and—'

'Becca, are you all right?'

I looked up. Riley stood in front of me with a face full of concern. Drew's voice exploded in my ear.

'Who the fuck is that?'

Bollocks.

I mouthed a quick 'sorry' to Riley. He nodded and went back inside.

'It's, erm, I'm away for a while,' I said.

'You're away? What – on holiday? With a guy? I never knew you were seeing anyone.'

'I never knew you were banging my best friend, Drew, but here we are.'

I didn't correct him. I wanted Drew to think I was with someone. I hoped that he felt that sting of jealousy, to know how it felt, even just a little bit.

'Becca, it wasn't like that. I thought Adam told you. Rae and I, it wasn't just a fling. We were serious. We were going to get married.'

That's so much fucking worse, I wanted to scream. I took a deep breath.

'So I hear, and I was apparently going to jump on board and be your bridesmaid? That was a lovely surprise. I really would have needed some notice so I could have caught the bouquet.'

'You would have done it. You'd have been the bridesmaid. You'd have done anything for her,' he said.

'I guess now we'll never know.' I ended the call with a shaking hand.

10

TEN YEARS AGO

It didn't take long for Drew to kiss me for the first time.

A group of us from work went to the pub one evening. There was a football match on, so Rae invited Mickey, the chef she couldn't stop talking about, to come along. They were getting serious pretty quickly and Rae was besotted with him. Meanwhile, he completely ignored her in favour of the screen for the full first half of the game. He was either shouting at the screen or texting on his phone.

Rae and I sipped our ciders and giggled with each other instead. I'd left an empty seat beside me. Drew arrived after finishing his shift to claim it.

Mickey glared at Rae when she snorted at something I'd said. She sighed and went to the toilet.

'That guy is a tool,' Drew said. 'Why did he even bother coming if he was just going to ignore her or roll his eyes at her?'

My insides tightened. Drew seemed so concerned about Rae. He glared at Mickey as he downed the last of his pint.

'Don't say anything,' I warned. 'Rae will flip if you do. Just leave them to it.'

'It's her life, I'm not going to say anything. But the guy is just fucking rude.'

'Who's rude?'

Mickey looked up, narrowing his dark eyes at Drew. He'd clearly caught on to the fact Drew had been talking about him. And he was not happy.

'Who's rude?' Drew said. 'You're fucking rude, mate. She's made the effort to invite you along and all you can do is sit there and ignore her. Why didn't you go somewhere else to watch the game?'

'Who the fuck do you think you are?'

Mickey stood up, narrowing his eyes further, and pushed towards Drew, who got up to face him.

I leapt up to calm them both down. Mickey put his arm up to push me away.

Drew flipped.

'Don't you touch her. Don't you dare touch her.'

They squared up to each other, growling like pitbulls in the park.

'Oi! You lot, calm down or get the hell out of the bar.'

The bar manager rushed over to break it up, just as Rae arrived back at the table.

'What's going on?' she asked.

'Your "mate" here,' Mickey said. 'Clearly fancies himself as more than your mate.'

'Mr Whippy? I don't think so, Mickey. He's into Becca,' Rae said.

Mickey snorted. 'Oh aye, sure,' he said, sarcastically. 'No offence, Becca.'

My face burned.

'That's enough. Out, all of you!' the bar manager shouted, pointing at the door.

Drew swore under his breath and Mickey downed the last of his pint. Rae sighed and picked up her jacket. I trailed behind them all.

'Can't fucking believe I'm missing the second half because of your so-called mate,' Mickey complained.

'Go to hell,' Drew said.

Mickey went one way while Drew turned to go the other. Rae and I looked at each other.

'Text me later,' she called over to me, an uneasy look on her face as she tried to put an arm around Mickey. He shrugged her off.

I nodded and followed Drew.

'You don't need to come with me, Becca. You could probably get back into the pub, if you wanted.'

'I probably could, yeah. Or I could go and third-wheel it with Rae and Mickey.'

'Well, I'd definitely pick me over that loser. The prick.'

He bared his teeth and spat on the ground.

'Lovely,' I remarked. He stayed silent, pacing forward, and I quickened my pace to keep up with him.

The evening sun bounced playfully off the deep blue lake as two men threw stones into the water, prompting ripples to break the stillness every few seconds. Drew and I walked along without a word. His anger hung between us, I could practically feel his adrenaline pumping. I had to ask. I couldn't let it remain unsaid any longer. Rae was always going to be around, looking as good as she always did, and I couldn't let myself fall any further for him. I had to know.

'Do you like Rae?'

I blurted it out before I could change my mind. He stopped and looked at me.

'Seriously?' he said, arching an eyebrow. 'You're seriously asking that question?'

I turned my back on him to face the lake. The water sparkled under the light but remained calm and still, stretching into the distance. Why did he have to answer the question with a question? It was obviously just a stalling tactic so he could figure out how to let me down gently.

'I am seriously asking that question. You really stood up for her today. Mickey thought it too. Maybe you were jealous?'

'Fuck, Becca. We've been – I mean, I thought we were – but maybe I'm wrong . . .'

He touched my shoulder and gently pulled me around to face him. I tried to look away but he reached out and cupped my chin so I was looking right into his eyes.

'I don't like Rae. I mean, I do like her, obviously. She's cool.

But, since I met you, there is literally no one else. Nothing else. I can't stop thinking about you. Only you, Becca.'

It felt like the air had been sucked out of my body.

How do you respond to that? I blinked. He leaned in towards me and the world fell into place as we kissed. And we didn't stop for a very long time.

11

I lay awake for most of my first night in Bellinder Cottage. Not that it came as any surprise. I leafed through the pages of Riley's book under the covers, just in case he happened to fling the door open at three a.m. shouting 'aha' when he caught me in the act.

As I flicked through the familiar words of his debut, I pictured him penning the novel in his office while Ivy played with her dolls in the living room. I pored over the three steamy scenes (yes, I counted them), wondering how on earth Riley managed to write them from a woman's perspective. I blushed. I cried again when I read the part where Alice's partner passed away and she finally got together with Leroy, her true love.

'Becca?'

I sat bolt upright in bed, my hair standing on end, realising I'd fallen asleep at some stage.

A light knock on the bedroom door followed.

'Erm, yes, I'm here!' I called back.

'I'm just taking Ivy to nursery for the day. I'll be back in ten,' he called.

'OK doke!'

OK fucking doke. Who even says that? I cringed and flung the covers back, pulling my favourite hoodie over my PJs. I waited until I heard their chatter stopping and, when the front door clicked to close behind them, I dashed to the bathroom. After a lightning-quick shower, I looked at myself in the round mirror that sat above the sink to assess the damage. I needed make-up, ASAP. Particularly concealer to hide the dark circles under my eyes. I dashed back to the bedroom, dressed quickly and grabbed my make-up bag, rubbing my foundation in as quickly as my fingers could handle. I poked myself in the eye while flicking mascara on my upper lashes as I heard the door click open again.

I grabbed my laptop and dashed into the hallway, laptop under my arm.

'I'm ready,' I said.

He threw me a lopsided smile. 'Erm . . . congratulations?'

'Seriously, let's get this writers' retreat on the road.'

Riley hung up his keys and pulled off his hoodie, revealing a tiny section of his tanned stomach.

Focus, Becca.

'Relax,' he said, as I followed him into the kitchen, my bare feet cold against the wooden floors. 'I only called in to let you know where I was going, in case you wondered. It's no drama if you want to stay in your room, sleep or whatever you want. It's not boot camp.'

He flicked on the kettle.

'Book camp!' I exclaimed. 'That's a great idea. We could start with drawing up a timetable of what to do when, like I do with my pupils in school. Lesson planning is my forte.'

I felt geekishly enthused by the notion of drawing up a timetable and ran to grab my notebook from the office. As I came back and laid it out on the kitchen table, Riley smiled.

'Works for me,' he said, as I made a start on mapping out what we'd talked about at the dining table: discussion time, writing sprints and slots and tea/lunch breaks. Riley passed me a coffee and gazed at my efforts over my shoulder.

'Do I need to ask to use the toilet?' he teased.

'Yup,' I replied. 'And you're only allowed to talk just now because it's "discussion" time. Silence during sprints.'

'You're strict,' he remarked, sitting across from me as he sipped his coffee.

'You better believe it,' I replied.

'I have an event to schedule in,' he said.

I arched an eyebrow. 'We're only just getting started here and you're asking for a break?'

He grinned. 'I've been asked to an author event at a bookshop in Dublin in a couple of weeks. It's part of a literary festival. I'm not the main act – some bigshot thriller writer is the big attraction, but it'll be great. Fancy it?'

My mouth fell open. 'Fancy it? Oh my God, yes please! I'd love to come!'

I sounded like a complete fan girl. Way to play it cool, Becca.

'Grand,' he said. 'My agent, Katrine, is coming, so you'll get to meet her; she's based in Dublin.'

'Check me out. I've just arrived and I'm already planning on living it up with the great and good of the literary world in Dublin,' I said, trying to stop myself from jumping up and down. 'Although of course, I know you'll be far too busy being famous to speak to the common folk like me. But yes, I'd love to come and see all you real writers in action. You can definitely have permission to be absent that day. I'll add it to our long-term timetable.'

Riley laughed. 'You know, I love what I've read of *Queen Bee* so far. You've got a really modern, distinctive voice. I'm sure Ivy will love it when she's a bit older.'

My heart fluttered a little.

'Well, I am obsessed with Alice and Leroy. Their story just lit up my life. Your story, I mean.'

I truly had gushed over the romance story and the will they, won't they tension he'd built between the two characters, Alice and Leroy, who had been each other's first loves, much to the disgust of her strict parents. They split up due to the family pressure and Alice went on to marry someone else, but Leroy never did. The pair eventually met again while Alice was caring for her terminally ill husband.

'A second-chance romance.' He smiled. 'It's a trope.'

'What do you mean?' I frowned.

'You haven't heard of it?' Riley asked, setting his laptop aside and sitting forward, with a semi-smile on his face. He was the master of that small smile that would put anyone at ease. 'It's a genre of romance. When a couple learn to love again years after their first encounter or after they've broken up. You also have other romance tropes, like opposites attract, fake engagement. All the stuff you see in films.'

'Wait, wait, wait.' I frowned, sitting forward in my seat. 'Are you telling me you romance writers all have these magical formulas up your sleeves to write best-selling books? Why don't I know about this?'

He threw back his head and laughed. A hearty laugh, like he was really enjoying our conversation. Riley, the romance writer, liked having me in his house. Someone was enjoying my company. I beamed inside.

'You do know about it.' He smiled. 'Everyone does, really. There's also the whole "one bed" trope, where a pair, usually one that don't really like each other much, end up in a situation where they've got to share a bed.'

I laughed. He was right, I'd read a book where that had happened. It was a thing.

'There's enemies to lovers, too, that's another trope. Oh and fake relationships, where they have to pretend to be in love for some reason or another and then they fall in love. I like the idea of writing one of those,' he said.

'I never studied creative writing or anything,' I said. 'And I guess I've never really thought about it, either. But now you mention it, that's totally a thing. And there's usually always a happily ever after, of course. Even though I don't agree with that.'

'After the grand gesture.' Riley smiled. 'Where one of the

characters has really fucked something up, big style, and has to come back and apologise. Maybe proclaim their love over a loudspeaker at a baseball game. Or here, it would be a Gaelic football game.'

'Oh, OK, what about a love triangle? Is that a trope?' I asked. 'Like in *My Best Friend's Wedding*. Oh, I love that film. Now, that's one of my favourites. You expect them to get together in the end, but they don't. It's much more realistic.'

His eyes crinkled at either side as he grinned at me. 'Cheers, I haven't seen that one yet.'

'Oops, sorry! I thought you loved romcoms? That's one of the best! I can't believe you haven't seen it.'

'Well, I don't really need to now I know the ending.' He grinned.

Just as I looked down, I saw Riley moving towards me out of the corner of my eye. I jumped back as his finger moved towards me and he rubbed a space just above my eyelid.

'What?' I exclaimed, leaning back and rubbing my own eyelid.

'Sorry,' he laughed, standing up. 'You had a bit of dirt or something above your eye. Shall we move to the office?'

'Mascara,' I said quietly, as I followed behind him, still rubbing my eyelid to ensure the mark had been removed.

I wondered how Riley felt so comfortable with me that he didn't mind pouncing on me to rub my face, while I was still tiptoeing around the place hoping he couldn't hear my heart thumping in my chest every time he happened to look at me.

As we sat down at our desks, just a few feet apart, I opened my laptop at the same time as he opened his. We sat still for a moment.

Silence.

'Tell me about this writing sprint thing then,' I said. 'I've put it on the timetable but I've no idea how it actually works.'

Riley sat back in his seat and looked over at me, crossing his legs. 'You have a set amount of time where you write, so say twenty minutes, and you just write for that amount of time. You might set a target, too, like to write five hundred words by the time you've finished.'

'Bet I can beat you,' I said.

'Not if I beat you first,' he said, pulling his chair closer to his laptop. 'Let's do it. Twenty minutes, five hundred words.'

'Make it thirty minutes,' I said. 'A thousand words.'

'Have you ever written a thousand words in thirty minutes?'

'Not a clue,' I replied, opening the timer on my mobile phone. 'But fuck it, let's see where we get to. Ready, set, go!'

I blew an imaginary whistle as Riley and I started typing furiously on our keyboards. At first, I had no idea what I was actually writing. I'd read the most recent chapter of my book on the journey over and studied my notes and chapter outline, but it didn't seem to be flowing the way I'd hoped. So I decided to take a leaf out of Riley's 'pantser' book and started a new scene where the lead character, Anna, overheard her sworn enemy, Rosie, announcing that she was auditioning for the same lead part in the school show. I could hear Riley tapping on the keyboard beside me. I threw a quick glance up but Riley didn't move his eyes from the screen.

'Eyes on the prize, kid.'

'Crap,' I muttered, as I continued with the scene.

My timer started buzzing after what seemed like only a few minutes.

'Pens and pencils down, please!' I said.

Riley tapped one more word on his keyboard and then raised his hands in the air. 'I'm done, I promise!'

'You'll be disqualified if you do that again, Mr Romance Writer. Now, tell me your word count.'

He stood up and stretched as though he'd just run an actual marathon.

'Six hundred and sixty-three words,' he replied. 'One hundred per cent likely to be a load of shite.'

'Six hundred and sixty-*two*,' I corrected him. 'I'm taking one word off since you wrote it after the whistle blew. What was that last one you just had to sneak in?'

'The,' he replied, feebly.

I snorted. 'Belter.'

'How did you do?' he asked.

'I tried being a pantser. I hadn't planned this scene at all but I've got about three hundred and forty-six good words and four hundred and fifty that are kind of shit. But it's the most I've written since . . . well, in ages. So I'm chuffed, actually. Maybe I could be a pantser, after all.'

'You should schedule some pantser time into your timetable,' Riley quipped.

'Oh ha ha,' I retorted. 'Very good.'

'I might even keep some of these words, you know,' he

mused. 'I've done writing sprints before with a group online. Everyone sits on a conference call and just writes until the timer stops. Then you read your work out at the end, if you want to. Or just leave the meeting. This is the first I've done in real life, though.'

'Wow. The secret seedy world of writers, eh? A quick hit, run and you're done.'

'Yup,' he said. 'I never read stuff out loud, especially not to people I don't know, in case they trash it. Look what happened to poor Kate that time on our writers' forum. She got torn apart.'

'I know, but you swooped in and stopped it! I was hiding behind my keyboard dying slowly on her behalf.'

'Writers can be brutal. Anyway, what does the timetable say now? Is it break time yet?'

'Nope,' I replied. 'We have another half an hour. Let's try another sprint and see if you can beat your personal best. No more words after the alarm has sounded this time, cheater.'

'Slave driver.' He grinned as I set the timer again.

'Bestsellers don't write themselves, Riley,' I reminded him.

'Don't I know it,' he said with a sigh. 'OK, let's do it. I'm definitely going to beat you this time.'

'Not if I beat you first.' I grinned.

12

Bridget and Ellie arrived for dinner later in the day, bearing a basket of colourful fruit and two bottles of wine.

'We've brought grapes for Ivy and grown-up grapes for us,' Bridget called as she entered the kitchen.

I wasn't quite sure what to do with myself, left to my own devices in a house that wasn't mine. Ivy had managed to persuade Riley to take her to the park after nursery, and I'd volunteered to wait in for Bridget and Ellie's arrival. I wanted to avoid looking like the Utter Nutter, making myself at home in someone else's house, at all costs, and had shuffled around for a while. I concluded that loading the dishwasher was a safe move: helpful but not in a manic I'm-taking-over-your-lives-and-am-never-leaving kind of way.

But Bridget and Ellie didn't seem to care.

'We're so excited to meet you,' Bridget said, enveloping me into a huge hug. She was so warm and inviting, I had to stop myself from burying my body into her generous bosom. Her long, jet-black hair spilled down her back against her bright pink top and I realised she didn't look much like Riley, though they shared the same sparkling green eyes. She then kind of spun me around and Ellie gave me a hug, too. The one who thought I could be the Utter Nutter. She wore her blonde hair cropped neatly around her chin and was dressed primarily in black, from her tailored trousers to her square-shaped glasses.

'Lovely to meet you.' Ellie's hug was looser than her partner's, but her smile was just as warm. 'Riley tells us you're a children's writer.'

I blushed. 'Oh, I don't think I could call myself an actual writer . . . not like him, anyway.'

'Whatever you do, don't make his head any bigger.' Bridget rolled her eyes. 'He'll think he's Jackie fecking Collins.'

'He is very good though, isn't he, Becca? He's making quite a name for himself,' Ellie said, and I nodded. 'Even if his sister is loath to admit it, she's really his biggest cheerleader.'

Bridget shrugged but her beaming smile betrayed the sense of pride she obviously took in Riley's success. 'Let's just hope the second book lives up to all the hype. Riley said it's coming along really well. Flying along, he said. Isn't that just brilliant?'

I paused. I wouldn't exactly have described Riley's work as 'flying along', despite our attempts at writers' sprints earlier. After we'd finished, he confessed that a lot of his writing for the day was going in his 'backstory' folder as notes. It wasn't a complete waste of time, he'd said, but I wasn't one for bursting his sister's bubble.

'Isn't it?' I replied, grinning.

'Anyway, it's great to finally meet you, Becca. I hear you thought my brother was a yoga-loving, romance-writing woman?' Bridget teased.

I blushed. I had a feeling I was going to be the talk of the town already.

'Don't listen to her, Becca. She's always on the wind-up,' Ellie soothed, folding her arms while throwing Bridget an affectionate smile.

'Oh my God, I'm so embarrassed about it,' I said.

Their eyes shone brightly, delighted at the whole turn in conversation as we walked towards the living room.

'Do you want to tell us?' Ellie pressed, taking a seat on the couch. 'Don't worry if you don't.'

'Oh you NEED to tell us. Wait, wait, wait!' Bridget shouted, turning back towards the kitchen. 'Do NOT start without me. Literally, not a word. I'm going in to pour the wine.'

'Where is Riley by the way?' Ellie asked, looking around.

'I said WAIT!' Bridget called.

I laughed and sat back in the chair. Ellie had her finger over her lips as though that was going to prevent her from firing more questions over at me.

Bridget came back out balancing three wine glasses between her hands. 'Un-pause. Where are they?'

'Riley took Ivy to the park after nursery. He'll be back shortly,' I said.

'So, start from the very beginning,' Bridget urged. 'You met online, you thought he was a woman and—'

I laughed and started to tell the story of Riley and me connecting over critiquing our novels as they sipped their wine.

I skipped to the part where Riley invited me over for an unofficial writers' retreat, bypassing his whole writer's dysfunction dilemma. He was obviously keeping his cards close to his chest on that one and I was totally cool with that. I had more than a few secrets tucked up my own sleeve. Instead, I focused on what they wanted to hear: my reaction to realising Riley was actually a man.

Bridget's expressions were priceless. Her eyes lit up as she exclaimed and gasped the whole way through the story, lapping up all the drama as she threw her head back and barked with loud laughter. Ellie smiled along politely, her own eyes lighting up at Bridget's laugh.

'I can't even imagine our Riley's face when you started talking to him about your smear test,' Bridget laughed. 'He's totally squeamish, he would have hated that. I'm pretty sure he fainted when Jackie was giving birth.'

'Jackie. I take it that's Ivy's mum? He hasn't really said much about her.'

Bridget's face clouded over.

'The less said about her the better,' she muttered as the front door flew open and Ivy bounced into the room. 'She's been off the scene for a long time now.'

'They've started on the wine already,' Riley laughed as Bridget and Ellie stood to cuddle Ivy.

'How's my favourite niece?'

'Good,' Ivy replied. 'I managed to do the high monkey bars. The ones Daddy said I wouldn't be able to do 'til I was seventeen.'

'Woohoo!' Ellie said, giving her a high five. 'That's our girl.'

'Auntie Bridget, Auntie Ellie, are you drinking that grown-up juice again?' Ivy enquired.

'Now, now, Ivy. Remember what we said, we don't keep track of every sweetie you have so go easy on the grown-up juice chat,' Bridget said, kissing Ivy on the nose.

'But last time you had too much and fell into the—'

'Anyway, Becca,' Bridget interrupted, clearing her throat. 'Tell us a bit about Glasgow. I've never been before.'

Riley let out a loud chuckle as he went back into the kitchen to fetch the food we'd prepared earlier.

Bridget and Ellie listened intently as I explained a bit about where I lived in the south side and explained that Glasgow was often thought of as the 'people's capital'.

'But Edinburgh is just so beautiful,' Ellie said. 'Do you ever visit?'

It took me a moment to answer. My memories of Edinburgh were entangled with thoughts of Rae.

'Yes, I go quite a bit,' I said, quietly. 'It is beautiful.'

'Dinner is served,' Riley called from the kitchen at the same time. 'Head on outside and I'll bring it out.'

We stood up, clutching our wine glasses, and filed out onto the patio area. Ellie and Bridget chatted to Ivy about her dolls as she carried them out to the garden. Riley brought out plates of pasta, while Ivy took her dolls to play on the slide.

'Are you all right?' he turned to whisper in my ear as he placed a sandwich platter on the table.

The low hum of his words near my skin made the hair stand up on the back of my neck. I felt myself nod and he nodded swiftly and carried on as though nothing had happened. Bridget and Ellie made various appreciative noises about the food, although they were clearly more impressed with the wine.

'Becca told us the story of you guys meeting in real life,' Bridget said to her brother. 'What a laugh.'

'I'm glad you've decided to give it a chance though, Becca,' added Ellie. 'He's not a crazy person, I promise.'

'I don't know if we should promise that,' Bridget whispered to her partner.

Ellie laughed and playfully punched her partner on the arm, while Bridget let out a large yelp and rubbed it, grinning back at Ellie. I was fascinated, watching them gazing adoringly at one another as if they had just met and finishing each other's sentences.

I glanced at Riley. He was looking straight at me. He winked.

'You guys are just the perfect couple,' I said, drawing my eyes back to Ellie. 'Riley said you met while travelling through South America?'

Bridget and Ellie beamed at each other as they halved a sausage roll without any prior discussion.

'We sure did.' Bridget smiled wistfully. 'Love at first sight.'

'She sat down beside me on a long coach journey and we just clicked straight away,' Ellie confirmed. 'I almost missed my stop because we were chatting so much.'

'Ha! Unlikely. You've never been late for anything in your life, Ellie,' Bridget said. 'A bit like myself.'

Bridget laughed loudly at her own joke.

'You two talking too much? Never!' Riley teased. 'And yes, Bridget will be late for her own funeral.'

'Speaking of talking a lot, what about you two?' Bridget sat back in her seat and grinned. 'Firing messages back and forth all day.'

I didn't dare to glance at Riley as I felt my cheeks flush.

'At least you'll fly through the last couple of chapters of your book, Riley,' Bridget said confidently. 'Now Becca's here.'

It was Riley's turn to avoid my gaze. He fidgeted in his chair and I watched his face cloud over. I wondered how he'd managed to convince his sister that his writing was going well. He had a terrible poker face.

'Of course we will,' I replied, raising my wine glass. 'We'll have that book bashed out so quickly, we'll spend the rest of our time in the pub.'

Riley grinned. 'Sure, we might as well go now. Start as we mean to go on.'

'We still get our Ivy every week though, right?' Bridget asked. 'Even though Becca's here?'

'Ivy comes to our house for a sleepover every Thursday night. Without fail,' Ellie explained. 'We just love it.'

'Good practice for us,' Bridget winked.

'Why?' I asked. 'Are you guys planning to . . . Oh God, sorry. I can't believe I'm asking that.'

'It's no secret, don't worry, Becca. We are going to adopt.
We're actually already on a list waiting to be matched.'

Ellie and Bridget reached out under the table and squeezed
hands.

'That's just . . . amazing,' I said. 'I hope it happens soon for
you guys.'

'Thank you, we hope so too.' Ellie smiled. 'It would be lovely
for Ivy to have a cousin to play with. Or cousins.'

'Wow! One at a time,' Bridget laughed.

'Hopefully not much longer for us to wait for our new family
member,' Riley said. He raised a glass to his sister and Ellie.
And, even though I'd just met them both for the first time, I
crossed my fingers for them under the table.

And then they toasted me. Becca. The guest of honour, Riley
said. I gazed around at the sun beaming down into the garden
with me, the guest of honour, surrounded by these people who
had filled me with more warmth in the short period I'd spent
with them than I'd felt in a very, very long time.

'Right, so you'll come for our weekly walk and then on Sunday
evenings we have outdoor book club . . .' Ellie said.

It had been a lovely afternoon. The conversation flowed so
easily and by the end, I felt like I'd known Bridget and Ellie
for ages. Riley, too, obviously. Although I did know him,
technically. Putting everything together and attributing it to
Riley, the romance writer, as a male, was still a confusing
conundrum. It was hard to think of him as the person I'd

messaged before, sometimes into the early hours. It had been so easy then, the chat flowed freely between us, but I could feel any tension slowly lift as we eased our way back into our friendship. His sparkling green eyes seemed to agree. On more than one occasion, I had to tear my eyes off them after realising I shouldn't be looking at him so much.

'You need to bring a hip flask for outdoor book club.' Bridget nodded firmly. 'You can't just turn up empty-handed.'

'What about the book? Should I read it before I come so we can talk about it?' I asked.

They burst out laughing.

'Oh, shit, that's right! We're supposed to read a book.' Their chuckles vibrated around the kitchen.

'I can't remember what we are currently pretending to read,' Ellie confessed. 'But just come along. We usually just talk about themes and then go off on a tangent with our hip flasks. Anyway, I think we've had enough hilarity for one afternoon. We should really be on our way. Put those dates in your diary, Becca.'

'I will, thank you.' I smiled.

'Oh, and don't forget, the grand opening of our business! You need to put that in your diary,' Ellie said. 'We'll be working to get everything completed and then get the finishing touches in place over the next few weeks. I can't wait to show you around.'

Ellie and Bridget had told me all about their new business venture. They had been working for months, renovating former cottages to transform into a self-catering business, and had promised me a tour of the site. Bridget insisted Ellie was the 'brains' behind the operation, sitting up at night crunching the numbers, while she 'oohed and aahed' at cushions and bed-spreads. Ellie fixed her square glasses firmly on her nose and confessed to knowing nothing about interior design.

'Can I cut the ribbon at the opening?' Ivy asked. 'Pleeeeeease?'

'I'm sure you can,' Bridget replied.

Ivy danced around, pointing her toes in a princess dress, as Ellie and Bridget made their way to the front door. Riley followed behind.

'Thanks for coming over.' He hugged Ellie first, then his sister.

'Thanks for having us. It has been so lovely to meet you, Becca,' Ellie said.

'It was lovely to meet you both, too.'

Bridget whispered in her brother's ear and he rolled his eyes.

'Goodbye, Bridget.'

'Bye, Auntie Bridget and Auntie Ellie!' Ivy curtsied as they left.

Both aunties pulled her in and showered her with kisses and Bridget made loud noises about how much she loved her. Ivy giggled and wriggled away from her.

As the door closed, I waited for the house to feel empty without their presence. But it didn't. It felt normal. I helped Riley to put the plates in the dishwasher in complete and utter silence. But not awkward silence, wondering when he was going to speak or whether I should say anything. Just easy silence.

'I'm sorry if Ellie and Bridget said something to make you

uncomfortable earlier,' Riley said, eventually. 'I heard you kind of go quiet.'

'No, it was fine.' I shrugged. 'Your sister and Ellie are the most adorable couple I've ever met in real life.'

'They're some craic, the two of them,' Riley agreed. 'Bridget is bonkers, but Ellie seems to keep her in line, most of the time.'

'You've not told them that you're struggling with your book, though? Bridget thinks you're nearly finished. I didn't tell them, obviously, about our joint writer's dysfunction.'

Riley rolled his eyes and sighed. 'Ah good, thanks for that. I haven't really told anyone about that, apart from you. And obviously my agent knows because of the distinct lack of words. Bridget always worries about me, you know. I thought when my book was published that it was great because she wouldn't have to worry any more. I want her to think I can do this whole writing thing.'

My body surged with pleasure at the thought of Riley sharing his secret with me. Only me.

'You can do this writing thing,' I said.

'What if I'm a one-novel wonder though? Like Chesney Hawkes,' he asked.

I snorted. 'With the one and only novel?'

Riley groaned. 'I'm serious.'

'Stop thinking like that,' I said. 'You're putting too much pressure on yourself, Ches.'

'I know, I know,' he sighed. 'And Bridget and Ellie would always help, if I asked them to. They always offer to babysit so I can have more time to write. And Ivy adores them.'

'I can see why,' I said. 'I think I do, too.'

'I'm glad,' he said. 'But you don't have to go to all the stuff they asked you to. Only if you want to. Apart from the opening night – we'll all need to go to that. They've been working so hard on it.'

'Have you helped out with the renovation work?' I asked.

'Yeah, I've been over a fair bit, chipping in with building beds and furniture, mainly. We've managed to do a lot of it ourselves, just using tradespeople for some of the trickier jobs.'

'A man of many talents,' I said. 'Is there anything you can't do, Riley O'Connell?'

'I can't sing to save myself,' he confessed.

'Oh, I know that already. I heard you warbling yesterday in the kitchen,' I teased.

Riley, who had been washing a cup at the sink, turned around, splashing me with some water. 'Hey!' He smiled. 'I'll have you know, I was one of the lead roles in my school show when I was younger. Doc, the main dwarf in Snow White and the Seven Dwarfs. Belted out a great rendition of "Hi-Ho" with the rest of the crew. But that was before my voice broke.'

I laughed and flicked him with a tea towel as he looked around, before hastily grabbing a pair of oven gloves. He looked down at them and frowned, unsure of his next move.

'What are you going to do, bake me until I surrender?' I arched my eyebrow.

He let out a hearty laugh and grabbed the red–and–white checked tea towel from my hands.

'Right from under my nose!' I protested.

'Aha!' he delighted, flicking me with the tea towel. 'How the tables have turned. I have disrobed you.'

I blushed before meeting his gaze again.

'Pretty sure that means something else,' I laughed, dodging the towel. 'This isn't fair; I am unarmed in combat!'

He stopped, pulled open a drawer and threw me a cream tea towel sporting a picture of a bunny. I caught it in one hand.

'Fight!' he ordered, moving closer to me, his eyes narrowed. 'Or the bunny gets it.'

We stood inches apart, almost touching, as the door creaked open. I looked down at Ivy, who stood in the door frame. She gazed up at us, a hint of confusion in her eyes, before frowning as she glanced up at the kitchen cupboards.

'Mammy's,' she said, pointing up.

Riley stopped in his tracks.

'Mammy what?' He knelt down to look Ivy in the eye and tucked her hair behind her ear.

'Becca put Mammy's cup in the wrong place.'

I gasped. Was Ivy annoyed? Upset? Distraught? I searched her small, innocent face for a hint of her reaction to the mistake I hadn't known I'd made. Riley watched her intently, weighing up what to say.

'I'm so sorry,' I said, carefully, moving towards the cupboard to try to fix whatever I'd done wrong. 'I didn't mean to . . .'

'It's fine,' Riley reassured me.

He reached up and moved the cup to the row above.

'That better?'

'That's it.' Ivy smiled. 'Back where it should be. For when she comes back.'

I looked at Riley to catch his reaction. His body flinched slightly before he lifted Ivy off the ground and swung her upside down above his head. Her white tights and princess dress flopped above her head and she giggled and shrieked.

'Daddy! Put me dowwwwwn!'

'Only if you say I'm the best daddy you've ever had in your whole life,' he said, his eyes lighting up with laughter.

'You're the only daddy I've ever had,' Ivy giggled.

'Exactly so I must be the best!'

Ivy laughed so hard that I thought she might throw up. I couldn't help but smile at the infectious sound. But as I looked at Mammy's cup and thought of Ivy's reaction, I started to wonder what I'd managed to let myself get in the middle of here.

Mind you, whatever it was, it couldn't be worse than what I had been running away from myself.

13

'Yoga mat?'

'Check.'

'Water bottle?'

'Check. Dignity?'

'You might as well leave it here.' Riley grinned at me.

'Aw gawd, I know! I'll be terrible!'

'I'm joking! You'll be grand, Becca. There are other beginners here, I promise.'

Riley had somehow managed to persuade me to come along to his yoga class, after dropping Ivy at nursery. He said it helped with the 'flow of his writing'. I'd protested that it wasn't in our timetable, but he eventually wore me down. I wondered if it would help with the flow of my writing, too. We'd continued with our daily writing sprints and they seemed to be working; Riley was getting more done and I felt like I was contributing a little to his progress. I had added more to my word count, too, and felt like I was getting there. Somewhere, anyway.

I had to give him credit; it was the most beautiful setting for a yoga class I'd ever seen. Not that I'd been to any yoga classes before, but I imagined it would kick the ass of any others. Nestled at the foot of the mountains beside a small stream, it was like something out of some mindfulness magazine.

Maybe this would be just what I needed. Breathe, relax, think of my story and then write my ass off when I get back. That was my new plan.

'This is Eimear, our instructor,' Riley introduced me. 'This is Becca, our new recruit.'

'Nice to meet you, Becca,' Eimear said, her brown eyes sparkling in the sunshine. She adjusted her sports bra and laid her mat down at the front of the class. I'd never seen someone with such a flat stomach before. Maybe I did need to stick in at yoga, after all.

'You too,' I called to Eimear, moving my mat up to the back of the class.

'Where are you off to?' Riley shouted.

He was right up at the front, just under Eimear's nose.

Teacher's pet.

'I might have agreed to take part but I don't need everyone watching my fat ass while I downward dog, thank you very much,' I called.

Riley laughed, his green eyes sparkling. 'Have it your way.'

He turned to face the front and I watched him lie down on his mat and start stretching. He laughed easily with Eimear and the other members of the class – all women, and all of whom wanted to chat with Riley before class started. I felt

97

like charging for tickets and telling them to form an orderly queue.

'Riley! How's Ivy doing?'

'Great to see you, Riley! How's the book coming along?'

'Riley, you're looking super trim,' one woman winked. Actually winked.

I tried to stop myself from rolling my eyes. Mr Bloody Popularity. I tried to ignore the pang of jealousy threatening to rear its ugly head. How pathetic that I wanted to shout about the fact that I was living with him at the top of my lungs. As though he were mine, which he absolutely was not. I sat down on my mat instead and took a sip of water, wondering where I would pee if I needed to. We really were at one with nature. I guessed I would need to hide behind a rock or something. I made a mental note to limit my water intake.

'Are we still on for our date?'

My head flew up so quickly, I almost got whiplash. Riley was going on a date with someone? He hadn't mentioned it. I mean, of course, I would be totally fine with him going on a date. He was allowed, after all. I was only his writing partner. And friend. It was nothing more than that.

'Sure thing.' He grinned.

Of course he was talking to the gorgeous Eimear, with her washboard stomach, perky boobs and the Irish eyes that were most certainly smiling. Damn her.

It stung a little. He might not have shared any details about his relationship with Ivy's mum, but I thought he was confiding in me. I was the only one he'd told about his writer's dysfunction, after all. But he hadn't mentioned dating. Maybe it was for his novel, I realised. Maybe it was all part of his plan to feel inspired again. Research, you could call it.

I held on tightly to the straws I was metaphorically clutching.

'Looking forward to it,' she smiled. 'OK, class, if everyone wants to sit on their mats, we'll get started.'

I felt a lot more tense than I had when I'd bloody arrived, thanks to the instructor. I watched Eimear moving her bendy body into impossible positions, with Riley just one move behind. They would make the perfect couple, I groaned.

I rolled my eyes at the girl next to me as I struggled to keep up with the ups and downs and breathing and warrior poses. She smiled politely back at me, but I knew I was distracting her.

I hated the bloody downward dog. Everyone else seemed to take it in their stride, but I felt my whole body shaking beneath my pathetic pale arms. They'd never had any strength in them; even when I carried shopping bags for too long, my arms felt like jelly for ages afterwards.

But being reminded to breathe what felt like every sixty seconds – that was good. That's what I needed. Someone to remind me to breathe in and out. To clear all the thoughts from my mind.

Breathe. Stretch. Breathe. Downward dog (oh fuck off). Stretch it out. Breathe in and out. Stretch. As we progressed towards the end of the class, I did feel slightly better. My arms were reaching places they couldn't when the class first started.

I watched Riley from the back of the class. As did the rest of the women. I spotted a black tattoo peeking out from under his T-shirt as he stretched towards the sky. He bent forward in one smooth motion and struck another 'warrior' pose with such ease. I'd never seen someone of his build move so flexibly before and, despite my lack of skills and interest in yoga, I was impressed.

The woman next to me gazed at him, too, while the class winker was practically drooling at the sight of his tanned thighs flipping expertly between the moves. I inwardly tutted like a petulant child. I was used to having Riley all to myself. I knew women would want him, but seeing it in front of my eyes was a different matter. His mere presence seemed to dominate the whole class. Or at least, it certainly felt that way.

I would not be one of these women. I was Riley's friend, after all. I wasn't looking for romance when I came here, and I certainly wasn't chasing Rathcliffe's most eligible bachelor. And with Eimear around, I clearly wouldn't get very far anyway. As she called for the 'shavasana' at the end of the session, I lay down and hugged my legs into my body.

When I came to Ireland, I'd been expecting to find a woman who enjoyed stretching it out at yoga, loved her adorable daughter and was an accomplished writer but, most of all, made me laugh and feel calm.

And just because Riley had a penis didn't mean that I couldn't have all that. It just meant that I needed to reset my expectations back to what they'd been at the start.

I couldn't get carried away with it all.

Note to self: stop thinking about Riley's penis.

14

'It's for me, it's for me!! Daaaaadddy!! Daaaddddyyy!'

Ivy shrieked at the top of her lungs. I was barely awake, despite the whole still-not-sleeping-well thing, but flung back my duvet and bolted to see where the screams were coming from. I quickly located her, bouncing up and down at the front door, clutching an envelope. She beamed up at me, her tiny white teeth poking out from under her lips. She wore her pink dressing gown over her mermaid nightdress and small fluffy unicorn slippers.

I reached down to take the envelope from Ivy's outstretched hand, just as Riley flew from the bathroom, wrapping a towel around his waist, his tanned torso still dripping wet from the shower.

I tried not to look. But failed. Was that an actual *six pack*? Oh. My. Days.

'Jaysus, Ivy, what in the name of the wee man—'

He looked at Ivy then up at me. I raised my eyebrows.

'Sorry, Becca, I totally forgot you were here for a second,' he said.

'What in the name of the wee man?' I repeated, looking down at his towel and smiling at him.

He blushed and fixed it back around his waist. I averted my gaze back to Ivy's hands.

'I've never had post before!' Ivy screamed and jumped up and down, her face flushed with excitement. 'I. Can't. Wait. To. OPEN IT!'

'It looks like a wedding invitation.' I frowned, glancing at the silky ivory-coloured envelope.

'Woooow! Can I go?!' she asked, still bouncing up and down. I gazed down at the mat and saw another invitation, addressed to 'Mr Riley O'Connell and Ms Becca Taylor'.

What on earth . . . I leaned down to pick the invitation up from the mat.

'There's another one,' I announced. 'Addressed to . . . us.'

'Us?' Riley said, strolling forward to check it out, a hand clutching his towel to ensure it didn't fall off. He stood beside me, smelling of the citrus shower gel from the bathroom, and gently placed a hand on the small of my back. Surprised, I almost jumped at his touch.

'Sorry,' he said. 'Forgot my hand was wet.'

'No, it's fine. I just . . .'

Our eyes met and I looked away, not finishing the sentence. What I'd felt was chemistry zipping through my body. It was unmistakable. But Riley barely seemed to notice.

'Will you do the honours?' he asked. 'Just in case my towel falls down.'

He threw me a good-natured grin while I blushed, unable to form a sentence to reply. Ivy bounced up and down beside us, completely oblivious to my sudden hot flushes.

'It's for the opening of Bridget and Ellie's business,' I stuttered, as I read the invitation.

'Brilliant,' he said. 'They've been counting down the days.'

'Let's open yours, Ivy,' I said.

Ivy grinned while I read the details to her as Riley turned straight back to the bathroom.

'See you when I'm better dressed!' he called out.

'I hope Mammy's back for the party so she can see me cut the big ribbon,' Ivy mused quietly. 'I wish she was here. I miss her.'

I stood still for a moment, unsure what to say.

There was very little mention of Jackie in the house during the day, but at night time, as I lay awake pretending to sleep, I heard Ivy creep into Riley's bedroom in the middle of the night. He'd try to put her back to bed but she'd protest that she was scared. He relented and let her sleep in beside him when she said she missed her mammy.

I pretended not to have heard the same conversation over and over again every night since I'd arrived.

'I know, sweetheart,' I said, eventually. 'I'm here if you ever want to talk about it. I miss someone that I was very close to as well.'

'Who?' she asked.

'My best friend in the whole world,' I said. 'Her name was Rae.'

'Did she leave too? Like my mum?'

'She did,' I said.

'Will she come back?'

I swallowed the lump in my throat. Why had I brought Rae into this? I didn't know what Riley had told Ivy about her mum, life, death and everything in between. It was dangerous territory. I should have known better.

I looked into her eyes.

'No, she won't,' I said. 'But she's always with me because I always think about her. So I carry her with me in my heart.'

Ivy frowned, confused with the answer. She looked up at me with her big blue eyes and whispered, 'Can I tell you a secret?'

It was a real whisper. Not like the shouting whispers in the morning as she tried to wake me up while pretending not to try and wake me up.

'Yes,' I said. 'Of course you can.'

'You can't tell anyone. Not even Daddy. Cross your heart and hope to die?'

'Cross my heart,' I said, without hesitation, shaking her hand to seal the deal.

Ivy leaned towards me and, as we were just about forehead to forehead, whispered, 'Mammy's coming back for me. She promised. We'll all be a family again. So maybe she *will* be back for the party and see me cut the ribbon.'

'Oh,' I said.

I wasn't sure what else to say. I had to tiptoe very carefully around all my words and phrases with Ivy. It was a minefield. One wrong move and I'd blow everything up.

'Yup.' Ivy smiled confidently. 'Mammy said so.'

'When did she tell you this?' I asked, hoping it was a safe enough question.

She smiled sweetly at me. 'When I saw her yesterday.'

And with that, she skipped off to get ready by her 'own self in my room, because I'm a big girl now.'

15

I thought about Ivy's confession when Riley was reading her a story at bedtime that evening. I'd kept my promise and hadn't said anything to Riley. The more I thought about it, I realised it wasn't possible that Ivy had seen her mum. She'd been at nursery the day before, while Riley and I tried to concentrate on writing. I collected her from nursery while Riley got dinner ready. We watched a TV show together in the evening, while Ivy was in bed.

It couldn't have been a more ordinary day in the life of Riley and Ivy. Obviously, I was only gatecrashing for a while, but I knew there had been no mention of Jackie. Or much else, for that matter. I didn't ask questions and very little information was offered. I didn't want to come across like the obsessive house guest who kept tabs on everything. It was bad enough that I was living under his roof, contributing very little while trying to inspire him with his writing. I wondered if I was a bit of a bad influence on Riley. We kept going off on tangents about absolutely nothing in particular, to the point where I was almost late collecting Ivy from nursery.

He didn't ask me to talk about my problems and I didn't ask him about Jackie. It was our unspoken agreement. We were both protecting our own small pieces of heartbreak.

As the full day flashed through my mind, I realised there was no way Ivy could have seen Jackie.

The poor soul obviously missed her mum so much she was fantasising about the family coming back together. There was no harm in it, I guessed. It wasn't like Ivy was hurting anyone. She clearly knew not to mention it to her dad in case it upset him.

I decided to put it out of my mind as my phone began vibrating insistently in my pocket. I moved quickly across to the door leading to the garden, to answer without disturbing Ivy's storytime.

'Joanna,' I said. 'How are you getting on?'

'Your class are all angels,' Joanna said. 'But Mrs Pender is the actual devil. She's throwing her weight around, demanding all these extra lesson plans. The term's practically finished so I don't know what she's playing at!'

Reality coming back to bite again. This was why I usually avoided answering the phone. I'd been trying not to think about work since I'd arrived in Rathcliffe. I wanted to immerse myself in mountain air, writing books and applying facemasks with Ivy in the evening, while Riley gave her the bedtime countdown. Nice things.

I felt a wave of guilt every time I thought about the voicemails stacking up from Rae's mum, which I hadn't got around to answering at all. Not even a quick 'oh shite, the mountains are so large I can't hear you' text seemed to appease Linda.

'Sounds about right.' I rolled my eyes. 'She's such a bitch. I've not heard a peep from her. She never replied to my email.'

'We're all having to stay for hours after class time. She's out of control! Listen, your phone's cracking up. Can you hear me? Will I pop round to your flat?'

'No, don't come around. I'm not in the flat, Joanna. I'm . . . I'm in Ireland.'

I strolled along the path at the side of the house, glancing up at the mountains and around at the fields of green that danced all around me.

'What the fuck are you doing there?' she asked.

'Visiting a friend.'

'Oh. Well, I was thinking about speaking to the union. She can't make us do all these extra hours unpaid.'

My whole body felt heavy as she kept talking about work.

'I'm sorry, I have to go, Joanna. Good luck on the whole taking the bitch down thing. I'm totally behind you. I need to go though, I have a call coming through.'

I hung up before she had the chance to protest.

16

The scent of aftershave smacked me in the nostrils as I pushed open the front door at Bellinder Cottage the next evening. I'd gone for a walk to clear my head and give Riley some peace to write, while Ivy was at Bridget and Ellie's house for their usual Thursday sleepover. I thought about my own ideas for character development in my head as I pounded my feet on the pavements, trying to block out all I'd left behind at home.

Riley was singing at the top of his lungs in the bathroom, with a navy-blue shirt hung on the outside of the door. He was getting ready to go out. And, judging by the smell of aftershave and freshly ironed shirt, he was going 'out out'.

The pangs of jealousy that threatened at the yoga class came tumbling back as I pictured him all dressed for a big date. He was probably taking Eimear out for a fancy meal somewhere. I sighed.

Lucky me, I had the evening all to myself by the looks of it.

The bathroom door flew open as I passed it, whacking me on the shoulder.

'Shit!' Riley called. 'Sorry, Becca, I didn't know you were in.'

He stood in front of the bathroom mirror, again wearing only a towel, with a clean-shaven face. He'd missed a bit of shaving foam on his neck. I didn't tell him.

'It's fine, I've got another shoulder,' I called as I sauntered into my own room, like I didn't care where he was going.

He knocked on my door five minutes later, just as I'd scraped my hair back and pulled on my comfiest trousers and hooded jumper.

'Come in,' I called.

And there he was, this time wearing the blue shirt that had been hanging on the door, the one that was now showing off his tanned muscular arms, ready for his big date. I was used to seeing him in various Gaelic football tops, shorts and hoodies, which always looked good on him. But this was a whole new level. I gulped back the disappointment.

I wondered how he would break the news about his big date with Eimear. He would probably just casually mention that he was going out with her, as though it wasn't even a thing. No big deal. Not that it was a thing. I was only his house guest, after all. But still.

'Oh,' he said, looking me up and down. 'I didn't think you'd change so quickly.'

'Sorry, monsieur, were you expecting me to wear a glittering ball gown for my solo evening at Bellinder Cottage?'

110

I teased, sitting on the side of the bench. 'I take it you're off out for the night?'

'Solo? Don't you want to come out with me?' He frowned. 'You said the other day you'd like to get out and see a bit more.'

'And you said I should,' I remembered. 'But we didn't agree anything. You want me to . . . tag along tonight?'

'I said *we* should. Did I forget to suggest Thursday night? Shit. I did in my head.'

My heart began beating a little faster. He wasn't abandoning me for a hot date, he was inviting me to come with him.

'Erm, well, yes, I'd love to go out. Where are we going? Who are we meeting?'

'Great.' Riley smiled, his shoulders relaxing. 'We're not meeting anyone. I just thought you could do with a proper night out in Rathcliffe, while you're here. There are two pubs, so it'll take all of twenty minutes. You've barely been out apart from walking to and from nursery.'

'That's not true; I also go to the coffee shop,' I protested.

'Come on then, get ready,' he urged, grinning.

'What, no hoodie and pyjama bottoms allowed?' I joked, looking down at my comfy trousers.

'Whatever you like.' He shrugged, as though he couldn't care less what I wore.

As good as Riley looked, this was obviously not hot date territory. I'd guilted him into taking me out because he felt sorry for me always hanging around with nothing to do. It wasn't like the date night he had lined up for the lovely Eimear, I could bet.

'OK,' I called, as he left the room to let me get changed. 'I'll be ready in a minute!'

And even though it was another one of Riley's pity invites, I was looking forward to going out.

I didn't want him to think I was one of those girls who took forever and a day to get ready. I wanted to emerge after five minutes looking utterly fabulous in an I-woke-up-like-this kind of way. Obviously (and unfortunately) he knew what I looked like first thing in the morning. But this was a chance to show him what I was made of. Or could be. In ten minutes or less.

It was a bloody tall order.

He was wearing his 'out out' shirt, so I had to find something fancy enough to pass for a night out but not too over the top – I was in a small town, after all, and didn't want to be the talk of it. I flicked on my hair straighteners to heat up and flung my suitcase open, riffling through it. Had I even brought something suitable for a night out? I remembered packing my shortest skirt and heels when I'd been pissed and promptly removing them as the hangover kicked in. Aha! But I had replaced them with black skinny jeans, a long-sleeved cream blouse with jazzy gold buttons up the front and on the cuffs and a pair of sparkly heels. I pulled my hoodie over my head and started my transformation. Tugging at my hair, I willed it to straighten quickly, and then patted and prodded my face with make-up, finishing with a healthy dose of mascara and red lipstick, hoping I looked vampy rather than trampy.

Glancing out of the window at the early evening sky in Rathcliffe, I saw that the clouds were heavy and threatening rain, so once I was ready, I grabbed my jacket and sprayed on some perfume, throwing a dazzling smile to the mirror to see how my lippy looked.

I checked my phone. My look had been achieved in around twelve minutes, but as I surveyed myself, I was fairly content. It looked more of a fifteen-minute makeover, so that was something.

I stepped out into the hallway, where Riley was scrolling through his phone. He looked up at me. I'd hoped for his eyes to enlarge and pop out of his head, like a cartoon, but instead he just grinned.

'I'll be fighting the lads off with a stick when they see you tonight.'

Translation: I'm not interested, but other folk might be, I suppose.

'I can fight them off myself,' I quipped, breezing past him.

It was time to show Riley my confident side. I was *funny*. Or I had been fucking funny, at some point, I just couldn't quite remember how. Those conversations Riley and I used to have on messages had been funny. I'd made him laugh, I was sure of it. Tonight, I was determined to show Riley I could still be the me that had made him invite me here in the first place. I was more than just the zombie lady wandering around his house in various colours of hoodies.

I was going to sparkle again. I could do this.

'So a night out on the tiles in the bright lights of Rathcliffe,' I teased as we wandered up the road.

It wasn't my best line, but it was a start.

It was drizzling with rain as we left Bellinder Cottage. Riley whistled as we wandered along, waving every so often to cars that passed us. Everyone seemed to know Riley. I wondered how much he'd told them about me, his crazy house guest.

'Think you can handle it?' he asked. 'You big city girls probably have your pick of bars but this one is the best, I promise you. Not sure you'll be able to hack the country drinking though.'

'Is that a challenge?' I asked, raising an eyebrow.

He glanced at me. 'Would you accept it if it was?'

'Pretty sure I could drink you under the table, Riley O'Connell.' I nodded confidently. 'I'm always the last girl standing on any night out.'

'Is that so?' he asked. 'You should really put your money where your mouth is then.'

'Bring it on,' I replied. 'I bet you'll be on your back before I am.'

Riley cocked his head to the side and grinned. 'Promises, promises.'

'Oh!' My hands flew to my face. 'I didn't mean *that*.'

'Be still my beating, romance-writing heart,' he joked. 'Right, up this way.'

He gestured as we came to a fork in the road.

I frowned. The path he was pointing to looked like a muddy dirt road, far from the warm and welcoming pub in the town I'd passed a few times on my way to the coffee shop.

'Up there?' I raised my eyebrow. 'Are you planning to take

me up a muddy lane so you can murder me in a field and bury the evidence?'

'Absolutely,' he replied. 'After I've had a pint though, obviously.'

I glanced down tentatively at my heels. They very much weren't made for walking, never mind stomping along a muddy path. Going out on the town in Rathcliffe was clearly not the same as Glasgow. A pair of wellies may have been more appropriate attire. It was all right for men; Riley always went between his vast choice of two pairs of shoes: what he called his 'gutties' (i.e. his pair of trainers) and black boots; tonight was the latter.

Riley powered on ahead while I struggled to keep my wee toes out of the mud. He barely glanced back, strolling ahead confidently, promising we were about to uncover the town's best kept secret.

The rain started to intensify and I yelped. Before I knew what was happening, I felt my legs give way. I put my hands down on either side to try and break my fall but wasn't very successful. My arse cracked against something surprisingly sharp, and I toppled backwards into the mud.

'Help!' I cried out feebly.

I lay on the ground, unsure if I could move. The mud felt surprisingly cold and unsurprisingly slimy against my skin. Had I broken something? I felt stiff, sore and, most of all, absolutely fucking mortified. My face burned.

'Jaysus, Becca, what the hell happened?'

Riley appeared above me, frowning in concern as I lay there.

'Oh, no big deal, just decided to throw myself into the mud to see what it felt like. Look, I'm fine,' I insisted, tentatively moving my fingers and then my arms. 'I think it must've been a rock or something.'

I looked like I was trying to make a mud angel.

He leaned down, his face inches from mine.

'Do you think you'll be able to move?' he asked. 'I'm going to try and pull you up.'

Riley frowned down at me in concern. My arse was throbbing.

'Yes, go for it,' I said.

After a one, two, three he hauled me up and a sharp pain shot through my body.

'Aaaowch,' I screeched, but found myself in a standing position. My hand flew to the back of my head, and I realised my hair was caked in mud.

Just as I stretched my other hand to check how sore my bum was, the two gold buttons on my blouse popped open, exposing my bra and cleavage to the world. Actually, not the world. Worse, just to Riley, who copped an eyeful and then placed his hands over his eyes as though they were burning, while mumbling that he promised he hadn't seen a thing.

We both knew otherwise.

I hastily buttoned up my shirt, cursing the faded old bra that had been hiding beneath it. In my attempts to dazzle Riley and prove I could get ready quickly and still look utterly beautiful in ten minutes or less, I'd disregarded the idea of changing my bra and was sporting one that, at one point or another, had actually been cream but was now very much grey.

Zipping up my jacket to contain my cleavage, I winced, with Riley taking his cue to open his eyes again.

'Come on.' He moved towards me and gently took my arm as though I was an old lady. 'Do you think you can walk? What hurts the most?'

'My pride,' I admitted. 'And my arse feels like it's on fire.'

'Hot arse from Glasgow coming through!' he shouted, helping me as I hobbled towards the bar door. 'Come on, let's get you inside.'

'You just want your pint,' I grimaced as he opened the door to the pub. 'Maybe they'll let you skip the queue once they see your hot date hobbling in, covered in mud with a throbbing arse.'

'I'll take you home,' he promised. 'We'll get you a seat, then I'll nip home and get the car so you don't have to walk.'

Riley helped as I hobbled towards the bar, lifting my arm to help me sit on the tall bar stool. My right arse cheek stung badly.

'No chance, I haven't even had a drink,' I groaned, looking down at my jacket and jeans, which were caked in mud, in dismay. 'And now I look like I've been for a mud bath. But I'm here for a good time, not a long time.'

'Well, Riley, what's the craic?' the barman asked.

'Well, John, this is my friend, Becca. She had a bit of a fall on our way here, hence the mud,' Riley said.

'Welcome to John the Craic-tist,' John said.

Despite the shooting pain down below and my less than conventional appearance, I snorted. 'Excuse me?'

'John the Craic-tist. That's the name of the bar,' Riley explained. 'Like John the Baptist but, you know, with all the Irish craic. And this is John.'

'That's the best pub name I've ever heard,' I laughed.

John smiled. 'I like her already.'

I caught a glimpse of myself in the mirror behind the bar and was horrified to see mud marks all over my face. Even worse, they looked like shite. Actual shite on my face. And maybe it was; I wasn't sure what was in that field, after all.

'Oh!' I exclaimed. 'I better go to the bathroom and try and fix myself up a bit.'

'Do you want me to come with you?' Riley asked.

'No two people of the opposite sex in the bathroom at one time,' John said, sternly. 'It's a house rule.'

'What?' Riley laughed. 'Since when?'

'Unfortunate incident a few months ago,' John replied, shaking his head, with a grave expression etched on his face. 'My missus was left traumatised, so she was. Let's just say, there could be a baby John the Craic-tist on the back of it. If they name it after where it was conceived, I mean; not that I was involved in any way.'

His stern face turned pink as I tried to cover up the laugh that threatened to escape.

'Seriously?' Riley almost choked as John handed him a pint. 'That actually happened in Rathcliffe?'

'Some of the things I've seen would burn your eyes, my

boy,' John said, shaking his head. 'So none of that here. What are you drinking, Becca?'

'I'll have a pint of your finest Guinness please, John. When in Rome and all that,' I said.

I followed the signs to the ladies' bathroom. Checking my reflection close up in the mirror, I sighed. The one time I'd tried to make a bloody effort, I'd ended up with a half-cracked arse, looking like I had shite on my face. Typical. I tried to wash the mud out of my hair under the tap, ignoring the throbbing when I bent to the side, and watched the water run brown. At least I was alone in the bathroom, mind you.

So much for being 'out out'. I looked like I'd been in the bloody wars.

'You all right in there?' Riley knocked at the door.

'Yes!' I called back. 'You better get away from here before John the Craic-tist's wife thinks we're cavorting. You'll get barred for life. I'll be out in a minute.'

I tidied myself up and hobbled back out to the bar, where Riley had a seat in the corner.

'Are you OK, big city girl?' he teased.

'I'm fine, I'm fine. Just a cracked arse and bruised ego.' I shrugged, lowering myself carefully onto my seat. Luckily, it was cushioned.

We chatted easily, with the Guinness going down so well that I forgot about my fall from grace. The booze seemed to numb the pain, too. We exchanged drinking stories, mainly centred around our university days. I wondered if, after a few pints, Riley would mention Jackie, but he didn't. Not one word

I talked about Rae, of course, because every good night out had been with her. She was the life and soul of every party.

'Listen,' he said, clearing his throat and leaning in towards me. 'If you ever wanted to talk about Rae, I'm a good listener.'

I mirrored his move, edging myself in towards him and resting my head on my hand, inches away from him. Evidently, the Guinness had kicked in.

'I know you are.' I smiled and spoke softly. 'And I do want to say thank you. You've . . . it's really helped knowing I have you on the end of the phone and now, here, in real life. Even though it wasn't what I was expecting, I'm glad I've stayed.'

'Pleasure is all mine.' He gazed at me, fuelling some flipping feelings in my stomach.

I felt myself blush and the moment hung between us for a few seconds before Riley glanced around the room and took a swig of his pint.

'I think we should get going,' he suggested. 'Call it a night.'
I nodded.

'Wow,' I said, wobbling as I stood. 'Not sure if it's the Guinness or the fact that I may have broken my arse, but I'm not . . . as steady as I thought. I'm going to nip to the loo before we go.'

Had I imagined that flicker of something between us? It had quickly been extinguished when Riley looked around the familiar faces in his local pub, where everybody knew his name. Perhaps it was just the booze working its unreliable magic.

As I made my way back from the ladies' room, the door flew open and a seemingly endless succession of glamorous females sauntered into the bar, all chattering excitedly amongst themselves. The combined scent of their perfumes almost knocked me off my feet. And amongst them, I spotted a familiar face.

But this time, Eimear had her make-up carefully and expertly applied and her pert boobs were on display for all to see in a low-cut gold top. The girls were out to play for the night, too, it seemed.

I stopped, twirling my mud-streaked hair around my fingers, as Riley moved to envelop the golden ball of loveliness, who I'm sure smelled like delicious sweet sunshine, in a hug. It played out in front of me as if in slow motion. The group of women all gave Riley long, lingering smiles of recognition, before chattering in low voices amongst themselves. Eimear was fixated firmly on Riley.

'Riley O'Connell!' she exclaimed in a high-pitched voice, practically jumping into his arms for a hug. 'Fancy meeting you here.'

'Good to see you, Eimear,' he replied.

She held onto the hug far longer than strictly necessary, squeezing her eyes shut before they sprang open again.

'Ach, sure that's right, it's Thursday so Ivy's away! I *completely* forgot you usually come here.' She smiled, batting her eyelashes. 'You should've said. I could join you?'

'Becca's here.' He lifted his hand to point towards the bathroom, where I stood completely still.

Ah, bollocks. He'd outed me to the gorgeous Eimear and now I was going to have to say hello, mud and all.

Without skipping a beat, she bounced over to me, flicking her hair behind her shoulder.

'Becca!' she said. 'Lovely to see you again, although, gosh, what's happened?'

I grimaced, looking down at myself. 'I know, I had a bit of a tumble in the mud on the way up the road. Guess I wanted to get a taste of real country living, you know? I'll be out milking cows in the field next.'

'Riley, you didn't take the walkway? Silly!' she punched him lightly on the arm but looked utterly delighted that he hadn't taken me up the walkway. In fact, she was beaming. 'He always takes me on the walkway when *we're* walking home, don't you, Riley?'

Ah, the walkway was *their* walkway. I'd fallen in fucking mud to avoid using their sacred walkway.

Riley's eyes shifted uncomfortably and he frowned slightly. 'Well, I—'

Oh, the awkwardness. Eimear was clearly annoyed that her boyfriend had taken me on a night out without telling her. I could have told her it was a pity invite but decided to keep my nose out of it. She was hardly going to be jealous over someone with mud in their grey bra, after all.

'I was just leaving,' I announced. 'Need to get this mud out of my hair. Riley, you can stay here and I'll see you . . . back there.'

Eimear's eyes popped hopefully as she glanced at Riley, but he shook his head.

'No, no, I'll take you back, Becca. Night, Eimear. See you soon.'

'Always such a gentleman.' Eimear smiled through her gritted teeth.

And with that, we left her standing there, all dressed up with a scowl on her face, while I went home with her man. I could see her point; I'd be pretty raging too.

The cold air hit me as soon as I left John the Craic-tist, and I pulled my rain jacket around my shoulders. My feet were sore from my sparkly heels, so I took them off.

'Here,' he said, squatting down in front of me.

'What the fuck are you doing?' I frowned as he stuck his bum out even further.

'A coal carry,' he said. 'Jump on.'

I laughed. 'Do you mean a piggyback?'

'Becca, I'm still squatting in front of you. Shit or get off the pot.'

'You're the one that looks like you're on the pot,' I giggled.

He turned around and laughed. 'I'm trying to be a gentleman here. A human taxi.'

'I'll break your back,' I said. 'Are you prepared for that? Ivy will come back tomorrow and we'll be hobbling around with sore arses and broken backs.'

'Just get on,' he urged. 'I do yoga. I can take it.'

I burst out laughing. '*I do yoga*,' I repeated in a gruff voice. 'As if you're a body builder. I'm not sure yoga will save you from the wrath of me plus six pints of Guinness, but you have been warned.'

'Don't knock the yoga.' He grinned. 'It can save you from all sorts of mud-based injuries. Maybe if you'd done more, you would have gracefully slipped into the splits on our way here.'

'Maybe if you'd taken me on the walkway, we could have skipped the mud and I wouldn't have looked like a pig snorting into a pint in the pub,' I replied.

'Are you in or out?' He squatted again.

I jumped up once, twice and then leapt on his back.

'Arrgh,' he said, stumbling forward.

'Arrgh,' I said, because the shooting pain in my bum was back with a vengeance. 'Told you I'm heavier than I look.'

'You're as light as a feather,' he replied.

'Because of all your yoga.'

'Obviously.'

Once we got into the rhythm of the piggyback, it worked. I bobbed happily on his back, blethering about a Glasgow nightclub I'd spent my university nights drinking in called The Garage, which featured a yellow car sticking out above the front door. He said I'd have to take him sometime.

'You'd love Glasgow,' I said. 'It's full of good banter.'

'You're full of good banter,' he replied.

And I smiled happily, thinking I'd achieved my goal for the evening.

We reached the main road and he stopped to shuffle me up his back. He strolled home, with me on his back, all the way to Bellinder Cottage.

I jumped down off his back at the front door.

'Thanks for the lift,' I said.

'That'll be eighteen quid you owe me,' Riley said, bending down to let me off his back.

'You can add it to my tab,' I said. 'I do need to start paying you, for letting me stay here.'

'Absolutely not,' he said, unlocking the door to Bellinder Cottage. 'You're my guest. Now, hurry up and take a shower. You still look like you've got shit on your face.'

The warm water cascaded over me as the mud and make-up fell away. I scrubbed at my skin while inspecting the large bruise that had already started to form on my bum. It was deep purple with some sort of circle in the middle of it, like I'd tumbled onto a sharp stone.

'Tell you what, I definitely won the bet though,' Riley said, as we sat in the living room later, both freshly washed, wearing our pyjamas, still fairly full of Guinness while sharing a packet of biscuits.

'How's that?' I asked, shovelling another chocolate bourbon into my mouth.

'I had you on your back within five minutes of taking you out,' he quipped.

'Wouldn't be the first time,' I quipped, standing up to head to bed for another night of pretending to sleep. 'Good night, Riley O'Connell.'

'Good night, Becca Taylor.'

17

The next morning, I lay under my bright yellow bedspread waiting for sounds of life from Riley. My head was pounding a little, my mouth felt dry, and I really needed to pee, but I couldn't bring myself to get up. Riley revelled in his Friday morning lie-ins and I didn't want to wake him. Usually Ivy was up at the crack of dawn, with the cheeriest voice known to man, asking endless questions. He answered them all while fetching her breakfast, encouraging her to get dressed by herself before attempting to do her hair. I had taken over that job as soon as I'd seen his dismal attempt at pigtails.

He deserved a lie-in. So I crept around my room in my PJs, bundling all my dirty clothes into the corner before sitting down – carefully, to avoid any further bruising on my behind – on the bed to write.

I stared at the Word document on my laptop and read back the last thing I'd written in *Queen Bee*. The two girls, Anna and Rosie, were having a major argument, which led to Anna storming off to the side of the stage. Rosie's cheeks burned as she was left standing alone, centre stage. I started writing the next scene when my phone pinged.

Riley: Are you alive?

I smiled. I'd missed Riley's messages. We'd fired them back and forth constantly as friends, but now we were housemates, there was no need for the texts.

Me: No.
Riley: Shame. I'll just have to eat all these freshly made pancakes by myself then.

I sniffed the air and, sure enough, there was some sort of deliciousness floating through it.

Me: Ah, what's this? I'm ever-so-slowly coming back to life. Chocolate spread?
Riley: Hell yeah. I have a child, remember. Chocolate eating is her favourite sport.
Me: Mine too. Beats all that yoga nonsense. Extra strong coffee?
Riley: You knows it.

I pulled on my hoodie and dashed to the loo. As I was washing my hands, I checked my reflection in the mirror. I looked like a ghost, at best, verging on a zombie. The dark circles under my eyes threatened to expose my lack of sleep, so I

dashed back to the room and quickly smeared on some foundation to disguise myself before heading out to the breakfast table.

'Madame,' Riley greeted me, standing up at one side of the
kitchen table. 'Breakfast is served. Take a seat.'

In the centre of the table lay a stack of pancakes, strawber-
ries, butter, jam, chocolate spread and a steaming pot of coffee.

'I'm literally in heaven right now,' I declared, pouring the
black coffee into a cup and inhaling its delicious smell.

'I'm going to write my balls off today,' Riley declared,
spreading butter on his pancake. 'Get this show on the road.
My agent is pestering me. She sent me an email this morning
with the subject heading "Wherefore art thou, Riley?" I didn't
want to point out that wherefore actually means "why" and
not "where". Although, why is a good question, too, I guess.'

'Wherefore art thou such a literary geek?' I replied, grabbing a pancake and knife to spread all the chocolatey goodness
over it.

He sighed. 'A geek would know what to write. I wish I
could just write the way I did with my last novel. Leroy and
Alice just kind of came to life on the page. It was like I wasn't
writing it at all, you know? They were telling *me* their story.
I just had to shut up, listen and write.'

'I kind of know what you mean. My characters, Rosie and
Anna, they're constantly bickering. I feel like I'm in the middle
of it, like I'm actually the referee instead of the writer.'

'See, you do know! Other people don't get it. When I talk
to Bridget about my writing, she just tells me to get my head
out of my arse and get a real job.'

'She doesn't mean it,' I said, feeling more human with every sip of my warm coffee. 'She is bursting with pride over her baby brother with his glittering writing career. Have you told her you're struggling with your second book yet?'

'I'm not struggling today,' he vowed. 'Told you, I'm going to write my balls off.'

I hoped that was the case.

'I'm going to write in my room today,' I said. 'If you don't mind. I started and I'm kind of getting into it.'

I couldn't tell Riley that he was distracting me, just by being him. I thought the more I got to know him, the less attracted I would be. But, the truth was, it was getting worse. His kindness wasn't a one-off, he really was that nice. All the time. Plus, his jokes were getting *funnier*. Even his singing was starting to sound better, even though I knew deep down it was awful. Worse still, he was getting hotter. Every time he moved near me, I felt the hairs on the back of my neck stand on end. If he spoke too closely to me, my lips pursed and I felt a shiver up my back. When he picked up the TV remote and asked if I wanted to watch a film, it was all I could do to stop myself from throwing myself at his mercy. And he was completely oblivious to it all. He could still function, quite clearly, in my presence.

I had to snap myself out of it to be useful to him on our writers' retreat, but I'd been on a bit of a roll this morning. I gave myself a pat on the back for being so sensible and prioritising my writing career, as Riley shrugged back at me.

'Sure,' he said casually. 'Write wherever it works best.'

'Unless you think I'm your muse,' I said. 'And you'll struggle to write without me by your side.'

He grinned. 'I think I'll survive. I'm planning to do two thousand words by eleven a.m. Think you're up to the challenge?'

'Ooooh,' I said. 'Pretty sure I can. Let me just finish this heavenly coffee and we'll get straight to it, then I'll be ready to beat you.'

'Not if I beat you first.' He grinned.

As I settled down to write, I could hear Riley tapping on his keyboard from the office. I smiled and continued with where I'd left my story. I was completely absorbed by the time the alarm sounded, indicating it was eleven a.m. Riley appeared at my bedroom door and leaned against it.

'Pens and pencils down, class,' he said.

'Oooh, I was just getting to a good bit,' I protested. 'How many words?'

'Just short of target.' He grinned. 'You?'

I checked my laptop. 'One thousand eight hundred and ninety-eight.'

'Good going,' he said. 'Let's go again.'

But this time, I couldn't focus. Instead, I looked out at the view from my bedroom at Bellinder Cottage. It was so peaceful. So idyllic. So inspiring. I willed all sorts of creative prose to roll off my fingers onto my keyboard, but instead I sat back and scrolled through social media on my phone. That was another thing I couldn't really do with Riley around: skive off.

PLOT TWIST

Eventually, I gave up writing altogether. I strained to hear Riley's tap tapping of the keyboard, but the sound had ceased.

Me: How are your balls?

Riley: Flying off here.

Me: Great! But not sure I believe you . . . Haven't heard much typing since the last sprint.

Riley: You're right. I'm screwed. You?

Me: I've been watching videos of cute dogs on repeat. SOS.

Riley: Let's get out of here. Fancy more coffee?

Me: You read my freaking mind.

18

I knew the peace couldn't last forever. The email reply I'd been dreading landed in my inbox.

I'd tried to forget the message I'd sent to Mrs Pender about my sudden leave of absence, but the time had come to face the music. The one-word response danced on my laptop: 'Noted', with a link inviting me to an online meeting. I frowned. Could she ask me to attend a meeting when I was absent from work? I wasn't sure. I hovered over the button to accept before pressing it. I guess I had to, she was my boss after all.

Reality came back to bite when I least expected it. Reminders of what I was running from pinged constantly on my phone during the day, so I often switched it off. The mountains, standing proud and tall in the distance, came in handy when I was looking for an excuse not to converse with people.

'Reception is shite here', I'd tap on my phone at three o'clock in the morning, squinting at my screen in the dark. 'You'll probably get this message in the middle of the night. My phone seems to come alive then. Lol.'

Sometimes Adam responded, even as the shadows bounced around my bedroom in Bellinder Cottage. Linda had gone through old photo albums in the attic and he shared the pictures with me. My heart felt heavy flicking through the images of Rae. There was one of us together in our swimming costumes, arms draped around one another, in front of a paddling pool in their back garden. Adam stood awkwardly beside us, armed with an ice lolly, as Rae tried to block him out of the picture. When I closed my eyes, I could practically feel the sun beaming down on us as we took turns perfecting our cartwheels in the garden before cooling down in the pool.

I scrolled through my own pictures and forwarded them to Adam in response. I had several selfies of us grinning manically at the camera and pulling funny faces, along with days away, nights out and holiday snaps. Sometimes Adam and I commented on the pictures, united in our combined happy childhood memories, where Rae looked so happy. So alive.

Other times, we didn't say a word.

Continuing my tradition of blocking out my real life, I snapped my laptop shut.

I'd been looking forward to this day for ages. We were going to Dublin for Riley's author event and I couldn't wait to see him in action. I wasn't going to let my bitch-boss-from-hell spoil my good mood.

Riley dropped Ivy at nursery and returned, whistling away as he came through the front door.

'Whistling while you work there, Doc?' I teased.

'You better believe it,' he replied. 'Are you ready for the big event?'

'Can't wait,' I said.

'Let's leave in the next hour or so. We can wander around and go for lunch before it starts,' he said.

I'd never been to Dublin before. It had always been on my wish list so I couldn't wait to get there. I packed a bag with my writing notebook and laptop, as well as some snacks I'd bought for our road trip. As I took my seat in Riley's car, I set my bag at my feet and waited for him to lock up.

He climbed into the car and closed the door behind him, turning on the engine.

'Ready?' he asked.

'Yup.'

Despite having lived in the same house as Riley for the last couple of weeks, the smaller space of his car seemed more intimate. My arm tingled as it sat close to Riley's and I scolded myself. It was no different to being in the house, really. I rolled down my window to let some air in as Riley navigated the roads to the motorway like an expert. The greenery flashed by in a haze of beauty and I sighed contentedly. Everything felt so much more relaxed in amongst all the beauty. And I wasn't just talking about Riley.

'So what exactly happens at these author events?' I asked. 'What will you do?'

'There's a host at the event who introduces the authors and then hands over to me. I'll read an extract or two from *The*

Fall Out and then the host asks questions and then invites the audience to ask stuff too,' he explained.

'Is there anything you want me to ask you?'

'What do you mean?'

'I can be your mole in the audience. I'll ask anything you want so you can make the most of it. We could make you sound really good. I mean, you are really good, obviously, but we can say something to really impress your agent and the audience.'

He looked ahead thoughtfully for a minute and grimaced. 'You could ask what happens if I don't finish my book on time.'

I turned to look at him. He frowned as he indicated to move into the faster lane.

'Do you really think it will come to that?'

'I don't know,' he replied. 'I've been writing more with you here, but I just can't seem to get in the way of things again. I know it's amazing that *The Fall Out* was so successful, but it also heaps the pressure on for book two, you know?'

'Try not to worry,' I said. 'Although being told not to worry doesn't exactly help, does it? Is there anything else we could do to get the juices flowing?'

I wished I could take the words back. It sounded like I was propositioning him. My hand flew back down to my lap. Luckily, Riley barely seemed to notice.

'You're helping. Seriously, it does help having you with me talking about timetables and structure.'

'I'm a natural bossy boots, is that what you're saying?'

'Yup,' he agreed, grinning. 'A born teacher.'

'What did you do before you were a famous romance writer?'

135

I asked, realising I'd never even thought of Riley as anything but a novelist.

'Guess,' he said.

I sat back in my seat and tried to think. He'd mentioned helping Bridget and Ellie with renovation work, I wondered if he'd been some sort of tradesman.

'Nope.' He shook his head. 'I worked in finance for the public sector in Belfast.'

I burst out laughing. 'You did not.'

'I did. Part of the nine-to-five commuter crew. Went to work suited and booted for years.'

I couldn't picture Riley as part of the rat race, standing in the queue with a coffee waiting for the lift. It just didn't seem to fit him. He certainly didn't seem like a typical finance kind of guy.

'I thought finance folk with swanky jobs were all minted and a bit arsey,' I said.

'Not in the public sector,' he mused. 'Although I worked in a private firm for a few years before that. Gave that up so I could be home more for Ivy. The money was great but the hours were long. I barely saw her.'

'Wow,' I said. 'I can't imagine you all "buy buy", "sell sell" at a desk all day.'

'You better believe it. I took a voluntary redundancy package when it came up around the time I got my advance for my novel. That wasn't exactly huge so the money was to help get me set up as a writer. Problem is, if I don't finish this book then it's not enough to keep me going forever. I'll need to get a job, especially if I want to keep Bellinder Cottage.'

I gasped. 'You can't lose Bellinder Cottage!'

Riley smiled wistfully. 'I know, I love it too. But I can't afford its upkeep as a single parent, unless I really hit the big time as an author. I've probably got 'til the end of this year. After that, it's hi ho, hi ho, back to the big smoke I go.'

I watched his broad shoulders slump in defeat as he exhaled, turning the radio station over. I folded my arms across my chest. We had to get Riley back on track with his writing. Bellinder Cottage meant so much to him, and to Ivy. And I loved it too, even though I hardly factored into the equation. But his writing was part of who he was now, too.

'That won't happen,' I said, feeling determined. 'We're going to get that next bestseller ready to go in no time. I promise.'

'I hope you're right,' he sighed.

When we arrived in Dublin, Riley took me for a walk along the wide pavements of O'Connell Street, which runs through the centre of the city. I made him stop every time we passed a street sign that said O'Connell to take his picture alongside his surname. He rolled his eyes but grinned every time or gave me a thumbs up. He pointed out various statues, the River Liffey, the General Post Office, offering up parts of his historical knowledge along the way.

I got Riley to take some pictures of me to send to Dad. He replied that he wished he was with me, but I was too excited to be homesick. We stopped at a small café. Instead of eating inside, I insisted we took our sandwiches out and we found a bench next to a tall grey statue.

We could hear someone playing the drums in the distance and the noise floated up the street, serving as a backdrop for lunch. Riley opened his chicken club while I stuffed my tuna mayo sandwich into my mouth.

'I'm starving,' I mumbled. 'This is brilliant. I love Dublin. It's so vibrant.'

'We should've come for longer, made it a proper trip,' he said. 'Maybe next time.'

Next time. I grinned into my sandwich as I thought of Riley and his 'next time' promises. Plans. I loved the thought of making plans with him. As friends, obviously.

'Definitely,' I nodded, taking a sip of water. 'So how far away is the event from here? It starts soon.'

'Just around the corner, that's why I stopped here. We can head round once we've finished.'

Riley led the way as we walked down the street and turned a corner, locating the bookshop easily. I hung back as he walked in front and opened the door.

'After you,' he said, holding the door.

'You go first,' I urged. 'You're the author.'

I followed behind him as he walked through the busy store and made his way to the cash desk.

'Ahhh, Riley O'Connell!' a voice boomed from the middle of the busy bookstore. 'The man, the myth, the legend! Here he comes.'

The lady was tall with a mass of wild, dark curly hair, a pair of narrow glasses and wore a long leopard-print maxi dress, teamed with a pair of sandals and a chunky beaded necklace.

'Katrine, great to see you. Becca, this is my agent.'

'Nice to meet you, Becca. Riley has told me all about you!' Katrine exclaimed, enveloping me into a hug. 'He said you're helping him with his second novel. I can't *wait* to read it. Didn't you just love *The Fall Out*? It was one of our bestsellers last year. I'm sure the second book will be a-ma-zing. Are you ready to share anything with me yet?'

Riley looked to the floor. 'Well, um . . .'

'It'll be winging its way to you in no time.' I grinned. 'The opening chapters just need a little polishing. He thinks so, anyway. I think they're amazing. I thought nothing could compare to Alice and Leroy but it's another special one. Set to really tug on the heart strings.'

Riley met my eyes and I gave him a curt nod of the head, urging him to play along.

'Sure is,' he agreed.

'Fantastic! Oh, wait 'til I tell the publishers,' she exclaimed. 'They were worried you couldn't deliver but I've told them just to give you some space. Riley always meets his deadlines, I said. I knew you'd come up with the goods.'

Riley nodded. 'I've definitely got the goods.'

'Oh yes, all the goods,' I agreed, nodding along.

No wonder Riley was feeling the pressure. I felt it. I gave him a small 'it'll be fine' smile and he grimaced back as Katrine ushered us into a small room at the back of the bookshop.

'You can leave your things here. The thriller writer, Zander Bennett, is just about to arrive so we can have a quick chat beforehand with the host about the itinerary. Have you read any of his work? He is A-MA-ZING. So talented. I mean, I would say that because he's also a client but he's seriously so good. He's written eighteen novels now. Can you imagine?'

Katrine sashayed ahead, beckoning Riley to follow.

'No, I can't,' Riley mumbled, shooting me a helpless look.

'I'll leave you to it,' I whispered to him. 'Good luck!'

'Where are you going?' he whispered back, frowning. 'What if she asks me more about the second book?'

I touched his hand lightly. 'Just change the subject. Ask her about the other guy – Zander or whatever. He's obviously the favourite writer child.'

I patted his arm before turning on my heels to examine the books in the thriller section. I wanted to see what Zander's books were about. Eighteen novels was pretty impressive; I could barely write one.

'Have you read them?' someone asked as I located the row of Zander's books, which were packed proudly on a stand at the front of the store.

I looked up. The man standing in front of me had a shaved head with tattoos creeping out from under his black shirt and the side of his neck. He carried a black biker jacket and clutched his rucksack in his hand. He looked like he'd love a good crime novel. In fact, he wouldn't look out of place in the novel himself. As the actual murderer.

'No,' I said, examining the blurb on the back of the first in the series. 'Not really my thing. I don't think I could sleep at night reading some of these.'

I wasn't sleeping much at night anyway, but still.

'Ah,' he said. 'Shame, that. I wrote them, you see. I'm Zander, the author.'

Christ. I was dissing the star of the show.

'Ah, it's lovely to meet you. I'm Becca. I'm here with Riley, the romance writer. He's your warm-up act, I believe.'

He snorted. 'Romance writers get all the groupies.'

'Not a groupie. Just a friend. Actually, I'm an aspiring writer, too,' I said.

'Genre?' he asked.

'Children's fiction,' I explained. 'I'm a teacher.'

He nodded slowly, as though he approved. 'You know your audience, then. That's a start. And that Riley one clearly knows his. He's like some sort of boy band member, just needs to open his mouth and all the women fall at his feet.'

'Oh, well, he's a great writer. Have you read *The Fall Out*? It's wonderful.'

Zander snorted. 'As if.'

'Don't judge a book by its cover,' I said, frowning at him. 'Just because you're a crime thriller writer doesn't mean you go around murdering folk. At least, I hope not.'

He shrugged. I wondered if he was contemplating making his next victim a male romance writer.

'Anyway, nice to meet you,' I said. 'Hope the event goes well.'

I moved away from him as quickly as my legs could carry me, towards the children's section which was located upstairs.

Ahh, lovely. Grown-ups could be scary but this felt much more like home. I watched two children and their mum browsing the shelves, a child reading a book with his grand-parent in the corner and a lady looking at books on her own. I checked out some of the titles that would be comparable to *Queen Bee*, reading the blurbs on the back and trying to think of all the things Riley had told me about high stakes, conflict and resolution. I looked around, picturing *Queen Bee* on the shelves here one day. The thought sent shivers up my spine.

I picked a couple of comparable titles that looked good, as well as a picture book to read to Ivy later.

'My wee girl loves that book.'

It seemed like a very friendly bookstore, everyone wanted to talk. I looked up at the lady, who was smiling nostalgically, her short hair tucked behind an ear.

'Does she?' I smiled. 'I'm buying it for my friend's wee girl.'

'I used to read it to my daughter every night before bed,' she continued, as though she hadn't even heard me.

'It's a popular one,' I replied. 'I'm a teacher. I read it to the younger kids. They always love it.'

She didn't reply as she wandered to look over the balcony at the floor below and turned back round to face me.

'Are you here for the event?' she asked.

'Sure am,' I said. 'You?'

'I'll maybe just watch from here,' she replied, peering over the balcony. 'I'm not a big fan of crowds.'

I nodded. 'OK, well, I'll just head down and buy these downstairs.'

'I hope your friend's wee girl enjoys the book. What age is she?'

'Four,' I said.

She smiled. 'I'm sure she'll love it.'

Everyone I'd come across in Ireland was so friendly. Well, apart from the creepy thriller author who looked like he wanted to murder me and fold me into his backpack when I confessed I hadn't read his books. As I walked down the stairs, I realised the bookshop was starting to fill up as people were ushered to the front of the store, where a few rows of seats were set out facing a desk. Riley sat at one side, a red-haired older woman sat in the middle fawning over him (obviously), while Zander sat with a scowl on his face at the far end.

I went to the cash desk to pay for the books I'd selected.

'Becca, is that you? I *knew* you'd be here!'

I could tell who it was before I even looked up. Eimear appeared at my side, sporting a tight crop top and baggy jeans, with a pair of trainers.

'Hi Eimear, nice to see you.'

'Isn't it?' She offered me a wide smile as I paid for the books. 'Do you know Riley is really nervous about today, isn't that sweet? We were texting *all* night last night and I told him not to worry about it. We're all here to support him. You know?'

'I know.' I nodded, flinching at the thought of Eimear and Riley texting back and forth all night, while looking over Eimear's shoulder to catch a glimpse of Riley. The red-haired woman was apparently fitting a microphone to his chest and

I could see her grazing his abs as she did so. I rolled my eyes inwardly.

I was getting used to having Riley all to myself but the minute we headed out in public, it was a different story. No one could keep their hands or eyes off him.

I snapped back to Eimear, who was flicking her hair over her shoulder.

'So, I came for moral support. Not that he really needs it. I mean everyone loved *The Fall Out*, didn't they? Have you read it?' she asked sweetly.

'I have,' I replied, trying not to sound too smug as I continued. 'I was a beta reader for the book. I read it just before it was published.'

'Oh,' she said, taking a slight step back, with a hand on her chest. I wondered if she might fall over. 'I didn't realise he needed help with that kind of thing. I'd *love* to read for him. I'll offer up my service. Anyway, I've got a friend reserving my front row seat. I'd better go.'

She turned and skipped away, her perfect little bum wiggling in her jeans the whole way up to the front row.

As the event started, I sighed and took the last empty seat on the back row at the side, where I could hardly see a thing aside from Eimear's excited head bobbing up and down, blocking my view.

The event was a success.

Riley spoke confidently about *The Fall Out* and answered

questions from his legion of, mainly female, fans, who gushed over the book. As he read an extract from the novel, I smiled. He'd chosen the perfect part, where Alice and Leroy met again for the first time in years. The tension between the two characters was palpable, even from their first scene. I remembered reading it for the first time and being so taken in by their dialogue and chemistry. I grinned manically in my seat, as though I'd written the book myself.

Katrine watched with interest at the side and I caught her nodding along to his answers, and the audience gave him a loud round of applause at the end. Eimear let out a low whoop and I caught Riley grinning at her. I moved my head as far up as I could to try and catch his eye but I was too far back to be noticed.

Zander, the headline act, growled the whole way through Riley's segment, but as the attention turned to him, he sat back and revelled in it. He gave a surprisingly interesting interview, where he talked about the time spent researching his latest novel, *Bonetakers*. He talked about his former career as a jeweller and how he weaved his knowledge of stones and jewels in his novels. All eighteen of them.

Zander made a big deal about gesturing to his work on the shelves and I noticed Riley squirming in his seat, glancing nervously at his sole book on the table in front of them. Zander answered questions from the audience with ease and when the event finished, everyone offered up another huge round of applause, led by the red-haired interviewer. I watched Riley's face light up. He was glad it was over. Zander stood up and took an actual bow.

Eimear skipped to the front as soon as everyone started moving, while I got held back in the crowd. I looked up at the children's section and caught sight of the woman I'd spoken to earlier moving away from the balcony and heading to the stairs. I would have waved goodbye, but I was faced with Zander instead.

'Did you enjoy the event?' he asked.

I nodded enthusiastically. 'It was great. Your books sound really interesting. I loved how you used your knowledge from your jewellery career in your novels.'

'Interesting enough for you to read one?'

'I'm not sure I'd go that far.' I gave a low laugh. 'Maybe.'

'I'll take you out for dinner?' He posed the question bluntly, as though it was more of a demand.

'I'm, erm, thanks but I'm only over for a short break. I'm from Glasgow.'

'Ah. Murder capital of Europe in 2005. Maybe you could teach me something.' He let out a deep chuckle as he lifted his backpack onto his shoulder.

He turned to leave as Riley approached, with Eimear hot on his heels.

'Eimear was asking about going for a drink but we're heading back now, aren't we, Becca?'

'Sure,' I said, shrugging apologetically at Eimear, who looked like a sad puppy.

'Let's get out of here,' he whispered conspiratorially in my ear and brushed his hand against mine. For a second, I thought he was going to hold it but instead, he pulled my arm towards the door, waving goodbye to Katrine, Eimear, the red-haired lady and a legion of female fans.

'So, are you finally going to admit that all women love you?' I asked as we made our way back in search of Riley's parked car.

'Never mind that,' Riley retorted. 'Zander bloody Bennett told me he was talking to you. Offered to give you tips on how to write a series of successful books. Smug bastard that he is.'

'He was jealous of you, too, you know,' I replied, as we navigated our way along the busy street. 'Most of the audience was there for you. All the women with their tongues hanging out.'

'I'm not jealous of him,' Riley retorted through gritted teeth. 'He can write hundreds of books for all I care. Award winners, whatever he fancies. Good luck to him.'

'Channel that energy, Riley.' I grinned. 'We'll use all this adrenaline to get your novel in shape. Let's get home. I mean, back to Bellinder Cottage.'

I saw Riley smirk as we climbed into his car.

19

I lay awake into the early hours, this time thinking about the impending doom of my conference call with Mrs Pender. The knot in my stomach tightened the more I thought of it. I should have declined the stupid invite and let the summer roll on without any contact with her. But I couldn't, not really. I had to face her eventually.

In the morning, as Riley took Ivy to nursery, I pulled on a short-sleeved blouse and applied make-up. I had to appear calm and stable during the call, even though I was a bag of nerves at the very idea of even seeing her. I watched the clock in the kitchen crawl closer to the start time, pacing up and down.

Riley came back and hung up his keys, wearing his light blue Gaelic football long-sleeved jersey and shorts.

'A blouse and PJ bottoms?' he asked, glancing at my attire.

'I've got a work call this morning,' I confessed. 'With my boss.'

'The one that told the cleaner a five year old could do a better job with their eyes closed?'

'The very same,' I sighed.

'Jaysus. Right, you take the office this morning and I'll work in the kitchen. I'm here if you need anything.'

'Maybe you could just pop in and bat your eyelids at her, see if you can distract her from the lecture she's about to give me.'

'Don't take any shit, Becca. You didn't take time off work lightly, you just lost your best friend,' Riley reminded me.

I grimaced. 'Wish me luck.'

I made my way into the office and drummed my fingers against the desk's wooden surface, waiting for the call to start on my laptop, watching myself looking petrified on screen. My heart hammered in my chest and I swallowed the salty taste in my mouth.

The call clicked to life and there she was, bold as brass, sitting in her large office chair. She wore her usual stern look, verging on a growl.

'Becca,' she said. 'Do you mind if I record this call? I like to keep a record of all my staff admin.'

I had to stop myself from rolling my eyes. She was so dramatic.

'Sure,' I replied. 'If you want.'

'Thank you. I wasn't sure if you'd come,' she stated.

'I accepted the invitation,' I said. 'I thought you knew I was coming.'

She raised an eyebrow. 'Well, you also signed an employment agreement to indicate that you would come to work. Yet, here we are.'

We stayed silent for a second. My mouth fell open and I closed it again.

'Anyway, I wanted to enquire as to whether or not you have a doctor's note for this leave of absence you've taken without authorisation.'

'I . . . I haven't been to the doctor,' I replied.

Why the hell hadn't I gone to the doctor? It seemed to be such a simple solution now I thought about it. The doctor would have taken one look at me and signed me off.

'I . . . I haven't.'

She pursed her thin lips and raised her eyebrows, jotting something down in her notebook. I wondered why she was bothering to record the conversation and take notes. Surely that defeated the purpose, but I kept quiet. She gazed back up at me through the screen.

'Look, Mrs Pender, I'm finding my bereavement very difficult,' I said.

My voice shook as I spoke and I could feel tears threatening in my eyes. I didn't want to cry, not on the call. Not in front of her.

'I didn't know what the right thing was to do or to say,' I continued. 'But I knew that I wasn't in the right frame of mind to be in a class teaching children. I'm sorry if I've not done things by the book.'

'Ah yes, the email. Dear Mrs Pender, I'm afraid I am unable to return to work blah blah blah. Best kisses, Becca.' She looked back up at the screen. 'I assume you meant "wishes" when you sent it . . . in the early hours of the morning.'

'Yes, I meant wishes, sorry. I haven't been sleeping since . . .'

She bent her head down and scribbled more notes before looking up and staring me down on the screen.

'May I ask where you are just now, Becca?'

'Just now? I'm in, erm, the office.'

'In your home?' she pressed.

I stuttered, feeling trapped. If I said yes, I was lying. If I said no and confirmed I was in Ireland, I didn't know what she would say or do. Was I allowed to be out of the country? I had a horrible feeling the answer was no.

'I'm staying with a friend, actually,' I said, feeling the blood pumping through my veins. I didn't need to just lie down and take her questions, I could fight back. 'I didn't want to be on my own.'

'Yes, I heard. Look, Becca, I think you and I both know that you've crossed the line here so I'm giving you advanced notice of your disciplinary hearing . . .'

'My what now?' I blinked.

I expected her to continue with 'you do not have to say anything but anything you do say will be given in evidence'. What was she talking about, a disciplinary hearing? I felt my blood pressure rising.

'Your hearing,' she repeated. 'It will be hosted tomorrow . . . In the office. In person.'

'You're kidding,' I said.

'I can assure you, I'm not.'

'Well, I can assure you, I'm not coming to any disciplinary hearing,' I said.

'You have to come,' she said. 'As per your contract agreement, if—'

'I would need more notice,' I said.

'You wouldn't if you were in the country,' she replied, frowning sternly.

'I can't come into the office,' I said.

'You have to,' she demanded, her face screwing up. 'As per your contract . . .'

'Screw the contract. In fact, screw you. I'm not coming to the hearing because I fucking quit.'

Her eyes darted up to meet mine on the screen and her mouth curled at the edges into a small smile. 'I'm sorry?'

But I didn't let her finish. I clicked the button to finish the call. Her resting bitch face that took up the whole screen disappeared and I exhaled.

I sat for a moment in silence before putting my head in my hands. Sudden huge sobs escaped, my body shaking with the shock of it all. I should have gone to the doctor for a sick line. How stupid was that? I should have declined the call or asked for a union rep to accompany me. I should have joined the union in the first place, rather than just looking at the forms sitting on my desk.

I should have told Rae to come the following week, like we'd planned. Stick to the original plan, Becca. Be a plotter and stick with it.

The door flew open.

'Becca, what happened?' Riley said, kneeling in front of me, taking my hands in his. He leaned forward and wiped away one of the tears.

'I . . . I . . .' another huge sob escaped.

'Sshh,' he said, pulling me into his chest, making the soothing noises I'd heard him offer up to Ivy when she hurt herself. 'You're OK. Everything's OK.'

I nestled into the crook of his neck. His green sweatshirt smelled of his aftershave. I muttered muffled apologies and he rubbed my back, saying it was fine. It was all fine.

I pulled away from him and looked at my hands as I told him all about the call. He sat in the office chair beside me before rolling over to be closer to me, sitting forward in his seat.

'So you told her you fucking quit?'

He repeated it. Once he said it out loud, it sounded even worse. I'd just told my boss that I fucking quit on a conference call that she was recording. How could I have done that? I looked at Riley. His bottom lip shook a little and I realised he was trying not to smile.

And through the tears that were still glistening in my eyes, I whacked him on the knee and burst out laughing. He followed suit, offering up a loud cackle.

'Ahh, I can't believe you told her you fucking quit, that is legendary,' he said, still laughing. 'Good for you, sounds like the bitch had it coming.'

'It's not funny, Riley,' I protested, but I let out a laugh again too, wiping the tears from my eyes.

'We could call your friend Zander and ask him for some hints on taking revenge. He'd know just what to do.' Riley smirked.

'Or we could call Eimear and get her to help me deep breathe my way through my career crisis.'

'Do you know, that's not a bad idea,' Riley mused.

I rolled my eyes.

'It'll all work out, Becca,' he said, his face turning serious again. 'Honestly. We'll fix this.'

We. We'd become a we, all of a sudden. A team.

Riley looked straight into my red, teary eyes, our faces just inches apart. I held my breath. He cleared his throat and stood up, shaking his head as though trying to erase a spell I'd cast over him. He'd felt it too; I was sure he had. The feeling that there was more to this, more to us, than a friendship.

'We'd better get writing then,' he said, lifting his hand. 'If you've fucking quit your job, we'd better fucking write our fucking books. It's the only way out.'

I complied with his high five, having been placed firmly back in the friend zone.

20

The next morning, I felt like I'd been hit by an almighty truck.

Joanna texted to apologise. Apparently, she'd told another colleague in the staff room that I was in Ireland and Mrs Pender overheard the conversation. Adam and I had texted through the night, sharing more memories of Rae. Real life was coming back to bite me.

I started questioning my drunken escape plan. I was running away from a life I couldn't face: Rae's death and the bombshell that she and Drew had been a couple. I'd put my career at risk because of it. I hadn't been thinking straight and now I was backed into a corner. How could I go back to face it all? But how could I not?

My whole body felt heavy. Even moving to the bathroom and back felt like a monumental effort.

Guilt rattled around my body. Rae's death was my fault. I shouldn't have encouraged her to come to meet me that evening. Why couldn't I just have stuck with the original plan? Then she'd still be here.

Now, I'd acquired a new set of problems and feelings. I had promised to help Riley finish his novel, but he was still struggling and the thought of him and Ivy losing Bellinder Cottage weighed heavily on my mind. Why did I have to jump into everything feet first? I was clearly going to end up covered in mud again.

I heard Riley return from dropping Ivy at nursery as I pulled my duvet back over my head. For the first time since arriving, I didn't want to see him. I didn't want to see anyone. I couldn't face it. Every single interaction seemed to open up a whole new problem.

He knocked lightly on the door.

'Becca?'

I didn't reply.

'Can I come in?'

I realised I didn't have my own space here and suddenly I craved my own flat, my own bed.

'It's your house,' I mumbled.

He nudged the door open.

'What do you mean "it's my house"?' Riley asked, standing in the doorway.

I didn't move from under the covers.

'Becca, can you speak to me?'

I moved the duvet from over my head, revealing my make-up-free, tear-stained face.

'I've fucked everything up,' I said.

I let out a huge sigh.

Riley left the room without a word and came back moments later with my jacket and trainers.

'Get dressed,' he said. 'I want to show you something.'

The walk was steeper than I'd imagined. I skipped cautiously past the rams roaming around the fields and dodged the large and small piles of poo they'd left scattered all over the grass. We climbed up the rocks and stopped every so often for breath, turning to capture the view over Rathcliffe. I kept one eye on Bellinder Cottage as it faded into the distance the higher we climbed. Rain drizzled lightly above us and I pulled my rain jacket closer to my body.

Riley navigated his way up the mountain with ease, turning around every so often to point out Bellinder Cottage in the distance or offer up an interesting fact. He didn't seem to require any answers, so I largely kept quiet.

I was breathing heavily by the time we made it to the top. I turned to Riley, expecting him to be the same, but his breathing seemed steady.

'Wow,' I said, eventually. 'That view is . . . amazing.'

The town was still visible in the distance but the surrounding greenery seemed to stretch for miles, with an array of different shades of green. The clouds above us threatened heavier rain, but the view was so majestic I didn't even care.

'Yup,' he agreed, taking a seat on a rock. 'This is my favourite place, right here. I come here anytime I need to clear my head.'

'My dad used to take me on mountain walks when we came to Ireland,' I said, the memory filling me with warmth. 'But I don't think I've ever seen a view as beautiful as this.'

We took a seat, perching on the spiky grass, and stayed silent, surveying the scene in front of us.

'What was it like for you, growing up without a mum around?' Riley broke the silence.

I took a moment, unsure what to say.

The truth was, it had been lonely. Actually, it was worse than lonely. But how could I tell that to a man who was trying to raise his daughter single-handedly?

'It was different for me,' I said, picking up a stray stone and turning it around in my hands. 'My mum died when I was young. My dad struggled to get over it. To be honest, I'm still not sure he is over it. He still won't go anywhere near a hospital. And he's never been with anyone else. Not seriously, anyway. I guess that was the hardest bit, seeing him struggle so much.'

The words tumbled out of my mouth and he listened carefully.

'I worry for Ivy,' he said. 'She misses her mum so much. I feel so helpless sometimes. I wish I could just fix it all for her.'

Sighing, his broad shoulders slumped, and I realised he was carrying the weight of the world on them, too.

It was the first time he had actively brought Jackie up and I held my breath, desperate for more information, but it looked like that was all I was getting.

'Ivy's pretty amazing, you know. Plus, it's not like she's lacking in female role models. I can't think of two better women to show her how it's all done than Bridget and Ellie. Hip flasks and all.'

'I guess you're right,' he said. 'I just wonder if she's going to be traumatised by my lack of knowledge of, you know, lady life. Despite what you first thought about me.'

He expected me to say something smart back, but I knew this was important to him. No laughing matter.

'I've worked with kids who are traumatised, Riley. And I know that Ivy misses her mum, but honestly, she seems to be coping well from what I've seen. I think you're doing a pretty awesome job, too.'

Riley sighed.

'Thank you. I hope you're right. Sorry, I brought you up here to cheer you up and now I'm offloading all my worries on you.'

'Offload away, my friend. It's actually helping me to talk,' I said, realising it was true. 'One thing that really helped me was having Rae. I never had any siblings so I guess I kind of clung on to her a bit when we first met. She became like a sister to me. Rae was the one who told me about periods and sex and all that jazz. And I guess her mum was kind of like a surrogate mum to me, too.'

'I am not looking forward to those kind of conversations with Ivy,' he said.

'Only because she'll know more than you,' I teased.

'She's a smart girl.' Riley nodded.

'She is,' I replied. 'She's already keeping you right.'

I reached out for Riley's hand and patted it gently. To my

surprise, he placed his hand on top of mine and curled it into his. We sat there, silent, holding hands for a few moments.

'Shall we?' he said, standing up.

He turned around and pulled me to my feet.

A gorgeous double rainbow was in view somewhere towards the bottom of the hill. I pointed at it and Riley grinned.

'There must be a pot of gold at the end!' he declared, grabbing my hand. 'Let's go!'

Following him, I ran down the hill, until the rainbow disappeared somewhere along the way.

'I've never believed in that pot of gold bullshit,' I declared, out of breath. 'Seems unlikely to me.'

'You can be very cynical, you know,' Riley said. 'For a children's writer.'

'We can't all be dreaming up the happily ever afters, Riley.' I shrugged. 'Sometimes it's not as easy as that.'

'Don't I know it,' he eventually whispered into the distance.

21

TEN YEARS AGO

After a quiet morning, Rae wandered over at lunchtime, as usual, and we walked around the lake together.

'Want half of my sandwich?'

'Yup,' I agreed. 'The less we spend on food, the more we get to put towards Tenerife.'

Rae looked at the ground and tore her sandwich in half, before handing me the other half.

'What's up?' I asked. 'You still hungry? You can have it all if you want, I'll walk over and get my own.'

'It's not that,' she said. 'It's Mickey. He doesn't want me to go.'

Bloody Mickey. The two of them were always squabbling about something or other. He was making Rae miserable. But they always seemed to make up and Rae didn't seem to see the issue.

'Why not?' I demanded.

'Well, Drew won't want you to go either.' Rae shrugged. 'I mean, how would you feel if he told you he was going on a lads' holiday right now? You'd be raging about it.'

'I would not,' I replied, even though we both knew that was a lie. 'I would trust him and hope he has a great time.'

We stopped at our usual bench but it was soaking so we kept walking instead. Rae popped up her brolly and we huddled underneath.

'Well, Mickey said it's him or the holiday.'

'You are kidding, Rae? That's the whole point in us being here, to save money for it. You wouldn't have met him if it wasn't for the holiday. Tell him to piss off. We're going to Tenerife. No matter what Mickey says.'

She swallowed the last of the sandwich and scrolled through her phone, selecting the Rihanna song that we listened to every day. It seemed to cheer her up.

'Yeah, you're right. We're going. I bet this song is everywhere over in Tenerife just now,' she said, moving the brolly above us around to the rhythm of the beat. 'We'll dance 'til the sun comes up, Becca. It'll be epic.'

'We found love in a hopeless place,' I joined in with the song and Rae laughed as we made our way back to the ice cream van.

Rae's shoulders slumped. She was wearing the same uniform she'd been given at the start of the summer but there was no push-up bra in sight. She wasn't even wearing any lipstick. I frowned at her.

'Just tell Mickey you're going. Don't take any bullshit, Rae.'

'I know. I won't,' she said.

'Close your eyes.'

My spine tingled as Drew whispered in my ear and put his hands over my eyes.

'Where are we going?' I demanded.

'Patience is a virtue, Becca,' he said, guiding me along with his hand.

'Kidnapping is an offence, Drew,' I joked.

'Almost there,' he whispered in my ear. My whole body tingled in anticipation. The next thing, we stopped. 'Keep your eyes closed.'

A key jangled in a lock. He pushed the door open.

'Surprise!' he said, and I opened my eyes.

There were pink rose petals all over the four-poster bed of the honeymoon suite of the theme park's on-site hotel, and a bottle of Champagne chilling at the foot of the bed.

It was all so cliché. And I loved it.

'I can't believe you did this.'

He moved to kiss me. The Champagne remained unopened. My phone rang again.

'Leave it,' Drew urged.

'What if it's important?'

'This is way more important.' He nuzzled back into my neck.

'Hello?'

'Becca?' Her voice sounded strained.

'Rae, what's wrong?' I asked, sitting up on the hotel's bed, looking out into the dark night. The big wheel glittered in the distance.

'I need you. Can you come and get me?'

Drew stood up and pulled on his trousers and T-shirt without saying a word.

'Of course,' I said. 'We're on our way.'

22

It was book night. Ellie and Bridget saved me a spot in the middle of the two of them and handed me a hip flask.

'It's full.' Bridget winked at me.

I took a swig and gagged. It was also very strong.

'That'll put hair on your chest,' she giggled. 'I'm not exactly known for half measures, if you know what I mean. Go hard or go home.'

'How was the author event at the bookshop, Becca? Riley said it went well?' Ellie asked.

I nodded and filled them in on the author event, from Zander the creepy crime thriller author to Riley's legion of fangirls.

Bridget and Ellie laughed.

'Eimear from yoga came along,' I said, a hint of accusation in my voice.

I wanted to dig the dirt on what was going on between Eimear and Riley.

The date they had discussed the first time I'd been to the class didn't seem to have materialised. Not that I was stalking him. I mean, I lived with him so I just happened to know. But she did seem to be a fixture in his life. They talked about a date, had definitely been out for drinks together, they messaged, and she turned up at his author event.

Then there was the whole 'mum' conundrum, which I still hadn't heard about from Riley. I thought about what Ivy had said about Jackie coming back. The poor girl was fantasising, she missed her mum so much. I didn't tell Riley; aside from the promise I'd made, I thought it might just make him feel guilty. And he had enough stress on his plate trying to write his book.

'Ah, I miss yoga,' Ellie said, completely missing my point. 'I love going. I've not had much time, what with the renovation works going on and everything, but once everything is up and running, I'm definitely going back.'

No mention of Eimear. Ellie wasn't picking up on my gossip cues. I wondered if Bridget might. She was hardly Little Miss Subtle.

'Ach, you know, I can really take it or leave it.' Bridget shrugged, stretching her legs out. 'Prefer the old mountain walks.'

'We'll have to take turns exercising soon. Can't both be away at the same time once the business gets going.'

'True,' Bridget agreed. 'Especially now we don't have our receptionist lined up.'

'Receptionist?' I repeated.

Ellie sighed. 'Yes, we were meant to have someone starting with us, working part time in the office and helping with the bookings, cleaning, admin, all that kind of stuff. But she was offered another job yesterday so it's back to being just the two of us.'

'Not that we mind,' Bridget said. 'But if we do happen to get a call about adopting soon . . .'

'We might not be in the best position,' Ellie finished her sentence. 'We'll work it out though. I'm sure we'll find someone.'

'Me,' I said. 'I mean, what about me? Could I . . . apply?'

Ellie looked up at me in surprise. 'You want a job? I thought you were a teacher,' she said. 'You're a professional. We're really just looking for someone that's starting out for now.'

'Yeah, the pay isn't the best, Becca. In fact, it's a bit shit. You'll be used to earning way more than we can pay you just yet. And won't you be going back to your real job in a few weeks?' Bridget asked.

'Long story, but please,' I said. 'I'd really love to help. If you'd have me. I could take on the job until you find someone else to do it, you know, more permanently.'

'Well, if you're up for the challenge, we'd love to have you on board,' Ellie said. 'We hardly need to interview you. The job is yours, if you want it.'

'I want it,' I said firmly.

We all put our hip flasks in the middle and toasted my new job. I didn't tell them just yet that I was, in fact, free forever. One step at a time.

'That was a lot easier than I thought it was going to be,' I exclaimed.

'Cheers, to our new employee.' Bridget smiled.

'Cheers to my new bosses. You're already a million times better than my last boss and I haven't even started yet.'

'Just wait until Ellie goes through her cleaning regime with you,' Bridget whispered. 'You might not be saying that then. She's a hard taskmaster. She changes the cups in the dishwasher around every time I load it.'

'That's because you're shit at loading the dishwasher, Bridget.' Ellie rolled her eyes and grinned.

Bridget stuck her tongue out at Ellie.

'I'm sure I'll be able to handle it,' I assured them.

Book and wine club, minus the books, was about to start. I sat back and looked up at the early evening sky and pushed all the uneasy thoughts of my bitch boss to the back of my mind.

'We have a surprise for you tomorrow,' Bridget whispered, and Ellie grinned conspiratorially. 'You and Riley. Bring your laptops.'

I took another sip from the hip flask, wondering what on earth they had up their sleeves.

23

'Oh my God, you guys! This is so exciting!'

Riley and I had been instructed to meet Bridget and Ellie for a full tour of their self-catering cottages. They had shown me 'before' pictures of the old apartments before taking Riley and me around every cottage. The lovingly restored houses were now filled with character, charm and warmth. Every cottage was freshly decorated with a themed colour running throughout the space. We were in Teal Cottage, heading towards the last space: a luxury two-bedroom apartment.

We brought our laptops and notebooks, as instructed, so we could take notes along the way. I wasn't sure what notes I was meant to be taking but I was enjoying the tour experience.

'The last one has a special surprise,' Bridget promised, her eyes shining. 'Wait 'til you see it.'

My eyes flew open as we walked towards the last space. I was instantly transported back to the time Drew took me to the honeymoon suite. I shook my head to clear the memory.

Ellie opened the door to a bold navy wall taking prominence in the open-plan kitchen-diner, which then led to a beautiful crisp white room with ornate navy bedspread and an en-suite with small navy face cloths and a large fluffy white bath towel.

'Wow! I just want to move in,' I said.

'Well, it's not Bellinder Cottage but it is gorgeous,' Riley said, throwing me a grin.

'Keep going,' they urged, pointing to the French doors at the back of the main room.

Riley pushed the patio door, which opened out onto a small outdoor decking area.

'This is what they call small but perfectly formed,' Ellie said.

I gasped as I spotted the surprise they mentioned: a hot tub sat outside with beautiful, uninterrupted views of the mountains. I closed my eyes and felt the sun beaming down on my face. Now this was bliss.

'This is amazing,' Riley said. 'I could hop in there for hours and let the whole day wash away. Beer in one hand, book in the other.'

'Oh yeah, and then laze around inside writing for hours afterwards,' I agreed, looking longingly at the desk in the bedroom.

Bridget and Ellie smiled at each other.

'Well, I'm very glad you said that, you two. You see, we need a couple of volunteers to try out the facilities and we couldn't think of two people who deserved it more,' Bridget said.

'Wait, what do you mean?' Riley asked, confused.

'We need you to have the full guest experience, so we've

booked you in for the night. It's Thursday, so we have Ivy anyway,' Ellie grinned.

'No, wait, we can't ask you to do that,' I said. 'This would cost a fortune and—'

'It's free of charge, obviously,' Bridget said. 'You need to be able to chat to our guests about the full customer experience, Becca, if you're going to be our receptionist.'

'Yes, you just need to relax and enjoy. Ellie packed a swimming costume for you, Becca, and shorts for Riley,' Bridget said.

They were looking very pleased with themselves indeed.

'Plus, you already have your laptops and notebooks so you might as well set to work. Riley, you're always going on about needing uninterrupted time and space to work on your book and how much Becca helps you. Prove it. You must nearly have finished your book by now and we're so excited to read it! The hot tub is at the perfect temperature, now jump in,' Bridget continued.

'Are you serious?' Riley exclaimed, laughing. 'I can't just . . . I mean, we can't just . . .'

'Stop pretending like you've got anything better to do, you big lazy fecker. Just get in and enjoy,' Bridget said, pushing her brother towards the hot tub. 'The bag's over there with your swim stuff.'

And with that, the two fairy godmothers waved their magic wands and left us alone.

My mouth was still wide open as I walked around the hot tub.

171

'I was not expecting this,' I said, looking up at Riley. 'I can't believe it. I've not even got clean pants.'

'Me neither,' Riley said, picking up the bag they had left for us. 'D'you know what's funny though? You said you talked to me about smear tests and all that jazz when you thought I was a woman, but you still talk about stuff like that with me now.'

'Pants. I said pants. It's not like I went into great detail,' I said.

He peered inside the bag and pulled out a black swimming costume.

'Madame,' he said. 'Your bikini.'

'Wait, what? A bikini?' I wrinkled my nose. I was not about to wrestle into a bikini around Riley. 'No, that's not a bikini, Riley. That's a swimming costume. Thankfully.'

'I don't bloody know, do I? I'm not a woman, despite what you thought.'

'This is definitely not what I signed up to,' I said, looking around at the sunbeds adjacent to the hot tub. 'It is so much better.'

A white fluffy bathrobe was waiting for me in the luxurious bathroom, and I slipped on the swimming costume, which was too big around the chest area for me and a bit tight around the thighs. I moved it around my shoulders and walked towards the patio area, looking towards the mountains and breathing in and out.

Riley was already in the tub as I walked out, his head resting against the edge with the bubbles dancing around his broad chest. I pulled the bathrobe tighter around me as the cool air hit my legs. Summer in Ireland could clearly be every bit as cold as Scottish summer.

He opened his eyes.

'Hey,' he said. 'Surprise.'

He leaned over and handed me a glass of Champagne from the small table set up beside the hot tub.

I clutched onto it and took a sip.

'Cheers,' he said, raising his glass. 'Get in!'

I slipped the bathrobe off and clambered in, suddenly feeling very self-conscious in front of this person that I'd conversed with so freely for weeks now. My face flushed as I thought of the time I told him about going for a bikini wax. And the whole smear test thing. And flashing him my old bra on our impromptu night out. I'd mentioned childbirth at one point, in our messages, expecting Riley to go into elaborate details about it the way any woman who'd had a child seemed to want to do. I'd thought it was so refreshing when the comment had been ignored. Now I could see why.

'This is just so kind of them both,' I said. 'I can't believe they've done this for us. They've done such a great job with the place, it's absolutely beautiful.'

'Two bedrooms though,' Riley pointed out, raising an eyebrow. 'Not a trope in sight.'

He was thinking it, too. About us. Our friendship. Was he thinking about the possibility of more?

The bubbles continued to dance enthusiastically around us. I sipped my Champagne and took a seat. The water was deliciously hot. I looked at Riley. He closed his eyes and moved with the rhythm of the water.

'This is exactly what I need right now,' Riley exhaled. 'Not a care in the world.'

His leg brushed against mine in the hot tub and an electric current zipped up my thigh. I moved my body quickly out of the way. I shouldn't even think about confusing things with Riley. I was in a weird place. I was grieving. He clearly had all sorts of baggage too. While I loved spending time with Ivy, I knew that all she desperately wanted right now was her mum. I wasn't ready to get involved in anything else.

'I can't help but get the feeling that the two of them are trying to matchmake us,' Riley said, his eyes still closed. 'I'm sorry about that, by the way. I know you're not here for that. You came here to get away from all your problems, not to gain some more.'

We were still playing a big game of hide and seek with our baggage, only addressing things when we had to. He hadn't even told me his ex-wife's name. I'd had to hear it from Ellie and Bridget. I sat up a little straighter.

'And all you want to do is be able to write your story. I get that too. But I have a bit of a theory. It's been playing on my mind,' I said.

I gulped, wondering where my courage had suddenly come from. Perhaps he would tell me to mind my own business. But I had to take the chance, while Ivy wasn't around, to find out more about Riley. If he'd let me.

'Go on, then,' he said.

I took a sip from my glass and put it on the edge of the hot tub, brushing against him again on the way past.

'I think if you want to be able to write your romance novel, you're going to have to open up a bit more about your ex. And your past. I think it's holding you back from moving on with your story,' I said.

I watched closely for his reaction. He raised his eyebrows. 'You do?'

'Look, I'm not just saying this to be nosy. I really think so. Your first book was all about heartache. It captured all the raw feelings and emotions of a break-up and make-up but this second book outline is meant to be a new romance and you're struggling to write it. I think it's because you need to let go of your past first. Like your very own second-chance romance.'

'What, and jump into a new relationship, for the book's sake?'

'Oh no, that's not what I meant.' I flushed.

Gawd, he thought I was hitting on him. I absolutely was not.

'Look, I know you're not exactly going to have trouble with finding a new relationship. The whole yoga class flirts with you. The author event was full of women gaping at you. Mrs Rivers from down the road swoons so much when she sees you driving past that I think she might collapse.'

Riley burst out laughing. 'Are you mad?' he said. 'That's not true.'

I narrowed my eyes at him. Did he really not know?

'Erm, yes, I think you'll find they were. And I know you're seeing Eimear but when do you actually go out with her anywhere? I'll watch Ivy for you, if you want to go on a date, by the way. You just need to say.'

I tried to stop the words from tumbling out of my mouth but they paraded out, dancing in front of us like I didn't care if he swanned around with Eimear while I was left holding the fort at home like the Utter Nutter.

'You *want* me to go on a date with Eimear?' He frowned.

He moved his hand to shield his eyes and took a sip of Champagne with his other hand. His face flashed with annoyance, although I wasn't quite sure why.

'If you want.' I shrugged, trying to act like I wasn't bothered. I vowed to help Riley and, whatever it took, I was going to do it.

How could Riley be so naive to think the women in the yoga class, and pretty much everywhere we went, weren't interested in him? He was obviously just so wrapped up in the past, in Jackie, that he couldn't see what was going on around him. Couldn't see all the women ready to fall at his feet once he just opened his eyes.

'OK, so just for talking's sake then, you think if I open up a bit more about my past with Jackie, I might be able to write more about a new romance – or the possibility of one?'

Riley's bright green eyes met with mine. I nodded, excited that he'd finally uttered her name in my presence. This was progress.

'And I want to know what happened because I'm nosy,' I added, smiling at him.

He threw his head back and laughed.

'At least you're honest,' he said. 'I just struggle sometimes, you know?'

'Struggle with what?' I asked.

He looked down into the bubbles, as though he was searching for something he'd dropped.

'To know exactly where it all went wrong.'

24

TEN YEARS AGO

'I'll fucking kill him,' Drew said, pacing up and down in Rae's bedroom.

My arm was flung around Rae's shoulders on the bed and she was cuddled into my chest, like a small child.

'See, this is why I didn't want to tell him,' she said, rolling her eyes. 'He thinks he's fucking Rambo.'

I stroked Rae's hair. It made a change from holding it back while she spewed over a toilet after a heavy night out. I missed those days. I missed that Rae.

'Drew just wants to look out for you,' I said. 'Do you want to talk about what happened? Drew can leave, if you want to keep it between us?'

'I'm not going anywhere,' he said. 'Unless it's giving me free rein to hunt him down and kick his ass.'

'Like that would help,' Rae said, rolling her eyes. 'You need to calm the fuck down, Drew. He's not going to admit to anything. I don't think he even thinks he's done anything wrong. Let's just say it didn't work out between us and I'll move on. It's not worth getting all dramatic about.'

She curled up in a ball, like a broken doll. The slim, confident, tanned and beautiful girl that I aspired to be was lying in a heap. Her shoulder blades stuck out of her body underneath her vest top. How had I not noticed how skinny she'd become?

She hid it well, though.

And of course, I was so wrapped up in my own relationship that I hadn't noticed what was going wrong with Rae. All I'd cared about was Drew.

'I just feel like such an idiot,' she said. 'People told me he was nasty, but I couldn't see it. I was totally besotted with him.'

'You're not an idiot,' Drew said. 'It happens.'

'Drew, I think it's better if you just go,' I said. 'Rae and I need to talk this out. Girl time.'

'OK,' he agreed. 'If you need anything, you let me know, OK, Rae?'

She looked up and nodded sadly, reaching out her hand to hold his for a second.

'Thanks, Drew. It was good of you to come round. You're one of the good guys.'

'What time's your flight?'

Drew drummed his fingers on the edge of the counter. I'd

told him my flight time about four times already. I'd also sent him a screenshot with the details, but he hadn't responded to my message. I wasn't even sure if he'd read it. We'd barely seen each other over the last week. He kept agreeing to extra shifts and staying late after work. I kept myself busy, packing for holiday after work and shopping with Rae.

I already missed him and I wasn't even gone yet.

'Only five more hours to go and you'll be rid of me,' I joked.

He was barely listening. As his eyes darted around the room, I wondered what, or who, he was looking for.

My heart sank as I looked up and spotted Leila, Drew's new boss, sauntering towards us, her hips sashaying from side to side. Her boobs were so big that I wondered if they ever caused her to topple over. She flicked her long, flowing jet-black hair behind her shoulder and pursed her bright red lips, placing a perfectly manicured hand on her hip.

It all started to make sense. Leila Jackson had made her mark as soon as she'd started, batting her eyelashes at anyone who looked her way. Especially Drew.

'Drew.' Leila smiled widely. 'We could have a drink now, if you like? Talk about your career progression plans.'

Drew stood up.

'You don't mind, do you Becca? You've got to get going for the airport now, anyway, right?'

'Right,' I said, standing up. 'Of course.'

'I'll walk you out,' Drew said. 'Give me five minutes, Leila.'

She grinned and walked back towards her office.

'Wow, five minutes. Thanks,' I muttered as we began walking to the door.

My stomach clenched.

'Don't be like that, Becca.'

'You can get back to your drink with Leila.'

I knew I was pushing it. Him. But I couldn't stop the words from tumbling out of my mouth.

The last thing I wanted was to fight just before I left for our holiday. I planned to spend the whole time cheering Rae up, not the other way around. But I could tell by the way Leila looked at Drew that she had more on her mind than discussing his 'career progression'. I could spot it a mile off, but he seemed to be oblivious. Or was he?

'What do you want, Becca? You don't want me to have a drink with her? She's my new boss. She wants to talk about career development. I'm not like you and Rae. I've not got university to get back to. I need to try and carve out a career here. I know this was just a stupid summer job for you guys so you could earn enough money to book a flight and drink some shots, but this is it for me. I don't have a back-up plan. This is my plan,' he said, his voice straining more with every word he uttered.

I couldn't fix my face into a neutral position. 'Nice monologue,' I muttered.

Drew frowned back at me. He was looking at me like I was a stranger. I wanted to wrap myself around him again, sit on his lap and laugh about ice cream. But Rae reappeared and started pulling me towards the taxi that had turned up.

'Have a good holiday, Becca,' he murmured.

When he turned on his heel to leave, he didn't even glance back.

182

25

We whiled away the time in the hot tub for over an hour, talking about high schools and growing up.

'I was awkward as anything as a child,' he chuckled. 'I had big thick glasses, probably from reading too many books.'

'When did you decide you wanted to write?' I asked.

'Oh, I always knew that. As soon as I could think, it felt like I was writing. I was always people-watching and making up imaginary stories. I used to hide at the side of my bed writing stories and drawing pictures of characters. What about you?'

'Well, I'm obviously not as advanced as you with the whole writing thing. I remember my English teacher reading Seamus Heaney to us when I was in first year and I loved it. Then I did a creative writing exercise when I was doing my teacher training. I just loved hearing everything that the kids came up with. I loved all their stories and helping their imaginations to come to life. Then I realised if I wrote stories that might help spark their imaginations too.'

'Did you always want to be a teacher though?'

'Yep, for as long as I can remember,' I confirmed. 'It's the only thing I've ever known.'

I stretched out my hands in front of me. My fingers were getting wrinkly. The sun was hiding behind a large cloud in the sky but I could feel it on my skin.

'I should really have sun cream on,' I said. 'Bloody Scottish skin.'

I stood up to get out of the hot tub and Riley groaned.

'Nooo, I've been enjoying chatting,' he said. 'If we get out we have to write.'

'I thought that's all you ever wanted to do,' I teased.

'It is, but not right now,' he said. 'This is the most relaxed I've felt in a long time.'

I grabbed the sun cream from my bag and wrapped a towel around myself.

'That's great,' I said, throwing a towel in his direction. 'Now, tell it to the reader. We need words on the page, my friend.'

'Slave driver,' he mumbled with a grin.

I turned my back to avoid catching him emerging from the hot tub like an Irish mythical god again. Focus, Becca.

The writers' retreat and hot tub turned out to be a winning combination, for Riley at least. As soon as he dried off and dressed again, he started tapping away on his keyboard with a determined look on his face. His tongue was sticking out a bit at the side while he sat at the desk area in the living room.

Cute.

I shook my head. Concentrate, Becca.

'Shall we try a sprint?' he asked, raising his eyebrows.

'Sure,' I agreed. 'Bet I can beat you.'

'Not if I beat you first,' he quipped.

Riley set the timer and I blew the imaginary whistle. I looked down at the blank page in front of me. My story wasn't flowing at all. The writer's dysfunction had well and truly set in. I was propped up on the couch trying to write the pivotal scene, where Anna and Rosie are at drama camp and agree they'd be better as friends than enemies. All girls wanted at that age was to have a solid friendship, someone they could really rely on. I remembered that feeling so well. Yet, I couldn't seem to form the words together to convey this on the page. Anna was coming across as a mouthy brat in my previous scene, while Rosie was being too passive. I frowned, wondering how to continue the upbeat pace of my opening chapters when I felt so exhausted all the time.

I draped a cover over me and picked up my laptop. The words jumbled in front of me and I closed my heavy eyes. There was something comforting about the tapping of the keyboard in the distance. Knowing that Riley felt inspired to write felt like a weight off my mind.

The rhythm continued as a backdrop and I pulled a blanket over me, with heavier eyes. I yawned. It was so peaceful here. And relaxing. And even though Rae was on my mind, as she always was, I wasn't panicking when I thought about her. Instead, I closed my eyes and let myself think of her face. The freckles that dusted the edge of her nose. Her loose curls that she worked so hard to maintain. Her tanned skin. Her wicked laugh, the dirtiest I'd ever heard.

I smiled at the memory. I didn't know how to bottle it up and send it to Adam to show him the real Rae; the one that I knew before all the bullshit happened. The confident, self-assured queen who was my very best friend in the whole world.

26

TEN YEARS AGO

I'd never seen Rae so drunk. She swung around the dance floor as 'Party Rock Anthem' blasted out of the speakers. It was following us around everywhere we went and she would go wild every time she heard it.

'Let's dance! Let's do another shot! Come on, Becca!'

I was exhausted trying to keep up with her. It was the fourth night of our holiday and all I'd wanted was to recover from the previous nights, order some pizza and curl up in bed. But Rae insisted. We were here for a good time, not a long time.

Drew and I were messaging but not calling each other, apparently. He'd texted when I'd arrived in Tenerife saying to enjoy the holiday, not to worry about anything and that he hoped I had a great time with Rae. He said he loved me.

'The bastard,' Rae said, rolling her eyes.

I knew she was kidding. She said Drew was a freaking saint compared to Mickey.

'You're so lucky with him, Becca. You need to stop thinking about Leila and all the things that could go wrong and just enjoy being with him. Mr Whippy loves you,' she slurred on the first night at the edge of the dance floor. 'Now, let's find me a man.'

She went to get a drink from the bar and twenty minutes later, I was still sitting on my own scrolling through social media.

I hesitated before typing her name into the top of my feed. *Leila Jackson.*

Did I really want to do this to myself? Rae wasn't here to talk me out of it. I looked around the room and located her having a deep conversation with two guys at the corner of the bar. She'd found people to do shots with her, at least.

Bingo. I spotted her profile, and ginormous accompanying boobs in her profile picture, alongside the words 'Single. Very single'. Classy. Plus, her page was public, which meant I was free to scroll through every picture she'd ever posted. I sat up straighter in my seat and tugged at my dress, wriggling around to get comfortable. Buckle up, Becca. You could be in for a long night.

My eyes were drawn to the first picture – 'Me and My New Team' – followed by a series of kisses. Yuck. She was clearly one of *those* people. I scrolled through the pictures. Leila with Kevin at the Ferris wheel. Leila in a tight top standing behind the bar pretending to pull a pint, with a big toothy grin. Leila and Drew at the ice cream van.

Wait. I scrolled back and studied the picture. Drew was inside the van, smiling – no, actually beaming – at his customer. Leila was posing outside the front of the van with an ice cream at her ruby red lips and a sly, sexy smile. She'd captioned the picture 'Drew AKA Mr Whippy is going soft on me' with a winky face.

My heart thudded in my chest. I zoomed in on Drew's face. He was practically drooling. The bastard.

'What are you doing there, pretty lady?' Rae's voice interrupted my social stalking.

She appeared back with the two guys from the bar, one at each shoulder, and plonked herself across from me.

'I need a shot,' I replied, putting my phone in my bag.

'Glad to be of service.' One of the guys stretched his arm out to me, with a small frothy shot glass.

I downed it in one and slammed it on the table.

'Let's have another then,' I said, wiping my lips.

Because, after all, if you can't beat them, you may as well join them.

27

I woke up with a start and looked around. The light bounced around the room, and I realised time had crept into the afternoon. I wondered how long I'd been asleep for. I was in a bedroom, too. How had I managed to get in here? The door lay wide open and there, sitting in the same spot I'd left him, was Riley. The side of his face was lit by a small table light. He paused every so often to think and then kept going, tapping away on his keyboard. It was no wonder the Rathcliffe ladies were falling at his feet. I could have watched him work for hours.

'Hey.' My voice cracked as I attempted to catch Riley's attention.

He looked up.

'Sleeping Beauty,' he smiled.

He stood up and walked towards the bedroom. My stomach flipped.

'Definitely sleeping, I don't know about the beauty part,' I said. 'What time is it?'

'It's nearly three o'clock. You've been asleep for a good couple of hours.'

'I can't freaking believe it. I feel like I've won the lottery.' I smiled up at him as he sat down on the bed beside me. 'I don't sleep. I mean, obviously I do for a while. Sometimes, at night. But two hours in the middle of the day is totally unheard of. Did you carry me into the bedroom by the way?'

'Yup,' Riley said. 'You were snoring so loudly it was putting me off my writing.'

I gasped. 'Noooo! Seriously?'

'I'm only teasing. Your neck looked like it was getting sore and you were so out of it, you didn't even hear the sprint alarm going off. I could see the four-poster bed just begging for you so I threw you on top of it. It wasn't exactly how I'd pictured going to bed with you, mind you.'

The fizzing in my stomach cranked up a notch. Had he really imagined being with me? I thought of Eimear and her washboard stomach. Of course he hadn't. He was obviously just a flirt, the way he was with every other female in Rathcliffe. Probably on the planet. I had to stop taking everything so literally.

'Thanks,' I said. 'I feel so much better for it. How's the writing going?'

'I've had a bit of a breakthrough.' Riley grinned. 'I think what you said earlier helped, actually. I've been trying to work out what the Grand Gesture should be.'

'I'm delighted for you,' I said. 'Although the grand gesture is a load of BS.'

'I'll have you know, Becca, it's not a load of BS. It works.'

'Oh, does it now? It's not realistic, though. I mean, men usually just say "fuck it" and pull out a dating app instead. Move onto the next thing.'

'I'm shocked and appalled that you feel that way,' Riley said, clutching his heart. 'You've never had a man fight for you before? Like, declare his undying love by hiring an aeroplane to spell out your name?'

'Nope,' I replied. 'Because Grand Gestures don't happen in real life. Have you ever done one?'

He thought. 'Well. I spelled out Ivy's name in Alphabet Letters last week.'

I laughed.

'That's cute. So, what are you thinking your Grand Gesture will be in the story?'

He shrugged. 'Dunno. Maybe I'm better concentrating on something else.'

We sat inches apart on the bed. His fingers twitched and I looked up at him. He reached over and took my hand in both of his, like a sandwich. I remembered Ivy asking me if a 'sandwich' was actually a 'sandwhich', like a choice of what to have right from the start. I smiled.

'Becca,' he started in a low tone.

'Do you remember Ivy talking about a sand–which the other day, like which sandwich would you choose? Because there's always a choice of them. That was so funny. She's so sweet.'

'She is.' He nodded, clutching my hand. 'I'm glad you think so.'

'I really do.'

I avoided his gaze. I didn't know why but I couldn't bring myself to look him in the eyes. My hand was almost certainly shaking in his and becoming all sweaty.

'Look, I just wanted to say, I think you're right about the whole thing with Jackie. I will talk to you about it all.' Riley looked into my eyes as he spoke softly.

'You don't have to talk to me. I didn't mean specifically me. I meant someone. Anyone.'

'Right,' he said. 'But I do want to talk to you about it. Specifically you.'

I allowed myself to look at him. His eyes were incredible, dancing as he spoke. And suddenly they were coming closer towards me.

'Eimear.'

I blurted her name out, my heart hammering in my chest. I had to get it all out in the open. This couldn't happen until I was sure he wasn't cheating on the flat stomach of Eimear with the not-so-flat stomach belonging to me.

'Pardon?'

'What about Eimear?' I asked.

'Why are you so focused on her? I don't get it.'

'You're the one who's focused on her,' I replied.

He paused. 'I'm not,' he said in a low voice.

But he had definitely paused. Aha. I knew it. I knew he was too good to be true.

'I do have Ivy, though. And a past. And it's all a bit unre-solved, I guess you could say,' he said, slowly.

193

I shouldn't let myself get involved in this. It wasn't a good idea. But my body was screaming something completely different, and I ignored the nagging in my mind. He pulled me into his arms, moved his head to one side and kissed me. Confidently. No hesitation.

It felt like I hadn't been kissed in a million years. It was hardly the top of the to-do list recently, with everything that had been going on. But as he pulled me closer towards him, I realised I needed it. More than ever. I didn't want him to ever stop. His hands slid into the roots of my hair and a tingling sensation spread across my body as he pulled me closer to him.

My mouth melted into his as he let out a low groan. He paused for a second and I looked into his eyes, wondering if he was going to stop. Instead, he smiled and cupped my chin and moved his lips back towards mine slowly. I smiled back, leaning into the kiss with ease and his strong arms held me for a moment before he pulled me towards him, as though he just couldn't wait any longer. He wanted me. Riley wanted *me*.

I couldn't believe this was actually happening. Since I'd first clapped eyes on Riley, I'd had to block these thoughts from my mind. Time and time again, I'd imagined him kissing me like this, feeling the warmth of his body next to mine, touching me tenderly. My whole body felt like it was on fire. I didn't have to blink the thoughts away this time, I could do everything I'd dreamed of with him.

The kissing intensified. Riley pulled away at one point. I almost gasped, ready to beg him to continue.

'I've wanted to do this for ages,' he murmured in a gruff, husky voice. 'Becca, I—'

'Sssh,' I said, putting a finger over his lips.

I didn't want to talk. I needed action. I pulled his mouth towards mine again, drinking Riley in, my hands grabbing at his toned, tanned back to bring him as close to me as humanly possible. He slid my top off and I leaned into his muscular body, kissing him hungrily. Our clothes lay in a heap on the floor as the sheets tousled around us. I couldn't let him stop; I wouldn't. Our bodies merged together, fast at first, before settling into a slow and steady rhythm.

It was all I'd thought it would be. And then some. My head felt dizzy as his body pressed closely on mine and he continued to kiss me tenderly throughout, his green eyes gazing intensely into my soul.

Afterwards, I lay in his arms under the covers. He kissed the top of my head gently. I looked up and caught him grinning down at me.

'All in the name of research,' he joked.

'Oi,' I said, punching him on the shoulder. 'Judging by that performance, Mr Romance Writer, you don't need any help when it comes to research. I'd say you're fairly well versed in that department.'

'Why, thank you.' He grinned. 'But I can't take all the credit. It takes two to tango.'

'I'd like to tango with you all day long,' I murmured as I leaned up to kiss him.

And then his phone rang, the shrill ringtone bursting our bubble. Who even had their phone on these days? He pulled away.

'Ivy,' he said, grabbing his boxer shorts as he moved towards the door.

Ah yes, people with children needed to keep their phones on.

My lips were still on fire. I moved my fingers along them. They were screaming at me, wondering why it had stopped. The abruptness of the ending left me dizzy.

'Hello?' he answered in the living area. 'Wait, Bridget, just slow down. What do you mean she's not there?'

I sat up straighter on the bed, wondering what was going on.

'Just slow down, Bridget. Tell me exactly what happened.'

He came back into the bedroom and stood at the foot of the bed, covering his mouth as he listened intently to what was being said on the other end.

Riley's phone thudded like a dead weight beside me on the bed as he pulled his T-shirt over his head and flung his jeans on.

'It's Ivy,' he said, his voice strained as he pulled on his jeans. 'She's not at nursery.'

I sat bolt upright in bed and pulled my clothes on, as quickly as my hands would allow.

'What do you mean she's not at nursery? I dropped her off there earlier.'

Riley grabbed his car keys, before swiftly collecting his phone again from beside me. I stood up and followed him as he paced towards the front door, grabbing my trainers in the process.

'Bridget just went to pick her up and some new teacher said she's not there. Said someone already came by to pick her up.'

'What? But we're here. Maybe it was Ellie?'

'Nope, Bridget checked with her already.'

The stones crunched beneath our feet as we dashed to the car.

'Well, they can't just have anyone walking in to pick her up, Riley. They must have a list of people with permission to do that, surely? They're not just going to give her away to a random stranger.'

He opened the car with a flick of his keys.

'Not a random stranger, no,' he said, turning back round to face me. 'I think Jackie's back.'

28

Riley slammed his car door behind him and the engine roared to life.

Shit. Shit. Shit. So Ivy hadn't been telling stories. She obviously had been in contact with her mum. But how? I considered telling Riley what Ivy had told me, but how could I break the news now, when he was driving full speed along the road, his face etched with anxiety? Instead, I kept quiet.

'Would Jackie take her somewhere?' I asked, tentatively. 'Or are we going to the nursery?'

Riley frowned, as though he was annoyed at the question, but I realised he was contemplating the answer. He was trying to think logically. Good luck with that.

'I need to speak to the nursery. Bridget is there but she's all over the place. I think she's in shock. We're only two minutes away anyway.'

Given the speed Riley was driving, I estimated we would be there in way less than that, but I kept my mouth shut and clung on to the edge of my seat. He turned expertly into the nursery car park, as he'd clearly done a thousand times before, and parked in the disabled spot. He turned off the engine and ran in, leaving the driver door wide open.

I wondered what on earth I was meant to do now. Should I follow him in? See if Bridget was OK? Or give them space? I'd never felt like more of a stranger.

Coming to Rathcliffe suddenly seemed like the worst idea in the world. I was totally imposing on Riley and his family, getting in the middle of things I didn't understand. Riley didn't want to open up to me about Jackie and now Ivy had gone missing. I didn't even know how bad it was that Jackie had Ivy; was she some sort of psychopath? I couldn't even let myself think about what Riley and I had just done, either.

Riley and Bridget came flying out of the front door towards the car.

'Sorry, I didn't want to get in the way,' I said. 'What did the nursery say? Is she with her mum?'

'Come on, sis.' Riley nodded to Bridget, and she scrambled into the back seat of the car as he started the engine again. 'We need to go to the station.'

Gawd. The police station. I pictured Ivy's innocent wee button nose all scrunched up when she smiled. All I wanted to do was gather her into a big bear hug and never let her go. If I felt like that after knowing her for such a short time, I couldn't imagine how Riley must feel.

Was Jackie really dangerous? She wouldn't harm Ivy, would she? I shivered.

But some mothers did. It was unthinkable, but I knew it was true.

As the engine roared back to life, Riley cocked his head to one side and bit his lip. His green eyes shone black and I felt like I didn't know him at all. Not really.

Traffic lights. Riley banged on the steering wheel and swore loudly at the car in front for, I assumed, adhering to the law of red lights. He rolled his window down to get some air. I shivered.

'Oh my God, I can't believe this is happening!' Bridget exclaimed from the back seat.

'It'll be all right,' I soothed, although of course I had no way to know that. But it seemed like the right thing to say.

I wished I'd offered Bridget a space in the front, where she belonged. I felt so out of place here, with this family who had more secrets than they were willing to share with me.

And worst of all, I hadn't told Riley about Ivy's claim that Jackie was coming back and they'd all be a happy family. I slid further down in the seat, looking out at the people whizzing past on the pavement as we made our way through to the small town I'd driven through on my way to Rathcliffe. Maybe this was all my fault, too.

So many people walking. It would be so hard to locate one small missing person. I mean, if Jackie had taken Ivy and she had legal rights or whatever, or had a passport perhaps with her name on it, and she was actually Ivy's mother, could she just take her away somewhere?

I gulped at the thought and stole a glance at the side of Riley's head. His cold, hard stare at the road in front was nothing like the easy smile that had leaned in to kiss me just moments ago. I shivered again.

The silence in the car was deafening. Bridget had never been so quiet before. Words tumbled out of her mouth more easily than they did for anyone I'd ever met. And she talked to everyone and everything. Last week, I'd overheard her having a conversation with a bird in the garden about what was for dinner that night. There was a discussion about worms and all sorts and I'd hoped I wasn't being invited to their house for a meal. I looked back to check on her in the back seat, but she was gazing out of the window with a pained expression on her face.

Riley flicked the indicator and I caught a glimpse of a sign for a police station. I wondered if I might be asked to give a statement. I mean, I would probably be under suspicion immediately, as the random house guest no one knew who had taken up residence in their house just as Ivy happened to go missing. I was here, obviously, and had clearly not actually taken Ivy, but maybe they would think I was some sort of accomplice. I'd been in bed with her dad when it happened, after all, like some kind of slutty temptress. They were bound to take up useless time investigating me and that was just pointless. But how was I supposed to clear that up without sounding guilty as charged? I was definitely going to raise some eyebrows.

The loud jangling tune of 'Girls Just Want to Have Fun' broke the silence, as Riley drove around in search of a space in the police station car park. He muttered under his breath as Bridget searched for her phone and then answered it in the back seat.

'Ellie, what's going on?'

She listened intently and hung up a few seconds later.

'She's at Bellinder Cottage, Riley. Jackie's got Ivy and they're waiting for you there. Ellie went round to check and found them bouncing together on the trampoline outside.'

'Oh, thank God,' Riley said, pulling over into a parking spot.

He sat completely still for a second before inhaling and exhaling with deep breaths. His hands shook against the wheel and I looked back at Bridget, tears stinging my eyes and hers.

Ivy was safe. Well, she was with Jackie. Somehow, that didn't seem to add up to the same thing, according to Riley and Bridget.

Riley flipped the key and started the car again. This time, he switched the radio on to a channel where they were having some sort of phone-in. He let the noise rumble on quietly in the background but still didn't say much.

Bridget piped up. 'Thank God she's OK. I couldn't believe it when nursery said she wasn't there. I just looked at the new girl and she looked so confused, like I was going mad or something, when I asked for Ivy. The panic in her eyes was unreal. I should phone the nursery and tell them we found her, actually.'

Riley grunted in reply and Bridget made the call in the back.

'It was her mother that took her . . . Yes, she was probably on the list. I'm not sure if she should be removed. I'll check with Riley and let you know . . . Yes, I know, we all got a big fright too. We weren't expecting her mother to be back, you see. No one knew,' Bridget said down the phone.

I knew. I sat still and closed my eyes.

Riley sped along the road and turned into Bellinder Cottage. Home sweet home.

29

Riley hugged Ivy so close to him that she struggled to breathe.

'Dadd-ay!' she protested with a little squeal. 'You're hurting me.'

'Ivy, I think you should come with us, love,' Bridget said, stretching her hand out.

All eyes were on Jackie. I frowned, realising she looked familiar, with short dark hair which was tied into a messy bun, hooded jumper and jeans. She was beautiful, in a very low-maintenance kind of way. Jackie didn't look stressed at all. In fact, she looked pretty chilled about everything. Like she snuck into nursery and took a child without permission every day.

'Riley,' Jackie said in a low, lilting accent. 'Good to see you.'

'Jackie,' he said, keeping his tone steady as he looked down at the little girl between them, smiling up at her parents.

And then I remembered.

'The book store,' I said, turning to her. 'You were at the author event.'

Jackie looked up and met my eye. 'Hello again.'

'Sorry, what?' Riley said, looking at me and then Jackie. 'You came to my book event?'

I knew inside he was a bubbling ball of rage. I could see it in his eyes.

'I was in the area.' She shrugged. 'So I popped along.'

Riley frowned.

'In the area,' he repeated. 'You haven't been "in the area" for over two years, Jackie. You should have told me you were coming. And you should definitely have told me you were going to pick Ivy up from nursery.'

'She's my daughter.' She shrugged. 'I brought her straight here but you obviously weren't home so we've just been waiting around outside. Anyway, I don't have your number.'

I blinked. How could she not have his number? The father of her child? I stole a glance at Bridget, who shook her head while staring at the ground.

'I'll take Ivy home with me,' Bridget announced. 'Let the two of you talk.'

'No!' Ivy protested. 'I want to stay and be all together as a family again. Just like you promised, Mammy. See, I told you, Becca.'

Ivy looked up and beamed at me. Riley frowned and I died a little bit inside.

'Nice to meet you again, Becca. I hear you've been staying. Ivy's very fond of you,' she said.

Her voice was strained when she addressed me and I realised, to Jackie, I was the elephant in the room.

'Er, nice to meet you, too,' I replied. 'Look, I'd better go. Somewhere.'

'You can come back to ours,' Bridget said. 'Stay with us tonight.'

'Thanks,' I mumbled in appreciation.

I tried to catch Riley's eye, but he was preoccupied, sporting a deep frown. His broad shoulders slumped in defeat. I remembered his carefree smile as he'd closed his eyes in the hot tub earlier and all the writing he'd managed to do that afternoon. The words had been flowing, he'd said. Now, with his ex back on the scene, I wondered how long that would last.

I thought of his mouth on mine. The tingling that spread across my body as we touched.

It felt like I'd imagined the whole thing.

'Come on now, Ivy. Let's leave Mammy and Daddy to talk things through here,' Bridget said.

'Aaawwww,' Ivy protested. 'Mammy said she would tuck me in tonight.'

'Tomorrow night, baby girl,' Jackie said.

Riley's eyes widened in surprise, but he said nothing.

'Come on, let's leave them to talk,' Bridget said quietly, pulling at Ivy's hand.

Ivy pouted but, reluctantly, nodded and leaned up to give her mum a cuddle. Jackie knelt down and gathered Ivy into her arms, inhaling the scent of her hair.

'Will you stay for the whole night tomorrow?' she asked. 'Bathtime and bedtime too?'

'I will,' Jackie said. 'I promise.'

Riley raised his eyebrows but again, said nothing.

'Right, we'll be off then,' Bridget said, leading Ivy away. 'Night. Text me later, Riley.'

I followed dutifully behind. Riley put a hand in the air to wave goodbye. Then he walked into the house with Jackie following closely behind.

Wait, what? They were letting Riley and Jackie stay together? Overnight, in the same house? This clearly was not a good idea. I mean, he'd been all fired up with me just an hour earlier and now he was in a house on his own with his ex? But no one seemed to think it was the wrong thing to do, apart from me. And I didn't seem to have a vote.

Ivy walked in the middle and asked us to swing her all the way to Auntie Bridget's house. She chattered about her day at nursery and how her mammy had turned up to take her home. Again.

'What do you mean, again?' Bridget asked, trying to sound casual.

'She's been coming to visit me when I play outside,' Ivy explained. 'I saw her yesterday. She stood on the other side of the gate and we talked.'

'And what did she say?'

'She said she's coming back to Bellinder Cottage.'

'Oh, is she now?' Bridget replied, frowning. 'Well, that's good to know.'

Ellie was waiting for us outside as we arrived.

'Sorry, I came back as soon as I saw her there,' she explained. 'I didn't want it to get too overcrowded and overwhelm Ivy.'

Bridget nodded and gathered Ellie into her arms.

'Jaysus, Ellie, I got such a fright. When I heard someone had just lifted her from the nursery . . .' she whimpered into Ellie's shoulder.

'Hey,' Ellie soothed. 'It's OK. She's safe. She's here.'

Ivy squeezed my hand.

'I don't know what everyone's making such a big fuss about,' she said to me. 'It's just my mammy.'

'I know, Ivy.' I smiled at her. 'Why don't you show me where you sleep when you're here? I'd love to see. We can have a special girlie sleepover tonight. I can paint your nails.'

'Yeeaaah!' Ivy exclaimed, pulling me into the house.

Bridget and Ellie shot me a look of gratitude and I followed Ivy into the house, feeling very much like the other child in the situation. I might as well just play with Ivy and let the grown-ups sort it all out.

If I was honest, it suited me fine. I was tired of having to be grown up all the time. Painting our nails and plaiting hair sounded much less stressful right now. Ivy showed me the spare bedroom, with all her teddies lined up on the bed, while Bridget and Ellie stayed in the kitchen, talking in low voices.

Ivy threw some toys on the ground and placed others on the bed.

'What did those poor guys do to you?' I asked, looking at the group on the floor.

'You said it was a girls' night,' she explained. 'They're the boy teddies.'

'Oh, I see. Well, we don't have to discriminate. They could stay. I'm sure they'll not get in the way.'

Ivy shrugged and put them in the corner.

'Do you think everyone is mad with me?' she asked, without looking up at me.

'Ivy, no, why would they be mad at you?'

'Because I went with Mammy. I just wanted to see her.'

Her whole face crumpled as her eyes filled with tears that quickly began to drip down her face. The more she blinked, the faster the tears fell.

I gathered her into my arms and her little body shook in mine. No matter how articulate she was, she was really only a baby. And while she understood what was going on, how could she possibly understand the implications of it all?

I wiped away her tears as she started to hiccup.

'I really, really hope Mammy and Daddy are back together. That's my biggest wish in the whole world,' she said.

I cuddled her into me without replying. What could I say? A few hours ago, I had been kissing Riley . . . and the rest. My stomach flipped at the thought of it, partly with guilt, while the other half was willing it to happen again. But things had changed drastically in the past few hours.

I wondered if there was a trope about being a homewrecker.

Ivy crawled off my knee and wiped away her own tears. And just as quickly as she'd started crying, she seemed fine again. Over it. She started humming as she set to work, tucking her teddies into bed, one by one.

'I promise I'll do bath and bedtime tomorrow night,' she

whispered to each of them as she kissed them on the head before wishing them sweet dreams.

I sighed and wished someone was tucking me into bed, too. And some of those sweet dreams would be lovely right about now. In fact, any dreams would do.

With Jackie back on the scene, I had a whole new layer of worry to add to my pile. I just kept heaping things on top, without resolving anything. As the pile got bigger and bigger, it was bound to tumble over at some point.

'Ivy,' I said. 'What is that song you're humming?'

She grinned up at me.

'It's my favourite nursery rhyme,' she explained.

'Oh really, what is it?'

'"Let's Get Down to Business",' she replied. 'We dance to it on a Friday at nursery.'

She sang the Tiësto song in a deep voice while her little body swayed to the off-key rhythm. I threw my head back and laughed harder than I thought I could right now.

This wee girl deserved the whole world. She was sweet, sensitive and absolutely hilarious. There was no way I could stand in the way of her happiness. And she wanted her mammy, not some wannabe replacement.

Whatever Jackie had done in the past, she was back now. But where the hell did that leave me?

30

We sat down for 'grown-up talk' as soon as Ivy was asleep. I wasn't planning to make this all about me but I had to tell them, at some point, my doubts about staying any longer. How could I stay? I dreaded going back to Glasgow but I couldn't remain here forever, pretending. I'd inadvertently stolen Jackie's life, but now she was back, I had to go.

What was that expression Riley had used? Shit or get off the pot. I had to get off the pot. It wasn't mine.

'You could stay with us,' Bridget said. 'You don't have to go, you know.'

It's what I wanted to hear but the niggling feeling in the pit of my stomach reminded me that I couldn't. I'd gone too far with Riley. I should have waited to hear what he had to say about his relationship with Jackie. I had no idea what I was getting myself into here.

'I'm sorry. I know I promised to help you out with your new business. And I'd really like to. But I came here thinking

I was staying with a friend and, well, it's not exactly turned out like that.'

'I thought you and Riley were getting on well. He said you were even funnier in real life,' she said, and then her voice dropped to a low whisper, making sure Ivy couldn't hear. 'He seems to really like you, Becca.'

My whole body tingled as I thought back to a few hours ago on the bed at the cottage. His smile. His kiss. Everything that followed. I shook my head.

'It's not that,' I said, taking a sip of the wine that Bridget had just handed me as she headed back to the kitchen. 'I really like him too. But if he's going to make it work with Jackie, they'll need space, not a lodger.'

'You like him too? Wait . . . Did something happen between you and Riley?' Ellie asked, leaning forward.

'Wait, wait, wait! Do NOT answer that until I'm back in the room,' Bridget called from the kitchen.

I hesitated. Should I tell them what had happened at the cottages? It didn't feel right to tell Riley's sister. Not like I had gory details or anything, but to break the news when her ex-sister-in-law had just returned out of the blue . . . I took a gulp of red wine. It was just as well Bridget wanted me to wait. I didn't know what to say.

So I ignored the question.

Ellie opened her mouth to speak.

'I SAID WAIT,' Bridget called, rushing back into the room and plonking herself down on the sofa. 'OK, I'm back now.

Spill the tea, sister. We need details. I'll pretend he's not my brother when it gets to the juicy bits. Or I'll cover my ears. Go.'

'Bridget, maybe she doesn't want to talk about this . . .' Ellie suggested.

'It's fine,' I sighed. 'He said he'd tell me a bit more about what happened with Jackie. And then you called. So maybe you could tell me what happened between them? So I know how much I'm . . . getting in the way.'

Wine in hand, I was desperate to hear everything now. All the details.

'God, where do I start with Jackie?' Bridget asked and Ellie rolled her eyes. 'I never thought they were compatible. She wanted to party all night and sleep all day. He was never one of those people. He enjoys the odd drink but she needed it. And worse. She was into drugs, too. Couldn't have a night out without something. That was it, at first.'

'Yup,' Ellie joined in. 'She was off her face every time I saw her. She was putting stuff up her nose. And she didn't seem to know when to stop.'

'No way,' I said. 'That can't be true. She seems so . . . normal.'

Bridget snorted. 'Huh, yup, that's our Jackie. But it got worse. When she found out she was pregnant, she was horrified. She really struggled. It was just awful but I think she managed to stay clean. Just about, anyway. And then, when Ivy was born, she went missing from the hospital.'

The plot thickened. My mouth fell open.

'What?'

'Yup, literally hours after she'd given birth. Riley said she just kept asking for medication to take the edge off and then she just took off while his back was turned. When she eventually turned up again, she was off her face. But Riley kept it a secret from everyone. The doctor diagnosed her with post-natal depression. But she was too far gone at that point.'

Poor Riley. And worst of all, poor Ivy.

I couldn't believe they'd had to go through all that. And how could anyone feel like that when they had such a beautiful baby girl? It was an illness though. Jackie was clearly ill.

'That's not all, though,' Bridget continued. 'When Ivy turned two, she told Riley she was leaving him for someone else.'

'Brian, his name was.' Ellie picked up the story. 'I think he was a dealer. Either way, he was into it all too. And Jackie seemed relieved when she finally told Riley she was leaving. So did he. Riley, I mean. His nerves were shot with it all. He didn't even seem to care that she was with someone else by then. Said she wasn't the person he thought she was. She didn't even say goodbye to Ivy. She just left one night and didn't come back.'

I couldn't believe it. I wasn't a mum, but even as a teacher, I couldn't imagine doing that to a child – leaving them without any explanation. No wonder Ivy was so confused about her mum. No wonder she wanted her back so badly.

'That's just awful,' I said, putting my glass down on the coffee table.

'I mean, we joke about drinking wine and all around Ivy, but we'd never do anything to—'

'I know that, Bridget. You don't need to explain anything, believe me.'

We all sighed. Poor Ivy. I wished there was something I could do to help her. And Riley.

'And now she's back,' Bridget said, exhaling. 'Riley really wasn't expecting her. She's not called, not texted, nothing. Just went completely off-grid. A friend of a friend said they thought she was in London for a while but nothing was ever confirmed.'

'What do you think Riley will do? Do you think she wants to get back with him?' I asked.

Second-chance romance. I wondered if he would take a gamble on his own trope.

'I bloody well hope not,' Bridget almost shouted.

Ellie shrugged, ever the practical one. 'He never wanted a broken family, though. He's angry with her, but he really loved her once upon a time. Plus, she's Ivy's mum, and you know what Riley's like, he's a dreamer. A sucker for a happy ending.'

My stomach twisted in a tight knot. Ellie was right, Riley was all about the happy endings. I knew he loved Ivy more than anything, too. She was his priority.

The thought of Riley and Jackie being in Bellinder Cottage together overnight to 'talk' suddenly filled me with dread.

31

TEN YEARS AGO

Rae kicked the bright orange and yellow leaves as we walked along the path. Tenerife seemed like a lifetime ago. I had barely seen her since we got back. I'd gone back to university and was preparing for my school placement. I was basically burnt out. I spent every waking moment plotting, planning and studying. I dreamed about lesson planning, reciting the class register in my sleep.

I barely had any time for Drew, either, and he was sulking. Big time. He was pulling long shifts working at the theme park and Leila was dangling the possibility of a promotion under his nose to get him to work extra hours. They stayed late after work together most nights for a 'drink'. He'd never told me that, but I saw it all over her social media pages – which I checked religiously. Obviously.

'So, I've got some news,' Rae said.

She was wearing a small black hat, her hair tumbling in waves beneath it.

'Oh?'

'I'm back with Mickey,' she said, avoiding my gaze. 'We're going to try and make it work.'

My heart sank. She'd spent the whole time in Tenerife off her face, determined to get over Mickey. She'd sworn she would never go back to him, revealing things that she'd never told me before as we staggered home in the early hours of the morning. She'd promptly forget what she'd disclosed the next day. But I remembered.

'So has he apologised for everything then? You know, all the stuff you told me about on holiday? He makes everything seem like it's your fault, Rae, when it's not. You told me he was emotionally abusive . . . And what about the time he . . . he hit you. You told me about that, remember? In fact, you said he punched you. In the side of the head.'

There. I'd said it. I couldn't not say it.

She looked up, shocked.

'I did not,' she whispered, her eyes suddenly darker.

'You did. You were pissed, but you told me.'

'I was obviously exaggerating, Becca. I was being my usual drama queen self because I was pissed.' She forced a laugh. 'As if he hit me. I'd never let someone do that.'

'It happens to women all the time, Rae. You wouldn't be the first. It's nothing to be ashamed of. There are people that will help you. I can help you. I don't think you should be getting back with someone like that.'

She stopped dead in the middle of the path and looked over my shoulder, avoiding my stare.

'Becca, I'm telling you right now, you've got the wrong end of the stick. If I said that, I was lying. Looking for sympathy. It's absolutely not true. And I'd really like it if you didn't bring that up again, actually. And I hope you've not told anyone that. Not Drew. No one. The last thing Mickey and I need is people trying to cause problems for us,' she said.

Her hands were shaking. I pulled one of them into mine and then linked her arm again but she tensed and pulled away from me.

'Of course I've not told anyone. I just want you to be careful. To be sure. You are so funny. And smart. And beautiful, obviously. You could have any guy you wanted.'

'I want him, Becca,' she replied. 'Yeah, sometimes he can be a bit jealous or whatever, but it shows he cares about me, doesn't it?'

'I don't know, Rae,' I said, doubtfully. 'I mean, if he's possessive and aggressive, there's a lot of big red flags waving around.'

'You want to talk about red flags, Becca? What about you constantly stalking your boyfriend's boss online? You're crazy jealous! You're worse than Mickey. If I found out he was doing that to me, I'd freak right out.'

She had a point. I fell silent, my cheeks burning. Maybe it was a pot-calling-the-kettle-black kind of situation.

'OK,' I said. 'Point taken. Maybe he's changed, anyway. Like you say he has. I just hope everything works out.'

She smiled with satisfaction at winning the argument. I was

a crazy jealous stalker, too. Who the hell was I to argue with that? It was true.

I was sure it wouldn't last between Rae and Mickey, anyway. They would have another blow-up and Rae would declare that they were over in no time. There was no point in pushing it with her, when their relationship was bound to come to a natural end point, anyway.

What was the point in ruining our friendship over something that would never last?

32

I checked my phone notifications and found I had a voicemail from Rae's mum, asking me to call her, and a text from her. Rae had always been tenacious too. Like mother, like daughter.

Ellie and Bridget were in deep discussion in the living room, so I went outside, wrapping a cardigan around myself. It was time to call her back. I couldn't keep ignoring her. I'd have to face the music eventually.

She answered after one ring.

'Oh, Becca. It's so lovely to hear your voice. Finally.'

'You too, Linda. I'm sorry for not calling before now. I'm in Ireland. I've been busy.'

'Oh, I know, love. Adam told us all about it. Living with the man you thought was a woman. How's it going?'

'It's fine, thanks,' I said, although of course it was far from fine, but that's just what you say. 'How are you?'

'You know,' she said. I could hear her voice crack. 'Just wanted to check in on you. I felt so awful after the funeral and everything that happened with Drew . . . I just wanted you to know that Rae didn't plan to be with him, Becca. They bumped into each other in Edinburgh when she moved. They didn't even plan to meet up. It was a while before anything actually happened, too . . .'

'It's fine, Linda,' I said.

I didn't have the energy to talk about it right now.

She sighed. 'Fair enough. I also wanted to let you know that we're holding a memorial for her. For Rae. On her birthday. I hoped you'd be home for it.'

'A memorial? What, like another funeral?'

'Well, I suppose. More of a remembrance thing. Maybe let off balloons into the sky or something. I don't know exactly yet. I need to confirm it with Drew, too. But you'll come, won't you, Becca? We couldn't have it without you there. When will you be back from Ireland?'

Confirm it with Drew. I rolled my eyes. As if he needed any more of an excuse to act like he was so important, so involved in everything. The prick.

'I'm not sure yet,' I replied, honestly. 'But I'll let you know when I do.'

'OK, love. Jim sends his love, too. And Adam. He's been keeping me in the loop with all the stories about Rae you've been sending him. Thank you, Becca. I think it's really helping him.'

'He's been keeping me smiling too,' I said. 'Thanks, Linda. Good night.'

Bridget came out to see me as I hung up the phone, leaving

me wondering if she'd been eavesdropping. Her eyes darted around nervously.

'Oh, thank God you're off,' she said. 'I need to ask you a huge favour. Come inside.'

'Of course.' I smiled, following her in. 'Ask me anything.'

'Will you watch Ivy for us in the morning?'

'Of course I will,' I replied.

'Thank you,' she said.

Ellie appeared by her side.

'Ask me why,' she said.

'What do you mean?' I asked.

'Ask us why we need you to look after Ivy,' Ellie said.

Their eyes danced in front of me.

'The adoption agency called,' Bridget burst in. 'They think they've found us a match.'

The two women clutched each other's hands and Bridget squealed. Loudly. The next thing I knew, I was joining in.

We hugged and jumped around.

'Wow, this is amazing! Tell me everything. What did they say?'

We gathered around their kitchen island for the update.

'That was all they said. They couldn't give any more details over the phone,' Ellie explained.

'It was like getting a call from a secret agent. We put her on speaker phone and asked a million questions, but she said she'd tell us everything in person tomorrow. Oh, Ellie, this could really be it!' Bridget beamed.

'The only problem is, of course, the timing with the new business. Would you stay and be our receptionist, Becca? I think we have something that's going to convince you.'

'What?' I raised an eyebrow.

'Well, while you're working for us, you could stay in one of the apartments while we sort everything out with Riley and Jackie and all the rest. You would have your own space, your own job and come and go as you please. For as long as you like,' Bridget said. 'What do you think?'

Ach, shite. The pair of them were so excited about everything. They'd obviously dreamed of this moment for so long. I couldn't ruin it for them. They were relying on my help and I had promised them I would take on the job.

I took a deep breath in before exhaling.

How could I tell them that I had to leave now?

'I'm sorry, guys. I am so over the moon for you both. But I just don't think I can stay. I don't think it's fair on Riley. Or Jackie. And most of all, I don't think it's fair on Ivy. She's so excited about her mum being back. If there's even the slightest chance that they might get back together, I need to step aside and let that happen. I can't be a homewrecker. I won't,' I said, firmly.

There. I'd said it. I watched their faces fall as I spoke, but they nodded reluctantly.

'Don't worry, we'll sort something else out,' Ellie said, although her worried expression betrayed her true feelings on the matter.

'I'm sorry,' I said, again.

'It's fine, Becca,' Bridget said. 'But just so you know, you've put Ivy first more times than her own mum ever has.'

I felt my eyes fill unexpectedly with tears as Bridget leaned over and squeezed me into a tight cuddle. I buried myself into her cosy bright red cardigan and reminded myself to breathe. Everything was happening so quickly. I blinked back the tears and cleared my throat.

'Do you know, you're the only one that's never asked us,' Bridget said.

'Asked what?' I frowned.

'Why we're adopting. You know, instead of going down the sperm donor route,' she said.

I blinked.

'People actually ask you that?!'

'All the time!' Bridget replied, laughing, waving her hand as though shooing a fly away. 'We're used to it by now. The whole of book club has asked at one time or another. Discreetly, most of the time, at least. Pete from the walking group even offered to be a sperm donor for us, after a few too many whiskeys on our Christmas night out last year. Can you believe that?'

'Noooo!' I replied, holding my face behind my hand to stop myself from giggling. 'But he's about sixty.'

'Sixty-four.' Ellie nodded firmly.

'I have to say, I'm not sure if I could have resisted that offer,' I said. 'He's got a cracking set of thighs on him. They might even be hereditary.'

Ellie and Bridget laughed.

'See, why are more people not like you?' Bridget said.

'They're all usually asking six million questions. Do we not want to carry our own child? Is there a problem with one of us? Both of us? Who would carry the baby, if we decided to go down that route? One person even asked me if we were thinking of adopting to make everything feel more even, because the one that carried the baby might feel like more of the mum than the other!'

My hand flew to my mouth. 'Nooo!'

'Yup.' Ellie nodded. 'As if, you know, a dad feels like less of a parent than a mum or something. Most people are understanding and supportive of us as a couple but it doesn't stop all the questions. But you've never asked us why. You just accepted it.'

'Of course,' I replied. 'But if you'd told me Pete from walking club with his super sperm was willing to get involved, I might have tried to get in on the action myself.'

'I think the reason you haven't asked is because you're a bit like us,' Ellie said. 'You want to help kids, too, right? You love working with the children in your class, don't you? We want to see if we can help a child that's already here and welcome them into our home. If we can't, then we'll look into having our own.'

I gave a tight smile. I did love the children in my class. It was my horrible boss spoiling it all that was the problem.

'Who could ever argue with that?' I said. 'And by the way, I think you're both going to be the most amazing mums in the world.'

'You too, Becca. One day. Maybe with our Riley.' Bridget winked.

I rolled my eyes but inside, my heart felt heavy. That ship looked to have well and truly sailed.

33

Ivy woke at the crack of dawn the next morning, asking if we could have pancakes for breakfast. We crept into Bridget and Ellie's kitchen and set to work, gathering all the ingredients from various cupboards. We managed to find everything we needed, despite the messy drawers, and having no idea where anything was in the first place.

Ivy giggled with excitement as I urged her to keep her voice down. We set about flipping the pancakes and laid out fruit, chocolate spread (of course) and maple syrup. I cooked bacon in the frying pan while Ivy sat at the table colouring in the card.

Just as she was putting the finishing touches to it, Bridget and Ellie came in, wearing matching dressing gowns.

'Good morning!' Ellie said.

'We barely slept a wink, we were so excited,' Bridget confessed.

I'd heard them whispering into the early hours.

'We made you pancakes.' Ivy grinned. 'Becca said we're

celebrating. She helped me make this card. Is it someone's birthday?'

She handed them the card that I'd supervised her making. She had drawn a picture of Ellie, Bridget and a sunshine and we'd written Good Luck on the front.

'Ooooh, this is so gorgeous, thank you, Ivy,' Bridget said, kissing her niece on the head.

'What is the good luck for?' Ivy asked. 'What's happening today?'

'Do you remember we told you that we're hoping we'll be mummies and you'll have a cousin to play with?' Bridget said. 'We're going to find out more about it today, but it looks like it might be happening soon!'

Ivy squealed with excitement and hugged her aunt Bridget.

'Is it a girl or a boy? Can you choose? What age is she? Or he? When will they move in? Can I still sleep over on Thursday nights?'

'Wow, wow, wow,' Bridget laughed, kissing Ivy on the forehead. 'We don't know the answers to any of that yet. Except one.'

Ivy glanced up at her auntie with wide, excited eyes.

'Which one?'

'You staying here on Thursday nights. You always stay here on Thursdays,' Bridget confirmed with a smile.

'Yeah!' Ivy laughed. 'I can't believe all my wishes are coming true. Mammy's back, Becca's here and I get a cousin!'

I was touched that she squeezed me into her wishes.

I could already picture Ellie, Bridget and a child sitting

happily with cousin Ivy every Friday morning at breakfast time. I wondered if the same joy was being felt over at Bell-inder Cottage this morning. I thought about Riley and Jackie all night while tossing and turning in the blow-up bed in the spare room. It was a whole new nightmare scenario to add to my growing repertoire.

I just wanted everything to be OK, for Ivy's sake. But I couldn't imagine how that could possibly happen, given everything Bridget had told me about Jackie.

But there had obviously been some attraction between them. What if Riley had caved in and they'd spent the night together? Like, together together. What if she'd managed to change his mind? Ellie was right; Riley loved the thought of a happily ever after. He'd admitted it himself. The thought gave me a knot in my stomach.

'It is very exciting,' Ellie said. 'We've got to get going now. You stay with Becca, and we'll let you know as soon as we know anything, OK? We've got to get ready for the big meeting about it this morning.'

They barely ate a bite of their breakfast, putting it down to nerves. Instead, Ivy and I finished off the pancakes as they left to get ready. When they came back, they were grinning like Cheshire cats and clutching each other's hands.

'I can't believe this is happening,' Ellie said.

'Right, you two, off you go then. The sooner you leave, the sooner we get the news about your new family member,' I said.

Bridget let out a loud squeal and clapped her hands like a five year old.

'If you get to choose,' Ivy said, 'I'd like a girl cousin. Same age as me. With bunches.'

Ellie and Bridget burst out laughing.

'We'll see what we can do.' Ellie nodded.

Ivy and I kept ourselves busy while Bridget and Ellie were out. We got dressed, tidied the kitchen and folded the washing. Just as we started dancing to Taylor Swift, the music blasting from my phone, the side door opened.

Riley.

I spun Ivy around, feeling dizzy myself as my heart began thumping in my chest, as he offered me an apologetic smile.

Had something happened with Riley and Jackie? Riley looked exhausted. His eyes usually lit up as soon as he laid eyes on Ivy, but today they remained still, even as Ivy threw herself into his arms. I wanted to do the same, but I didn't. I stopped dancing instead and watched him closely.

'How are things?' I asked.

'Where's Mammy?' Ivy asked at the same time.

Riley smiled at Ivy. 'I'm going to bring you over to see Mammy now. If that's OK with you, Becca.'

'With me? Why would it not be OK with me? It's absolutely nothing to do with me, when Ivy sees her mum,' I said. 'So of course.'

Why could I not stop bloody talking?

'Go and get your bag, Ivy,' Riley urged, and Ivy fled glee-fully from the room, ready to pack up and see her mum again.

'I'm so sorry,' he said, as soon as she left.

He moved slowly towards me. I kept my hands in my pockets.

'It's fine.' I shrugged, trying to offer a smile. 'Of course it is. It's not your fault. It's not like you planned it.'

He stood in front of me and looked straight into my eyes. I shifted uncomfortably.

'I need to let Ivy see Jackie now. It's just a really . . . delicate situation. But Ivy has the right to see her mum and I guess I've got to let that happen.'

'It's fine. I'm fine. You don't need to explain. Of course you need to go and see her.'

No he didn't! Exes are exes for a reason. That's what Riley said before we'd even met, when I said Drew had been at Rae's funeral. Back in the good old days when Riley was just my friend, before I even realised he was a six-foot-something drop-dead gorgeous guy. One who kissed me in a way that felt like I'd never been kissed before, or would be again.

'Where are Bridget and Ellie, by the way?' he said, interrupting my thoughts.

'Oh, didn't they tell you? They have a meeting with the adoption people this morning. They got a call last night to say they might have found a match.'

Riley's mouth fell open. 'No way! That's brilliant news!'

'It is.' I smiled. 'It really is.'

I shuffled from one foot to the other, suddenly unsure what to say.

'You can come back to Bellinder Cottage with us, if you'd like?'

'No, no. I'll leave you to it,' I said.

He leaned towards me, lowering his voice. I could almost taste him and held my breath as he edged towards me.

'Becca, yesterday was—'

'Daddy!! Becca and me made pancakes for Auntie Bridget and Auntie Ellie this morning and a good luck card. They're going to get a cousin for me!'

'I know, it's very exciting. But it's Becca and I,' Riley corrected her grammar.

'That's what I said,' Ivy retorted.

Riley rolled his eyes and kissed Ivy on the cheek as they turned to leave.

'I'm sorry, Becca. Can we talk later?' he asked, throwing me a quick glance over his shoulder.

'Of course,' I replied.

I could hear Ivy's chattering all the way along the path as they walked through the garden.

'So now all my dreams are coming true,' was the last thing I heard Ivy proclaim before they were out of earshot.

34

'Twins! We just can't believe it. It's better than we'd ever hoped for. A boy and a girl. Damien and Lucy. Can you believe it?'

Bridget and Ellie came back from their adoption meeting floating on air with their news. I listened to them telling the story over and over again and shared the delight with them every single time. The one-year-old twins were coming to live with them as soon as all the paperwork was signed off.

As Ellie left to call her parents and tell them the big news, Bridget turned to me. Her face fell.

'They've come from a terrible background though, Becca,' she confided, whispering. 'I mean, I know they're young but they've been in care for months now. I wonder what that will have done to them, you know, emotionally.'

'You're offering them a stable home now, though. You just need to focus on the future and plan to make things better for them. I'm sure the adoption agency will give you support too?'

'Oh yes, they gave us leaflets to read. So many leaflets.' She gave an uncomfortable laugh.

'It's natural to be nervous, Bridget,' I whispered. 'This is a really big deal.'

'Do you think so?' she asked, wringing her hands together. 'It's all we've ever wanted but now it's here . . . Well, I'm shitting myself. I can't tell Ellie because she'll think it's because I'm getting cold feet. I'm not, but I am so nervous. What if we can't handle it?'

I took her hand in mine. 'Look, Bridget, you can do this. I promise you. Nobody knows what they're doing at the start, I'm sure, but you'll find your way. The first time I stepped foot in a classroom, I felt like hiding under the desk until a real teacher came in to take over. You're going to be amazing parents. I have every faith in you.'

Bridget exhaled and gave me a quick hug just as Ellie walked back in.

'Ellie, I'm shitting myself,' Bridget called to her wife. 'There, I said it. I'm so freaking nervous now.'

'Oh Bridget, me too!' Ellie exclaimed, running to her partner. 'I just said the exact same thing to my sister. I didn't want to tell you in case you thought I was backing out, but it just hit me all of a sudden and I'm totally shitting myself now.'

They both laughed and then moved towards each other for a huge bear hug. It looked so cosy, I could have jumped right in the middle.

'Well, now everyone agrees that we're shitting ourselves, I'll leave you both to it,' I said, giving them each a hug in turn.

'But you're both going to be amazing parents. Damien and Lucy are lucky children.'

I waved goodbye to them both and went for a walk to clear my head and give them some space to talk about their plans and future together. While I contemplated mine.

I could go back to Glasgow and beg for my job back. Apologise. Suck up to my bitch-of-a-boss. Or I could appeal or whatever it is you do when you tell your boss to fuck off and quit your job. I wasn't sure that was covered in their policies or manuals though, which was a bit of an issue.

I wandered along the road, past Bellinder Cottage, and took myself for a coffee in a café. As I sat back in my seat, looking out at the quiet streets of Rathcliffe, I realised I could get used to this kind of laidback lifestyle. Glasgow's streets were busier and everyone was always in a hurry. Rathcliffe folk just seemed to stroll through life. I wished I could shrug it all off and stroll too.

I sipped my coffee. Ellie and Bridget were going to have their work cut out for them in the coming weeks and months with not one but two children to look after, while Riley and Ivy had to navigate their new normal with Jackie back on the scene. I didn't quite fit here any more. Not that I ever really had in the first place, but now it was different. I was an extra piece of an uncertain puzzle. I felt a lump forming in my throat. This had been my refuge, my escape route, my safe space. My mind wasn't any clearer than it had been when I arrived here, and I felt panic looming at the thought of returning to 'normal'.

'I'll have a cappuccino, please,' a familiar voice echoed

through the small coffee shop, snapping me out of my day-dream.

Same flat stomach and perfectly tiny little bum. Eimear was practically bouncing at the till, with her yoga T-shirt and skin-tight purple leopard-print leggings, waiting for her coffee. Her little body practically disappeared to the side as she turned around and spotted me.

'Ah, Becca!' she exclaimed and proceeded to skip, actually skip, over to me. I sighed inwardly.

'Hi . . .' I gestured to the seat opposite, secretly hoping she wouldn't take me up on the offer. But her face lit up at the prospect of a chat and she placed her perfect little bum on the seat across from me.

'How are you? I meant to try and catch you after our yoga session the other day. Riley said you're enjoying it a bit more?'

I actually didn't like it at all. All the downward dog and warrior poses and breathing in the world wasn't going to help fix my problems.

'Yes, it was great, thanks,' I said, instead.

She smoothed either side of her head and pulled her long hair back into a perfect ponytail. Every strand of hair in place with the flick of a wrist. I subconsciously patted my own mane and wondered when I'd last washed it.

'Anyway, listen,' she said, pulling her seat closer to me. I groaned. So much for my peaceful coffee. She leaned in to whisper. 'I don't mean to pry, but there's a rumour flying around town and just as I saw you, I thought I should really get it straight from the horse's mouth.'

I raised my eyebrows. Had Eimear just called me a horse? To my face? I opened my mouth but closed it again. Now wasn't really the time to debate with her.

'Cappuccino, Eimear. Do you want a cup if you're sitting in?' the barista interrupted, placing a takeaway cup in front of her.

'No, that's grand, thank you. I'll have it in this.' She gestured at the cup and smiled before leaning closer to me as the barista walked away. 'The woman who lives three doors down from me was speaking to Maeve, whose sister Gina works along the road from the nursery. She said Jackie's back.'

Ah, so it didn't take long for the whole town to be talking about Riley and Jackie. I couldn't say I was surprised.

'Erm, well . . .' I stammered, unsure what to confirm or deny. This wasn't my story to tell, after all.

She crossed her legs in her shiny purple exercise leggings and leaned in further to dish out more gossip.

'And I texted Riley last night, just by coincidence of course, to ask about our yoga book and he didn't text me back,' she continued, as though that confirmed it.

'What yoga book?' I asked. I'd never heard Riley mention anything about that.

'He didn't tell you?' she frowned, looking hurt. 'The one we were meant to meet to talk about. I wanted his advice on writing a book about yoga. He said we'd get a date in the diary but it's not happened yet.'

Ah, the date. I doubted that Eimear had any interest in writing a book about yoga. I could bet she was keen to try some new positions with Riley, though.

237

'Anyway, is it true? Is Jackie back?'

My phone rang before I could answer. Saved by the bell.

'Sorry, I need to get this,' I apologised, standing up.

Eimear's mouth fell open, as though she wanted to lie down on the ground like a toddler and throw a tantrum. I felt a little bit guilty as I lifted my phone to answer it on the way out of the café, waving goodbye on the way out.

'Hello?' I said.

Somehow, I knew it was him before he even replied. I felt it somewhere deep down in my gut.

'I'm sober now,' came the reply. 'And I wondered if we could talk.'

35

NINE YEARS AGO

'They're planning this big opening do. A black-tie swanky event. Leila said I might get to go.' Drew's eyes danced as he spoke.

He was wearing a perfectly pressed suit. Again. Did he think he was impressing someone? It certainly wasn't me. I preferred him when he looked normal. Acted normal. The Drew I'd met at the ice cream van last summer wouldn't have cared about a black-tie event. He'd looked like he rolled out of bed every day and pulled on his crumpled T-shirt, shorts and trainers before strolling into work. If he'd been asked to a swanky event, he'd have run a mile.

Now, since his promotion, he was all 'dress for the job you want, not the job you have' and all this corporate mumbo jumbo about sales potential and exponential growth. He credited Leila with his newfound success, of course. He thought the sun shone out her backside. They'd gone for drinks to celebrate his promotion, which she'd labelled on social as 'Bye, bye Mr Whippy, helllllllo Mr Suave Boss Man. Same level as me now. Even-stevens' with all the clapping emojis that followed.

I'd had to pretend to be surprised when he'd called me with his promotion news. The next day.

'That's great,' I said. 'When is the black-tie thing?'

He looked away.

'When?' I pressed.

He had that shifty look that I'd seen before, the one that he used when he knew I was going to give him trouble. I knew there was more to this than met the eye; I just hadn't quite figured out what it was.

'Next Thursday,' he said quickly, as though he was hoping that the faster he said it, the less likely I was to realise what that meant.

A quick reflection and my reflexes kicked in.

'You'd miss my graduation day.'

He let out a huge sigh. The secret was out. I'd scuppered his plans.

'I know, but Becca, we can go out and celebrate just the two of us, especially now my promotion has been confirmed.' He smiled hopefully at me, looking over his shoulder and around the restaurant.

He was hoping I wouldn't cause a scene.

I took a sip of my wine and narrowed my eyes at him. I was about to burst his bubble.

'My graduation is a very big deal,' I said, slowly, hoping he'd intervene and say of course he was coming. He wouldn't miss something as big as a graduation. My graduation. The thing I'd been working towards for the past four years. He couldn't possibly miss it.

Partners went to graduations. They took pictures standing outside with big cheesy, proud grins, jostling for position against the graduates' parents, who would insist on pictures without said boyfriend/girlfriend because parents knew it was unlikely to work out.

I'd only been given two tickets for graduation. I only had one parent. Drew had to be there.

'This is a big deal to me, Becca,' he replied. 'It could shape my whole career. Leila said they're talking about a Head of Sales job for me in future. She said she'd love to see me in that position.'

I knew what position she wanted my boyfriend in. And he was falling for it, hook, line and sinker. She knew she could lure him away from me with the promise of promotions but really, she was working towards her long-term goal. Girls like that don't give up until they have exactly what they want. That's what Rae said. I guessed she was right.

'Rae could come,' he said, 'To your graduation ceremony. I bet she'd love to. She'd stand up and whistle when your name was called. She'd give you a "woop woop" from the crowd.'

That was actually very true. But it wasn't the point.

'She's graduating on the same day,' I reminded him. 'Linda and Jim are going along. Her aunts are even trying to get extra tickets to come and see her. Even her brother wants to come, and they don't even like each other. Because it's a big deal, Drew.'

The aim was to make him feel more guilty. Pile the pressure on. But he didn't seem to blink.

'What about your cousin? The tall blonde one?'

'Stop!' I shouted, banging my hand against the table.

Drew jumped and looked around, his face flushed at the tone of my voice.

'If you don't want to come, don't come,' I said. 'But don't expect me to just bring anybody along in your place. I want you there. You and Dad. That's it.'

He sighed and rolled his eyes. It must be a complete inconvenience for someone to love him so much. He knew how hard I'd worked to get my degree. He'd witnessed the hours of stressing over essays and school placements and pupils who I wanted to support. He knew I was invested in their futures, in helping them to be the best they possibly could. Drew knew. How could he not want to be with me on the biggest day of my life?

But he didn't care. That's what it came down to. Or perhaps he cared about his career more. Or Leila. I'd never seen such a freaking beautiful elephant in the room as Leila Jackson with her big boobs and her flawless smile and her stupid social media posts about every freaking day of her life. I had been glued to her feed for months now, after all. I could even tell what time she was taking her lunch break every day.

'OK, I'll come,' he said, letting out a huge sigh in the process. 'I'll just tell them I can't make the event.'

Our food arrived and the waiter placed it in front of us. Fish and chips for me, seafood linguine for Drew. When we'd first started going out, he would only eat pizza or burgers. Now, he was intent on 'exploring the menu' to advance his hospitality career.

We sat in silence as he quickstepped away. Drew lifted his fork and started twirling the linguine around on his plate. I shook vinegar on my fish and chips, followed by salt.

I broke the silence eventually.

'I'd rather you didn't come at all than me having to drag you there. Go to the event that's going to catapult you to the top of your hospitality career. That's obviously your priority.'

'I'll fucking come,' he said.

'You fucking won't.'

'OK, I fucking won't.'

'Is this about Leila?'

I said it. He dropped his knife and it clanged loudly against his plate.

'What's that supposed to mean?'

I exhaled. It was the conversation I'd been holding back for months but the anger was coursing through me. I'd had enough.

'You obviously like her.'

'She's my boss, Becca.'

'Not any more,' I pointed out. 'You're the same level now. Even-stevens. That's what you said.'

'I never said that. I wouldn't say that. That phrase,' he said.

Shit. Shit. Shit. He hadn't said that. It was Leila. It was on her social media page.

'Oh,' I said.

The penny dropped right about then. I could see it all over his face as he realised.

'You've been looking at her social media,' he said.

'What? No.' I shook my head.

Deny to the death. That was my new plan. How had this suddenly turned on me? He was the one in the wrong, not me.

'Becca, don't lie to me.'

He placed his fork on the plate and looked me dead in the eye.

'All right, Inspector Fucking Morse. I look at her social media every so often. It's not a fucking crime. And do you know who's a star guest on it? You.'

His face flushed a deep shade of pink. Embarrassment, I thought at first, but when he spoke, I realised it wasn't. He was angry. Really fucking angry.

'She doesn't even tag me in pictures. You must actively go on and seek them out.'

'Every girl does it, Drew.'

'Oh wait, because Rae does it then it means it's normal? Mickey is an asshole, Becca. Don't put me and you in the same category as him. Them.'

'At least Mickey wants to come to her graduation,' I pointed out. 'He might be a horrible person who has sucked every ounce of confidence she ever had but at least he wants to support her on the most important day of her life.'

'Enough!' Drew's chair flew back to the floor as he stood up. He threw his napkin down on the table. 'Becca, I can't deal with your insecurities any more. There is nothing going on between me and Leila.'

'Yet,' I muttered under my breath but also loud enough for him to hear. 'You do know this is exactly what she wants, Drew. She's been after you from the minute you first met.'

'Oh God, Becca! What, she wants you to stalk her on social media and then accidentally slip up and tell me what she's saying so we break up? Is that it?'

'Are we breaking up?'

My eyes filled with tears at the words coming out of his mouth. I'd pushed him to it. I knew that.

'I think we are,' he said.

And with that, he walked away. I blinked back tears and took out my phone. I could barely see the words as I scrolled through mindless nothingness, just to look like I was doing something as the tables all turned back round to their conversations and the low chatter resumed across the room.

The waiter arrived at my side a few minutes later.

'Your, em, friend paid the bill before he left,' he said. 'And he left a tip. So no need to.'

Always following the fucking hospitality etiquette. That was Drew.

36

NINE YEARS AGO

'Look,' Rae said. 'I'm sorry, Becca. There's no easy way to say this. But he's lying. He is seeing Leila.'

I whipped my head up to look at her as we sat in the car, side by side. I gulped.

This couldn't be real, surely? Rae must have the wrong end of the stick. Drew had point-blank denied anything was happening between them. He'd just said it was all in my head. He'd accused me of being in the wrong. Surely, he couldn't have just acted his way through all that?

My heart thudded in my chest along to the low beat of the radio in the background of Rae's car.

'What?' I whispered. 'How do you know?'

She sighed. 'Someone I know saw them together. Like, *together* together. I was going to tell you, but I thought he might come clean. Clearly not. He didn't confess at all?'

I could feel my heart cracking, threatening to break into a thousand pieces. It was hanging by a thread.

'What do you mean together?'

'I wasn't going to spell it out . . . but they were full-on snogging outside one of the hotel rooms . . .'

My stomach dropped faster than the rollercoaster we'd gone on together so many times over the summer. I pictured us in the honeymoon suite together, Drew pulling my hand, begging me to ignore the phone call from Rae. Then I envisaged him doing the exact same thing with Leila, re-enacting the scene with his best moves. The pink flowers and all.

Out with the old and in with the new.

The bastard. How could he?

'You're sure?' I said.

She nodded and, unbuckling her seatbelt, reached over to cuddle me. Her leather jacket smelled like male aftershave.

'I think everyone knows, Becca. It's apparently been the talk of the theme park for weeks now,' she said.

'Why didn't you tell me?'

'Well, I didn't know until last night. I wouldn't go back to the theme park if you paid me.' She shrugged.

She wouldn't go back there because Mickey had pretty much banned her from going. She was allowed to see me on occasion but that was about it these days. But I didn't say that.

My cheeks burned at the thought of everyone knowing about Leila and Drew apart from me. How could I have been so blind? I mean, it had literally been there in front of my eyes. The pictures on her page. Him working 'extra shifts' so he could try and persuade them to promote him again. He'd just been promoted, how far up the ladder was he hoping to go? All the way up her skirt, apparently.

I shuddered.

'By the way,' she said, starting the engine. 'I'm moving to Edinburgh. Mickey and I are getting a place together.'

It took all my strength to form the vowel response in my mouth.

'Oh,' I said. 'Why Edinburgh?'

'He's got a job there. I'm young, free and jobless so might as well go with him.'

'You're sure about this?' I frowned.

'Oh look, can you stop picking at us all the time? You could be happy for me,' she pointed out. 'For us.'

She tutted and stopped at a red light.

'I'm happy if you're happy,' I said.

'Well, could you tell your face that?'

I turned away to look out of the window so Rae couldn't see the tears forming in my eyes.

37

'Becca, are you there?' Drew repeated. 'Can we talk?'

'What exactly do you think we're doing right now?'

He sighed.

I clutched onto the phone, waiting for his next move.

'It's about Rae,' he said. 'I've got something to tell you.'

My heart. My Rae.

'Well, what are you waiting for?' I spat. 'I don't have all day, Drew.'

I did have all day, though. As I walked along the cobbled streets of Rathcliffe, the ones that contrasted so drastically to my own hometown, I realised I literally had not one thing planned that day. All day. Not only was I alone, I was lonely. The realisation stung in my chest.

'We got a box of Rae's things from the police after the accident,' he said. 'And there was something in the pocket of her leather jacket for you. I just found it.'

I stopped dead in the middle of the street.

I should have gone to the doctor's, like Dad had suggested. I should have asked for the anti-depressants, or anti-anxiety, or anti-whatever-the-fuck-it-was that was going to stop my heart from thudding this hard in my chest and bring back the breath that suddenly escaped me.

I found my voice but it was a lot quieter than the usual bold tone I adopted when speaking to Drew. He'd finally knocked the wind out of me altogether.

'What does it say?' I whispered.

'I've not opened it, Becca. It's addressed to you. I presume she was planning to give you it when she met up with you that evening. You know . . . before she died.'

I desperately wanted to tear the letter open right now and devour her thoughts and feelings, the curly loops of her Ls and the line across her number sevens. Her terrible grammar. Her LOLs and her FMLs.

Oh, my Rae.

I wanted to grab the letter out of Drew's grubby stupid hands and run off with it so he could never lay claim to her again. She wasn't his. She couldn't be.

I weighed up what to tell Drew to do with the letter. I could ask him to send it to Bridget and Ellie's house in Rathcliffe. Not Bellinder Cottage. I wasn't going to stay there. Or I could tell him to hang onto it. I was going home anyway, wasn't I?

'Can you send it to me over here?' I found myself saying.

I hated asking him anything, like he was doing me some sort of favour. But for all I knew, he could be a real bastard and put it in a fire or something.

Then I'd never know what she had wanted to say to me that day. How she planned to tell me she'd decided to marry the love of my life. Or the former love of my life. Whatever.

'I can,' he said. 'Give me the address.'

'Can you send it next-day delivery?' I asked. 'Is that even a thing for letters? Or first-class post? Who the fuck even sends letters any more?'

'No one,' he said. 'Text me your address and I'll send it on.'

'OK,' I said. 'I'll do it now. Bye, Drew.'

'You're welcome, Becca.'

'I didn't thank you.'

'I know. You should though. Do you know how fucking hard this is? All I have left is a pile of her clothes, Becca.' His voice broke. 'Her leather jacket and a locket. The engagement ring I bought her is in my drawer. She never even got to see it in real life.'

The anger bubbled inside me. I wasn't willing to play this game. I wasn't buying a ticket to Drew's pity party. He had Linda and Jim and Adam and everyone else all clearly eating out of the palm of his hand.

'Goodbye, Drew.'

I hung up.

Head down and heart pounding, I hurried along the street, trying not to regret being such a cow. The guilt swam around in my stomach, entering every crevice. I shook it away. I found myself subconsciously drawn back to Bellinder Cottage. All my stuff was there, after all. I had to pack up and head back to Ellie and Bridget's. I texted Drew their address. I hated even seeing his name again on my phone, it had been absent for so long until recently.

He replied with a thumbs up.

Oh, fuck off.

I walked along the lane and up to the cottage. My car was still parked in the driveway, as though I belonged there, even though we all knew that wasn't true.

I went to push the door open but instead rang the doorbell.

Ivy opened the door.

'Becca!' Her little face lit up when she saw me.

'Ivy, what did I tell you?' a voice called from behind. It was Jackie. 'You don't just open the door to strangers.'

'It's not a stranger, Mammy. It's Becca.'

Stranger danger. I taught the kids about it in my class at school, how they should never go away with a stranger, even if someone claimed to know you or offered you sweets or a puppy or something amazing. I wanted to protest that I wasn't a stranger, ask Jackie to quiz me on the intricate details of Riley and Ivy's existence, but instead I felt my throat tighten as I leaned down to give Ivy a cuddle.

'Hi, Ivy,' I said. Ivy jumped into my arms, her hair spraying all over my face, smelling of the strawberry shampoo I'd picked up for her at the shops just the other day. How quickly things had changed.

'What can we do for you, Becca?' Jackie said, folding her arms.

She was like a guard dog, unwilling to open the door any further than absolutely necessary.

'I'm just back to get my things and then I'll head over to Bridget and Ellie's,' I said. 'They're preparing for their new arrivals.'

'Yes, we heard.' Jackie smiled down at Ivy. 'Isn't it wonderful? Damien and Lily.'

'Lucy,' I corrected her.

'I'm going to be a big cousin.' Ivy bounced up and down. 'Does Lucy have bunches?'

'She won't have much hair yet, darling. She's only one.' Jackie ruffled Ivy's hair affectionately.

I hadn't noticed before how similar they were. As Ivy gazed up at her mum, I realised her pretty little face was a carbon copy of her mum's. But Ivy was so innocent and sweet, while Jackie growled at me like a bulldog.

I was her Leila. With big bags under my eyes, instead of Leila's big boobs.

'I packed up your stuff already,' Jackie said. 'It's sitting in your bag outside the room. I'll fetch it for you now.'

'Thank you, that was kind.' I fake-smiled as Jackie disappeared from the front door.

'Daddy's away to meet his secret agent,' Ivy said. 'Is he a spy?'

I smiled. Riley hadn't mentioned a meeting but speaking with his agent was a good sign. He'd said he'd only call his agent if he had made enough progress on his work.

'Oh, that's good. I don't think he's a spy though. Although, I wouldn't really know because spies are good at keeping secrets, aren't they?'

'Like you,' Ivy whispered. 'You kept my secret about Mammy

coming back. Daddy said he's glad she's back now too. We really are going to be a family again!'

As selfish as it was, Ivy's words made me feel ill.

Riley was glad Jackie was back. Ivy had confirmed it. And they were going to work things out. It was exactly what I thought would happen, and maybe it's what should happen. They were a family, after all. But it stung more deeply than I ever thought it would. I reminded myself to mask my feelings in front of Ivy. I produced a wobbly smile to the little girl who deserved the whole world.

'I'm so happy for you, Ivy. I'm glad it's all working out.'

Just then, Jackie came back with two black bin bags, packed full of my stuff, and my suitcase and dumped them on the ground in front of me.

'Ivy, in you go and play for a second.' She smiled, and Ivy toddled off, grinning to herself.

'I just popped it all in, some of it's probably dirty.' Jackie shrugged. 'But I guess you can wash it at Bridget's. Or when you get home.'

'Thank you,' I replied through gritted teeth, lifting my suitcase into the back seat. 'I'll be off then.'

'Becca,' she called as I slammed the boot.

I looked up as she folded her arms across her chest.

'I know you've got a little bit of a crush on Riley, but most women do.' She smiled, as though it was all a bit silly. 'Trust me, it's always been the same. But we're working things out. Riley wants us to be a family again. It's what he's always wanted. So, I think it might be best if you go back to England and leave us to it.'

'Scotland,' I corrected her.

'Whatever.' She smiled.

I narrowed my eyes.

'I'm planning on it,' I stated. 'I just need to attend the opening party for Bridget and Ellie's business and then I'll be out of your hair.'

She replied with a thin smile as I turned on my heel.

I grabbed the keys from my bag and hopped in the car. I switched on the engine and drove away as quickly as I could, turning my head away from Jackie so she couldn't see the tears in my eyes.

38

I didn't tell Bridget or Ellie about my conversation with Jackie.

The next evening was the grand opening night of their business. The moment they'd dreamed of had finally arrived and I knew Bridget wouldn't exactly be thrilled to hear about the pair reuniting. I wasn't about to spoil it for them.

Since I'd left Bellinder Cottage, a whole new wave of heartache had consumed me. I wandered around in a trance, wishing it had turned out differently but knowing everything was exactly the way it should be. I was just a fleeting fancy to Riley, but Jackie was the mother of his child. And Ivy was his priority, his everything.

Just like it had been with me and my dad. But the three of them had the chance of a happily ever after and I had to respect that, no matter how much it hurt.

Bridget was on the verge of hysteria. She walked around, clutching an anti-bacterial spray in one hand and a banana in the other, claiming she didn't have time to eat. Ellie had written down a full set of instructions to help 'keep Bridget on track' but it didn't seem to be working.

'She's so nervous, she'll just run from room to room doing nothing 'til the party starts. This will help focus her attention,' Ellie explained.

They shouted orders from Ellie's to-do list as they passed each other.

'Is apartment seven's light working yet?'

'What time is the food arriving?'

'Where are the scissors?'

'Did you remember to invite that reporter that your friend knows?'

Everything had to be just perfect.

'It's almost like if we get this right then the rest will just fall into place. The twins will settle, they'll love their new life, and we'll all live happily ever after,' Bridget confided in me. 'And we've made the right decision, you know?'

'Of course you've made the right decision,' I said. 'How can two beautiful children ever be the wrong decision?'

She smiled and squeezed my hand. 'I'm so glad you're here, Becca. I don't know what we'd do without you. Thanks for all your help.'

'Thanks for letting me stay in your guest bedroom,' I said. 'I promise I'll be out of your hair after tonight so you can get ready for the twins coming. I'm not sure it would go down well with the agency if you told them you also happen to have adopted a thirty-something-year-old woman.'

'I hope you're not avoiding Bellinder Cottage because of

Jackie. Riley wouldn't want that, Becca. You were his guest. She's the one that turned up out of the blue.'

I shrugged.

I thought back to our messages before agreeing to stay at Bellinder Cottage. Riley was my friend long before I arrived and saw him in person. He took my breath away from the moment I laid eyes on him, of course. All women were the same, Jackie said. I was hardly different or special.

We should have stayed strictly as friends in the first place, just a summer romance. We should take the memories, say thank you very much, and move along. Forget about each other. That was probably for the best. For them, anyway. Riley had a child to think about, after all. A family.

Anyway, it had all been decided now. Agreed. He was moving on. Or moving back, if that was the same thing.

'I need to book my boat back home. Just haven't quite got around to it yet. But I know it can all be last minute, I mean, look at last time.'

'You definitely won't stay?' she asked, hopefully.

'No. I can't stay. I think I'm just waiting for a sign from the gods or something before I leave.'

I wasn't sure what was holding me back. I had nowhere to go but home.

'I'm going to hoover the bedrooms,' I announced, changing the subject. 'That's next on my list.'

'You are an angel, Becca,' Bridget said. 'How do you always seem to know what to do next?'

'Actually, it's hardly a coincidence. Ellie gave me a list, too,' I said. 'I'm working my way through it.'

Bridget rolled her eyes.

'Who's going to take time off with the twins when they arrive?' I asked. 'Have you agreed?'

'We've still got to look into it all but we're hoping to have shared parental leave. I'll take the majority of the time off to settle them in, with Ellie looking after the business side of things. But we're going to need to advertise for some help. We'll not be able to run all the cottages, do all the cleaning and admin and look after the twins. And we both want to bond with them; it's so important.'

I grabbed the hoover and made my way to the first cottage, zipping around to make sure it was spotless. There was something satisfying about cleaning: you could see the mess at the start and walk out at the end, confident you've achieved the job you set out to do.

It wasn't like teaching, which was a slow process and a series of wins so small sometimes you barely noticed them. But when you took a step back and reflected on a child's progress at the end of a term, whether they'd developed in confidence, skills or from an academic perspective, or all three, it was more rewarding than anything else I could imagine. I always missed the children over the summer holidays, but this time it felt so much worse. I didn't know if I even had a teaching career to go back to.

Trying to block out my feelings, I concentrated on weaving

the hoover around the rooms, with Ellie popping in every so often to pretend she wasn't freaking out about everything.

'It's looking great, Becca! Keep up the good work!'

I carried the hoover across the courtyard to the next cottage as my phone vibrated in my pocket again.

'Dad, how are you?' I answered.

'All good, Becca Bear. How are things? Is your man friend looking after you?'

I'd eventually opened up to Dad that Riley was, in fact, a male. But I hadn't gone into any further details. No high-speed chases to police stations with missing-child reports or return-of-the-ex stories. No point in worrying him.

'Look, I was in Glasgow for the day and I came past your flat to check up on things. You've got a few letters here. There are two from the NHS. They say they're not circulars so I guess you should open them?'

'OK, can you open it and send me it? A picture of it, anyway,' I suggested.

I couldn't think for a minute why they would be contacting me.

'OK, if you're sure,' he said.

'Go for it.' I shrugged.

He wrestled to open the letters on the other end of the phone. I listened closely as he paused.

'Are you reading? What does it say?'

He was silent. The suspense was annoying me rather than killing me. Why wasn't he just spitting it out?

'Dad, what is it? Just a leaflet about something? My doctor's surgery was getting work done the last time I was there, it could just be something to do with that.'

'I'll send you a picture, Becca. But it says something about the smear test you went for. They've been trying to call you. Something about abnormal cells. They want you to come back in for a colposcopy. Whatever that is. You've to call and arrange it.'

Dad's voice shook as he spoke. I knew he was thinking about Mum. I wished he wasn't thinking about that. I wished I didn't know him so well that I knew he was thinking about it too.

I wished I wasn't thinking about it either.

'Oh,' I said. Damn shaking hands. 'What does that even mean? Does it mean I have cancer?'

'I don't know, Becca. I don't think so, it doesn't say anything about that, it just says you've to call. You should do it now. Like, today. You need to come home.'

And just like that, the sign from the gods had come.

'OK, Dad, don't panic. I'll call the surgery and ask them for some more details. I'll Google around and get a bit more information, too.'

'Don't fucking Google anything, Becca,' he warned. 'You'll only panic. It'll say you're about to drop down dead.'

But we both knew that as soon as we hung up, we were going to Google the hell out of whatever it was in the letter. The colposcopy procedure. I'd never heard of it. It sounded like a colonoscopy, though, which I knew wasn't entirely pleasant. I wondered if it was similar. I shivered.

'I'm shitting myself, Dad,' I confessed.

Suddenly, Dad seemed too far away.

'Me too, Becca Bear. But we don't know anything yet. Let's read up on it and then decide whether to shit ourselves and we can do it together. Deal?'

'Deal. I'll phone you back. Send me the picture,' I said.

'I'm on it,' Dad said.

> **Colposcopy:** a simple procedure used to look at the cervix, the lower part of the womb at the top of the vagina. Often done if cervical screening finds abnormal cells in your cervix. These cells could go away on their own, but there is a risk they could eventually turn into cervical cancer if not treated.

Of course I fucking Googled it.

A simple procedure. Only a risk, not a confirmation, of cervical cancer. They just needed to have a wee look, that's all. It wasn't necessarily something to panic about.

But my heart pounded in my chest as I leaned against the beautiful armchair that took pride of place in one of the cottages. Apartment seven. The one that needed a light fixed.

I blinked and, before I could think too much about it, I called my doctor's surgery.

'Hello, Parkville Medical Practice,' the voice said.

I recognised her voice. It was Moira. 'Not to be fucked with' Moira.

'Hello.' My voice sounded much more confident than I felt. 'It's Becca Taylor. I am calling to book a colposcopy. I got a letter in the post.'

'Can I take your date of birth?'

The digits fell out of my mouth on autopilot, and she tapped them into her computer.

'Ah yes, here you are,' she said.

I wondered if my name came up with red flashing lights 'POSSIBLE CERVICAL CANCER: TBC' when she typed it in. What did my notes say? What exactly was the problem with the smear test?

'Maybe they didn't do it properly. The smear test, I mean. There was a student in. Maybe she made a mistake. She looked about twelve,' I said.

I hoped they wouldn't hold it against the poor student. I didn't want her to get marks off her assignment or anything, but she did look a little young to be playing around with possible cervical cancer.

'They've actually got a cancellation appointment on Wednesday. Can you make it?'

Wednesday. Four days away. If it could wait four days then it couldn't be that serious, could it? It wasn't like they were rushing an ambulance around to collect me straight away.

'What time?' I asked.

As if I wasn't free all day. My diary consisted right now of one thing: make sure you don't have cervical cancer.

It was amazing how quickly things could change.

'Two p.m.,' she said.

'OK, two p.m. it is,' I replied.

I called Dad back to say I was booking a boat for the

following day and that I'd see him once I got home. He sounded relieved.

And while I was on a roll, I called and booked my place on the afternoon sailing the next day.

I stopped when I realised. Rae's letter was probably winging its way to me right now, in the post.

I quickly typed Drew a text, hating that I had to contact him, as though I needed him in some way.

Did you send the letter from Rae yet? If you haven't, then don't. I'm coming home tomorrow. If you have, I'll get it sent back to my flat.

I watched my phone for a response, but nothing. After all the contact that I didn't want from him and telling him not to call and to leave me alone. The prick was completely ignoring me.

39

The launch event was in full swing. The courtyard dazzled, with fairy lights sprinkling soft magic all around and lanterns flickering in each of the corners. The waiters, wearing matching shirts and bow ties, served Champagne to the guests.

Ellie displayed before and after pictures all around the courtyard area on large boards. Guests wandered up and down, marvelling at the effort they had gone to. The doors to each of the cottages were open so visitors could have a look inside and admire the beautiful interiors.

Bridget and Ellie beamed as they posed for photographs outside. Ellie wore a floor-length, modest deep purple dress with a cowl neck, while Bridget's frock was cerise pink with a large bow at the back. Bridget beamed as people enquired who had done the interior design work, while Ellie explained how they juggled all the different trades and contacts in the building industry.

I smoothed down the black satin dress I'd borrowed from

Bridget, the one she had hanging in the back of her closet for 'skinnier times to come'. I had lost weight since coming to Rathcliffe, with all the fresh-air mountain walks and, yes, maybe the yoga classes had helped.

My heart soared as I caught sight of Ivy rushing towards me, bursting with excitement.

My eyes flickered up as Ivy hugged me, before she dashed off to find Auntie Bridget. My breath caught in the air as I saw him: Riley.

I'd never been a fan of a suit. Drew put me off the whole 'dress to impress' thing. I always thought he looked like a prat, like he was trying too hard.

But Riley. Riley was a different matter. His broad shoulders fit snugly beneath his three-piece black suit, teamed with a bright white shirt and black bow tie. He even made a dicky bow look good. As he strolled towards me, it took all that I had not to throw myself into his arms and beg him to kiss me again. He cocked his head sideways, revealing his freshly shaved face in all its glory and flashed me an easy grin as our eyes met.

Why did he have to come here looking like *that*?

I held my breath as he edged towards me. Inhaled the scent of his favourite aftershave as he slid an arm behind me, lightly placing his hand on my lower back, and pulled me into a close embrace. His scent was so familiar. So Riley.

I gulped as he bent down to whisper in my ear.

'You look amazing, Becca.'

I wobbled in my heels. Shit. Riley was literally making me

go weak at the knees. I steadied myself and took a couple of steps back.

'We don't scrub up too badly for a pair of struggling writers,' I replied with a nonchalant shrug. 'At least I don't have shit on my face this time.'

'You certainly don't,' he said, his eyes burning into mine.

I had to break this. Riley was off limits now; Jackie had made that perfectly clear. They were working things out, for the sake of their family. Riley was working towards his happily ever after and I didn't feature.

'Where's Jackie?' I asked in a low whisper.

'On her way,' he replied.

That seemed to snap Riley out of whatever world he was living in for a moment. I tried not to let him see my face fall in disappointment. The last thing I wanted was to see Riley and Jackie together, like one big happy family, but I had to suck it up.

I had more pressing things to deal with now.

I tore my eyes away from him and located Ivy, who was walking back towards us with a huge grin on her face.

'Auntie Bridget says I look like a princess!' she exclaimed, her whole face lighting up at the comparison.

'You certainly do. Four outfit changes later and you found the perfect dress,' Riley smiled with a small eye roll.

My insides felt like they were melting as Ivy grinned up at me, her baby teeth proudly on display as she cuddled into my leg.

'What's a diva, Becca?' she asked, scrunching her nose up at me. 'Daddy said I'm a total diva.'

'A princess that deserves only the best. Just like you, Ivy.'

I forced the smile as my heart broke a little inside.

God, I was going to miss her.

40

My eyes followed Ivy as she floated around, grinning while everyone told her how beautiful she looked. She already knew, with her pink, sparkly dress and matching sparkly shoes. Her hair, I noted, was styled to perfection in a French plait with small flowers woven in and out.

'Mammy did it,' she told me, with a curtsey, as I commented on how beautiful it was. 'And Daddy said it was a good job she was back to fix my hair for tonight.'

A salty taste took over my mouth and suddenly I felt totally exhausted, like I could curl up in a heap on the rock-hard beige bricks across the courtyard floor and fall fast asleep.

I just had to get through tonight before I would say my goodbyes. Riley, Ivy, Bridget and Ellie were all moving on with exciting chapters. Ivy would be starting school after the summer. She had already picked out her bag and pencil case.

Ivy probably wouldn't recall my existence in a few months, never mind years. Child development studies at school had taught me about infantile amnesia, the inability of adults to recollect early memories, and the rapid forgetting that occurs in childhood.

The memories I shared with her would be mine only.

I glanced up and spotted Jackie, sauntering towards Riley in a tight black dress and silver heels, as though she hadn't a care in the world. She placed her hand on his arm and leaned in to whisper something in his ear. His face remained expressionless. I'd become accustomed to Riley's hearty laugh, his easy-going shrugs and his wide, easy smiles. I looked away. It was none of my business.

I had to tell him though. I couldn't leave without saying anything to him at all. Not that he'd probably notice, given how preoccupied he looked with Jackie being back. But it was only courteous to tell him I was leaving, given he was the reason I was here in the first place. Now was neither the time nor the place, though. Lifting a glass of fizz in one hand, I straightened up and went to find Bridget and Ellie to see if I could help with anything.

A noise echoed around the courtyard as Ellie and Bridget called for everyone's attention.

Bridget held a microphone and, with a shaky hand, started to read out the speech she'd been stressing out about the evening before. I'd already heard her going over it approximately forty-six times. I crossed my fingers that she'd be able to get through it without stammering over her words.

I'd assured her everyone would be rooting for her, but that didn't help when all eyes were fixated on you.

She thanked everyone for coming and made a few special mentions: the catering staff; the cleaning staff (which was actually just me and Ellie, but she reasoned cleaning staff sounded more professional); everyone that had helped with the project, from plumbers to the local suppliers and shops. She gave Riley, Ivy and me a special mention, too. Then she turned to Ellie.

'Most of all, I want to thank Ellie, for putting up with me and being my partner in business and in life. We are excited to announce that we are now about to embark on another adventure together, this time as parents to two beautiful children who will join our family next week. So, I'd like you all to raise a glass and toast . . . to the future!'

An excited murmur made waves through the crowd as everyone raised a glass to toast their lovely news. Bridget's legs were shaking by the time she'd finished. Ellie was beaming and the two leaned into one another and embraced.

'Congratulations, you two,' I said, walking over. 'That was fantastic, Bridget. And everything looks amazing. You guys make the best team.'

'Ach, you think so?' Bridget said. 'It wasn't too over the top? Maybe I shouldn't have mentioned the twins. What if it's tempting fate?'

'Nothing's going to go wrong,' Ellie assured her. 'It's all going to be just fine.'

'I hope so,' Bridget mused.

I hesitated, wondering if my announcement would be classed as something going wrong, but I had to tell Bridget and Ellie my plans to leave. I couldn't hold off on breaking the news any longer, given I was leaving the next day.

'I'm booked to go home tomorrow,' I blurted out. 'I'm sorry to tell you on your big night but if I didn't tell you now, I wasn't sure when I'd get the chance. I'm sorry to let you down, too, just as the twins are arriving and the business is opening. I feel awful about it. But, I have to go.'

My eyes flew to Ivy as she danced in the middle of the floor like no one was watching.

The job as their receptionist would have been a dream come true. It could have solved all of my problems, for the short term, at least. But now, with a big dark cloud hanging over my head and Riley probably dancing somewhere close by with Ivy's mum, I couldn't stay.

'We understand,' Bridget whispered, although her puppy dog eyes betrayed her.

'We didn't just want you to be our receptionist,' Ellie said, placing her hand on mine. 'Just so you know. We'll miss you. I wish you could hang around and meet the twins. More than anything.'

Another two hearts I wasn't willing to tamper with.

'I'll miss you, too,' I whispered but the words were cut short as someone called my name. Ellie glanced down and murmured something about checking a cottage and Bridget followed swiftly behind her.

The music took on a slower pace and I watched the fairy lights glittering all around the dance floor. Bridget and Ellie were in the centre; Ellie swayed from side to side, then whispered something into Bridget's ear, who threw back her head and exploded into raucous laughter.

'May I have this dance?'

Riley stood in front of me, his hand outstretched.

I wondered if he was joking, but one look at his expression and I realised he was deadly serious.

'You've got to be kidding,' I said, folding my arms in front of my body.

'I don't kid, Becca. Not about dancing, anyway. Come on,' he said, grabbing my hand.

He pulled me in so close that I felt his breath on my cheek. Swaying from side to side to our own rhythm, I glided along beside him. I wasn't sure what the song was but as he held me tighter, I thought of Jackie warning me to back off.

And the cancer letter, burning a hole in the coffee table at my flat.

'Are you OK?' he whispered.

'Just thinking,' I replied.

His breath became hotter on my neck and his body pressed up against mine.

'It's so beautiful, isn't it?'

'You are so full of shit,' I whispered back, grinning.

'Ah Jaysus, Becca, give me a break. I'm a romance writer. I live for this kind of thing. Let me just soak it all up. The lights, the music, the mood, not having to debate with Ivy about her bedtime over and over again. It's everything I've ever dreamed of and more. And you look beautiful, by the way.'

'It's your sister's dress,' I replied with a shrug. 'I didn't pack anything this fancy.'

He twirled me around and pulled me closer again, his hand clutching mine. There were so many questions swirling around in my mind, I didn't even know where to start. But instead, we danced wordlessly and moved together in a perfect rhythm. It was all too intense for a man with a child. With a partner. And me, with possible cancer.

'I have to go,' I said, pulling away from him.

'Wait,' he said, pulling me back. 'I know this is all so fucked up, with Jackie back on the scene, but can we talk about it?'

'I'm sorry, Riley. There's just too much going on now,' I said. 'You and Jackie are still sorting things out and I don't want to confuse or disappoint Ivy. She's been through enough. When she told me she'd seen her mum in the playground last week before she came back and I—'

He stopped suddenly and frowned slightly, moving his hands away from mine.

'What do you mean?' Riley asked, staring me straight in the eye. 'When did she see Jackie in the playground?'

Shit. Shit. Shit.

I looked around the dance floor and wished we weren't in public right now. Riley searched my eyes for an answer. My mouth fell into an unattractive, vacant gape as I stared up at him, as the beat of the background music picked up pace and vibrated between us. Swallowing the saltiness of my stupid mistake, I knew it was time to come clean.

'Ivy said Jackie came along to see her a couple of times at

nursery and talked to her over the gate before she picked her up that day,' I summarised, looking down at my heels.

'And tried to kidnap her,' Riley finished.

'Well, I'm not sure I'd go that far but I mean, yeah, took her home without you knowing . . .'

Riley's whole face flushed as he put his hands over his eyes. 'She told you she'd seen her mum and you didn't think to tell me?'

The thudding of my heart matched the beat of the music as the dance floor began to fill around us. Someone bumped into Riley and apologised, but he didn't even flinch.

'I was going to tell you, but she asked me not to,' I stuttered. 'I thought about it, of course, but I really was sure it was just a wee white lie. You know she likes to make up stories. I didn't think for a minute she was actually seeing Jackie. If I thought that it was true, I would have told you. Of course I would have.'

But it looked like I'd got that wrong, too. He stepped back from me, towards the edge of the dance floor.

'I wish you had,' he said softly. 'I know you promised Ivy but she's just a kid. It's not in her best interest to keep that sort of thing from me. I was out of my mind worrying about her that day. You could have mentioned it then. Why didn't you tell me then?'

His frown creased his whole forehead. The only time I'd ever seen him so worked up was when Jackie was there. The realisation stung; I'd broken something between us, just like she had.

'I'm sorry,' I mumbled.

'I need to go . . . it's past Ivy's bedtime,' he said. 'I'll walk her home. Clear my head. This is a bit much just now. I'm sorry.'

'Riley, please don't go,' I said. 'I honestly didn't mean . . .'

He turned on his heel in his sharply pressed suit and, within seconds, he was gone.

The lights around the courtyard became blurry as I shuffled from one foot to the other. My body felt like it was deflating like a balloon as disappointment washed over me. The evening air was getting colder and I wrapped my arms around myself to keep warm. Riley and I had fought. The night before I was meant to leave. I hadn't even told him that I was going yet. I hadn't told him why.

The fluttering panic intensified in my chest.

Hello, anxiety, my old friend.

'Well, that was all a bit dramatic,' a voice said from behind me.

I spun around. And there he was, in front of my eyes.

What the actual fuck was he doing here?

41

'Seriously, Becca, do you just have that effect on men? What was that hissy fit all about?'

Déjà bloody Drew.

The wind felt like it had been punched out of me. Again. All smug-faced, fully suited and booted and full of shit. And he'd been creeping around, watching me, at a party with my friends . . . in a completely different country.

My eyes narrowed as I looked up at his annoyingly handsome face.

'What the fuck are you doing here?' I demanded. 'And don't dare tell me you were invited this time because that would just be a lie.'

The audacity of him turning up out of the blue. First the funeral, now here in Rathcliffe. In my safe space. Anger bubbled inside me. I didn't want to ruin Bridget and Ellie's evening or the launch party but I could literally strangle him to the ground. Now was not the time for his bullshit.

His outstretched arm gave me the answer. I sucked in my breath at the sight of her handwriting on the front of an envelope addressed to me.

'The letter,' I said.

My voice cracked. I looked away as he nodded, still clutching it in his hand.

'Have you never heard of a fucking post box, Drew?'

He looked down at the envelope and back up at me.

'I wanted to see you,' he said quietly. 'I needed to see you.'

'I didn't need to see you.'

Tears threatened in my eyes. This was just too much to take, my two worlds combining at the worst possible time in the worst possible way.

The letter hung between us. I couldn't bring myself to take it from him.

'I know. I'm sorry. I couldn't *not* come.'

'So that's why you didn't answer my text. You were planning to sneak up on me instead.'

'You gave me the address,' he protested. 'And then I tracked you down here. It's a small town, too. Seems like there's only one party happening here tonight. Trust you to be at it. You always did love a party. The two of you.'

I caught sight of Ellie turning the music down in the corner, while Bridget was chatting loudly to the caterers. Drew's brown eyes twinkled sadly.

He should stop trying to make me bloody feel sorry for him. I refused.

'I'm not opening it here,' I said. 'In the middle of a party.'

He nodded. 'Of course. Will we get out of here?'

I frowned as I realised that he was trying to call all the shots again and take charge of the situation. Mr Suited and Booted. My lip curled in annoyance.

'I'm staying at one of the cottages here tonight. And where are you meant to be staying, by the way?' I demanded.

'I hadn't really thought that far ahead yet.' He shrugged. 'I've got my car with me, if the worst comes to the worst.'

'The worst will most definitely come to the worst,' I said. 'Wait here and don't talk to anyone.'

'You're bossy in Ireland,' he said.

'You're a dick everywhere,' I replied over my shoulder.

Bridget caught sight of me marching over.

'Becca,' she called. 'Come and meet Paul. He owns the laundrette in town so we're going to keep him pretty busy with all our bedding and washing. And of course, you know Eimear.'

'Hi, Paul, nice to meet you. Hi, Eimear, I didn't know you were coming. Lovely to see you.' I nodded.

Eimear grinned back, looking like a runway model in a long, floaty silver number with a plunging neckline. She clung onto Paul the Laundrette Man's arm. He smiled smugly. No wonder; he was really punching above his weight with Eimear.

Focus, Becca.

'Bridget, is it OK if I go to my apartment now, or do you need it for people to view?'

'No, I think the viewings are all pretty much done, Becca, so you head on to bed whenever. The party will be finishing up soon anyway. Is everything OK?'

'Yes, I just . . . have a bit of a headache,' I replied, thinking about Drew. 'A big bloody headache, in fact.'

'We'll turn the music down soon,' she promised.

'Oh no, I didn't mean that. Keep the music playing for as long and as loud as you like and enjoy the rest of your evening. It really has been so lovely. I'll see you in the morning.'

I gave her a hug and waved at Eimear and Paul before heading back over to retrieve Drew.

'Follow me,' I ordered.

It wasn't the kind of tone you said 'no' to. Drew followed obediently behind as I fumbled with my key in the door at the cottage. He tried to help but I waved him away until I succeeded.

'After you,' he said, when I eventually managed it. I tutted in response as I walked in.

My overnight bag was set up on the couch and I moved it onto the floor.

'Sit,' I commanded.

'Becca, I'm not a bloody dog,' Drew said.

I sighed. The fight with Riley had taken me completely by surprise. The thought of him not speaking to me made me crumble inside. And the one person I really didn't want to speak to couldn't stop bloody talking and following me around. But I knew I couldn't keep this up. I had to talk to Drew civilly at some point.

I had to read the letter, too.

'I'm just so angry with you. Turning up here. This is my space, Drew. You can't just turn up without asking me.'

'I know,' he said. 'But I knew you wouldn't see me otherwise.'

'There are so many reasons why I don't want to see you,' I said. 'If I don't want to see or speak to you, you need to respect that.'

He sighed.

'You're right. I'm sorry, Becca. I just . . . I really want to know what the letter says. And I didn't think you'd ever see me to tell me.'

'You're right about that.'

'And you don't have to tell me what's in it, of course. It's just . . . I know it's going to be about me and Rae. About us. I've started doubting things. Like if it was ever real, you know? Everything is so mushed up in my mind. I'm not thinking straight.'

'It was clearly real, Drew. Everyone knew it was, apart from me. I was the one that was kept in the dark, not you,' I retorted.

He put two hands over his eyes and let out a deep sigh.

'I guess I wanted to know what she said about me. I need to hear it from her, maybe just one last time,' he whispered, his voice cracking.

'You just want to hear how wonderful you are.' I rolled my eyes. 'Fine. I'll read the letter. I just . . . I need a drink before I do.'

He nodded, his eyes checking the room for booze to ply me with so I could just get on with what he needed from me.

'Have you got some stashed in here somewhere?' he asked.

'Nope, but it's a free bar. I'll nip out and grab a bottle. Stay here and don't move.'

As I walked out to the courtyard on the hunt for a bottle of something, I couldn't help but feel a little . . . impressed. Drew, who had wanted so badly to read the letter from his late girlfriend, had instead travelled all the way over here so I could be the first to read the words. It was addressed to me, but still. I knew if the shoe had been on the other foot, things would have been completely different. I'd have read the letter then completely denied all knowledge, keeping the whole thing to myself. I really had kept my grudge against Drew for so long now, I didn't even know how to speak to him normally any more.

I located a bottle of sauvignon blanc and turned to go back to the cottage. My shoulder nudged someone's back. I flew around.

'Sorry,' I said.

'Sorry,' he said.

Riley.

'Oh, it's you,' I said, meeting his eyes again.

'You're back,' he whispered softly at the same time. 'I've been looking everywhere for you.'

Shit. Shit. Shit. How was I going to explain this now?

'I am back. But I'm just about to go to bed,' I said. 'Sore head.'

He looked down at the bottle of booze and then back up at me and raised an eyebrow.

'It'll be even worse in the morning if you drink that on your own,' he said. 'Look, I wanted to talk. Can we go into your room?'

Now, that's what I really wanted, more than anything. I

wanted Riley to come back to my room and continue where we'd left off. But bloody Drew was there and that was going to be a hard one to explain. And then there was Jackie. And Ivy. And the boat I'd booked home. I had to tell him I was leaving the next day. When would I even get the chance?

'Do you mind if we leave it tonight?' I asked, clutching the bottle in my hand. 'We can catch up in the morning, maybe?'

'Sure,' he said. 'We could go for the group mountain walk? I don't know if Ellie and Bridget will make it, but we could.'

I couldn't.

I thought of the appointment letter and the procedure. I thought of Drew waiting for me to come back to the cottage. I thought of Rae.

I thought of Riley. And Ivy.

'Riley, I'm sorry but I booked a boat home for tomorrow.' I let the words roll off my tongue like a robot, trying not to feel anything. 'I'm going home to . . . sort a few things out. My head included. And you need to sort things out with Jackie, so I think it's really for the best all round.'

His mouth flew open as his voice strained. 'Seriously?'

'I'm sorry,' I said, looking away from his intense gaze. 'I really am. But I think it's better if we both have some time and space to clear our heads, then maybe we can be friends again, at some point.'

'Friends,' he repeated, like a parrot. 'You want to go back to being friends.'

I looked away from him. 'I want you to be happy. You and Ivy. So this is what's best.'

'Becca!' called a voice from across the courtyard.

Shit. Shit. Shit. Not now, Drew. What the actual fuck.

'Who is that?' Riley asked, frowning as I turned around.

Drew stood waving from my cottage door, with his tie loose around his open collar and his shoes off.

Then Drew followed up with a loud: 'Did you get the booze? I'm parched over here.'

I sighed and placed my fingers on my temple. The sore head was becoming a reality.

'That's . . . my ex. Drew. The one that was going out with Rae, before she died. He just—'

Riley's eyes darkened. He frowned over at Drew, who put his arm above his head and leaned against the doorway as though he owned the place. Smug. He always looked so fucking smug.

'Good night, Becca.' Riley didn't even look me in the eye as he turned to leave.

'Riley, wait . . .' I called after him, but he refused to turn around. 'Riley!'

42

It took every ounce of strength I had not to chase after Riley and beg him to listen to me. But even if I did, even if I told him how I really felt about him and Ivy, about being here in Rathcliffe with them both, it didn't matter. They were a family now, with Jackie, just like Ivy wanted.

And my life had been flipped upside down. Tears threatened in my eyes but I blinked them away. I would not let my stupidly handsome and exceedingly annoying ex-boyfriend see them. I refused.

I marched back over towards Drew. My first love. I'd got over him, so I could get over Riley too. I sighed.

Drew offered up a crooked smile as I stomped past him into the cottage. He closed the door firmly, leaving the noise of the party behind us.

He walked over and sat on the edge of the bed, waiting for me.

Breathe, Becca.

'Don't get too cosy there,' I called. 'You're not staying in here tonight.'

I opened the bottle and retrieved two glasses from the cupboard in the kitchen area. He came to the door and took the glass that I offered. I turned my attention to the matter in hand. If I were even to think about Drew with anything other than contempt, I had to know the full story.

I let out a long sigh.

'I'm tempted to ask how and when the two of you got together. I presume she'll tell me that in the letter. But I'd like to hear your version first.'

I wanted to see if it would match up. Rae's version versus Drew's. Who had betrayed me more, my best friend or my ex-boyfriend? I guessed Drew didn't have as much to lose. But I couldn't stand the thought of Rae lying to me. I eyed up the letter, which he was still holding.

'You want to know everything?' he asked.

I nodded.

43

Drew cleared his throat.

'OK, well, she moved to Edinburgh with Mickey. I eventually broke things off with Leila, too. I did end up seeing her, Becca. I'm not going to lie about that. But it didn't last.'

I knew it. I knew as soon as we split up that Leila would get her claws into him. The thought didn't make me as annoyed as it once would have. In fact, it all seemed a bit stupid now.

'Well, I could have told you that.' I shrugged.

'Anyway, I bumped into Rae a couple of years ago. She was pretty wasted. Crying outside the men's toilets. Mascara everywhere. I took her home and slept on the floor in her bedroom. She and Mickey had been together on and off for ages, but she said it was over for good this time. Nothing happened that night between us, obviously.'

My hand shook as I took another gulp of wine, totally immersed in the story.

'She'd lost so much confidence at this point, Becca. She was a shell of herself. At first, I guess I just wanted to protect her.'

I shivered. I should have been the one in Edinburgh, picking up the pieces, not Drew.

'So, we started hanging out. Just friends, at first. It turned out she didn't live too far away from the hotel where I was working. So, she would come in sometimes and just hang around there. I'd walk her home when it got late. I liked having her around. At first, she reminded me of you.'

'Don't say that.' I shook my head as if that could erase his words.

'It's true.' He shrugged. 'But the more I saw her, I couldn't shake the feelings. I wanted to be with her all the time. It took a long time for us to get together. She was devastated about it. Kept wondering how she was ever going to tell you. The longer it went on, the harder it was. But our relationship . . . it was amazing. She was free and funny and beautiful, you know. Just so Rae. She turned heads in every room. I was so proud to have her on my arm.'

I knew he'd felt like that about Rae. I always knew he wanted her instead of me. Mickey had even predicted it. No offence, Becca, he'd said.

'She got to know the hotel staff and we all hung out together. We were so good together, Becca. I'm sorry, but we were. She said she'd never been so happy. The only thing she hated was the fact that she was lying to you. She beat herself up about that every day. I didn't want to see her upset, so I was annoyed that she was worried . . . I told her that you should just get over it. We'd been over for ages by that point.

'We talked about getting married. She was scared of your reaction. When she was coming to meet you that night, she was coming to tell you. But she wasn't planning to tell you face to face. She thought a letter would be better, so she didn't have to say the words. She couldn't seem to get the words out, she said.

'And this is the letter.'

We both stared down at it.

My eyes brimmed with tears. I wasn't upset because of Drew and Rae. It had never been about that. Not really. I just wished that there hadn't been a huge secret between us before she'd died. And I missed her so badly that it physically hurt.

I drained my glass and poured another large one. I reached over and topped Drew's glass up, too.

'I don't know if I can read it,' I whispered to him. 'It's easier to not know.'

'OK,' he replied. 'There's no rush.'

We sat in silence. I sipped on my wine while he tapped his foot lightly against the bedside table.

'That's annoying,' I said.

'Sorry.'

We stared at different parts of the room, each lost in our own thoughts.

'I never cheated on you, Becca,' he said. 'Just so you know.'

'It's water under the bridge now. I don't really care any more. I cared at the time, obviously. I was so upset about graduation and Leila. And breaking up. It was so stupid.'

He sat up a little straighter and cleared his throat.

'I started driving to your graduation,' he confessed. 'In the ice cream truck.'

'What?' I said, looking up at him with a smile playing on my lips. 'Are you serious?'

'I'm deadly serious. I asked at work if I could borrow it. I planned to drive outside and do an announcement on how sorry I was. But the bloody thing broke down on the way there. I was stranded at the side of the road in the Gorbals for about two hours. I turned around to call the breakdown people and when I turned back, I had a queue of folk waiting to get served ice cream.'

The Grand Gesture. It looked like someone had at least attempted one for me after all.

I couldn't keep it in. I buckled with laughter at the thought of people queuing up for ice cream at his truck while he was broken down at the side of the road.

'You're laughing,' he said, his face breaking into a grin. 'I was fuming. I was on the phone trying to sort everything out and next thing I knew they were all lining up with their pocket money asking why I didn't have the music on.'

But he saw the funny side too and we both laughed together. I snorted.

'So you decided not to go through with it then? After the ice cream van thing?'

'I tried things with Leila after it, for a while. But it didn't work out. I didn't get over you that easily.'

'Me neither,' I replied, sucking my breath in for a moment before exhaling.

Drew edged towards me slowly and took my two hands in his, pulling me into a standing position in front of him. I stared up into his deep brown eyes that I'd fallen in love with all those years ago. My heart thumped wildly in my chest as I remembered feeling his body close to mine, the scent of his aftershave, the promise of first love that could have lasted forever.

'We could try again, you know,' he said, in a low, controlled voice as he held my gaze. 'I mean, I know a lot has changed but we're still the same, deep down.'

I let him hold my hands for a second, allowing us both to soak up the feeling of hope. He leaned down towards me, with his lips parted. A part of me wanted him, wanted this, but my brain screamed that this wasn't what I needed any more. But could one time hurt? One night?

As his lips pressed against mine, I flinched and moved backwards.

'We . . . I don't think I can,' I stuttered, as I watched his face fall.

'Becca, you know how I feel about you.'

'Felt,' I corrected him. 'That's in the past. Everything's changed, Drew.'

He let out a low sigh. 'Is it because of him? The guy you're staying with?'

My shoulders slumped as I thought of Riley. I wished I could say that he and I were together, more than anything, but whatever we had was over the minute Jackie turned up.

'No, Drew. It's not Riley.' I shook my head. 'It's us. We're both grieving Rae. That's why you're here, doing all this. You miss her; I do too. But that doesn't mean we should go backwards.'

He sat down on the bed and sighed again, placing his face in his hands. I sat down beside him and tentatively rubbed his back. He sat up straighter.

'Can you say you'll think about it at least? Maybe you'll change your mind,' he said. 'And if not, I'd rather have you in my life as a friend than nothing at all.'

I sat back. I had been angry with Drew for so long, it felt strange not to retaliate with something mean or sarcastic. But I also knew it was pointless holding a grudge. If we'd learned anything recently, it was that life really is too short.

Would it be possible to think of anything more with Drew?

It didn't matter any more that we weren't together or that he'd been with Rae. He had tried to reconcile with me, ice cream truck and all. But he had gone on to make Rae feel secure and happy. That's what mattered now. In fact, I was glad she'd had him. Felt comfortable. Had the best of nights with the best of friends. I wanted her to be happy. That's all you ever wanted for someone you loved, wasn't it? I didn't know if it was the possible cancer speaking or the grief over Rae, but I felt that I was finally at peace with it all.

Did that mean *I* was willing to try again with him? I had loved him once. Drew could be my second-chance romance. Like Riley and Jackie. It was possible to forgive and forget, they'd proved that.

'I can't think about it just yet,' I said, eventually.

He nodded, placing his hand on my arm. I put my hand over his.

'So, are you going to read the letter?' Drew asked after a few moments of silence.

I stared at the outside of the envelope he stretched out in front of me, studying her handwriting. I smoothed my hand over it, feeling connected to her again. and soaked up all my memories of Rae. Her beautiful, confident smile, the mischievous look in her bright eyes, the sound of her loud laugh. I prised it open and held it in my hand. Drew sat still beside me, as if he was holding his breath.

Dear Becca,

If you're reading this, it means we've had yet another EPIC night out and I've loved every minute of it. We've probably danced until our feet are sore and laughed 'til we snorted. Our nights out are always the best when it's just the two of us.

That's why I don't want this letter to change anything between us. I've been so nervous to tell you this but please read it all the way through to the end.

So, I moved to Edinburgh to be with Mickey, but, as you know, it didn't work out. I felt really low for a while, like I just kept making all the wrong choices . . . But I did like my job here, so I decided to stay in Edinburgh anyway. Give it a go.

I bumped into Drew.

Yes, I know how much he hurt you. But there's something

you need to know — it was Mickey that told me he saw Leila and Drew together that night. He eventually admitted that he lied about it so you guys would break up. He thought Drew was interested in me. He thought every guy was interested in me. I'm so sorry I believed him and told you about it. I know it ruined your relationship.

I wish I'd never met Mickey, but that's another story.

Anyway, I planned to tell you that Mickey had made the whole thing up. But Drew and I started spending time together in Edinburgh.

This is the hardest thing to say to you. Drew and I accidentally fell in love, Becca. I don't know how else to explain it. I tried to ignore it at first. I tried to just be friends because I couldn't bear the thought of hurting you. But the truth is, I love him more than I've ever loved anyone. He makes me happier than I ever thought I could be.

We're living in Edinburgh together and we want to plan a future together. But, before we do, I had to tell you. The last thing I want is for this to get in between us. I'm trying to sort my head out and get my life back and telling you about Drew is the final piece in the puzzle. I've carried around so much guilt and anxiety already. I hope that by telling you all this, I can let at least some of it go for good.

I know it might take a bit of time to think through. Take all the time you need, and I'll be right here when you're ready.

I love you forever and a day.

Rae x

PLOT TWIST

Tears spilled onto the page. Drew sat beside me and wrapped his arms around me. And for that moment, we were united again in grief for our Rae, the love of our lives.

44

Drew sprawled out under a blanket on the couch, playing on his phone while I watched the clock ticking on the wall.

We'd stayed up talking into the early hours about Rae. Reminiscing. My heart felt a little lighter. Drew had been right when he said we were the only ones who really understood. We laughed, we cried, and we took long, comfortable silences while we gathered our thoughts. I texted Adam along the way with the memories I'd promised him.

Drew filled me in on stories of the two of them as a couple that I'd missed, too.

The New Year's Eve party and 'best time with the best friends' had gone on until six a.m. In the early hours, Rae insisted that everyone team up with a partner to sing duets. There was Sonny & Cher, 'Summer Nights' from *Grease* and 'Shallow' by Lady Gaga and Bradley Cooper. Rae insisted on singing the Rihanna and Eminem duet, convinced she was a rapper, so she took on the part of Eminem, while Drew warbled the high notes. He said they'd rapped the whole way home and slept until 2nd January.

He showed me a picture of the ring he'd picked out for her, too. A beautiful three-stone diamond ring, symbolising past, present and future.

He couldn't bring himself to tell me how he'd planned to propose to her. He choked up and lost the words. I didn't push it.

'Morning,' I called.

'Hey,' he replied.

The realisation hit me: I was going home today. I had to say goodbye to everyone and pretend I didn't have abnormal cells growing inside me. I gulped and pushed the thought to the back of my mind.

'I'm sorry, Becca,' he said.

'About what?' I quipped. 'Turning up unannounced, dragging me away from the party or trying to snog me?'

'All of it. I didn't plan to try and kiss you; that was a heat-of-the-moment thing. But I stand by what I asked. We could give it another try. It might not be perfect, but whose story is perfect, you know?'

'You're just lonely, Drew,' I replied, looking down at my hands.

'So are you.' He shrugged.

It was true. Having Drew sleeping in the same room as me was comforting, I couldn't deny that. Rae's letter also confirmed Drew hadn't cheated on me, and that mattered more than I'd ever thought it would. But did that mean I should take a chance and go back too? I wasn't sure.

'I am,' I admitted. 'Not sure that's a valid reason to start a relationship, though. But I guess I should apologise, too.'

'You should or you will?' He grinned.

I threw a pillow at him and he batted it onto the floor, laughing.

'I'm sorry for always thinking the worst of you,' I said, throwing him a grin. 'I think that sums it up. And I'm glad you came here, in a weird way, even though I was mad with you. It was so good to talk about Rae and read that letter, even though it broke my heart all over again.'

'I'm sorry for turning up out of the blue, too. But I wouldn't have changed talking to you about Rae last night for the world.'

I felt lighter, too. Like part of the weight had been lifted from my mind. Hating Drew had been so exhausting.

We sat in silence for a moment.

'What time's your boat back today?' he asked.

'This afternoon. Three p.m.'

'I'll call and see if I can book on, too.'

'OK.'

Drew left before me so I could say goodbye to everyone on my own. Bridget, Ellie and Ivy came to the cottages. Ivy had drawn me a picture of me pushing her on the swings. I held it close to my heart.

'Riley's not coming?' I asked, looking around.

I knew deep down that he wasn't. The look in his eyes when he'd seen Drew in the doorway of the cottages last night told me all I needed to know. But there was no point fighting it; Riley and I, whatever we were and whatever we could have been, were over. Everything had changed.

'Sorry, Becca. He said he'll be in touch. I don't think he could face saying goodbye,' Bridget said.

My heart sank. I couldn't believe he wasn't coming, after everything. He was the reason I was here in the first place. But I could also understand. I'd have found it difficult saying goodbye too. Almost impossible.

'Oh well,' I said, forcing a cheery smile for Ivy's sake. 'I'm sure I'll see you guys again soon.'

Ivy gave me her very best puppy dog eyes. 'Are you coming back?'

Bridget and Ellie looked to the ground.

I knelt down to speak to Ivy.

'We'll see,' I said, looking her straight in the eye.

I wasn't willing to make a promise in case I couldn't keep it. Not this time.

'You definitely have to come back and meet Damien and Lucy,' Ivy said. 'Daddy was so excited about getting a niece and nephew he barely slept a wink last night. He was tossing and turning all night.'

'Was he?' I asked, my heart hurting. 'I hope he starts to sleep a bit better soon.'

I leaned in for a big bear cuddle from Ivy. She smelled of chocolate and I breathed her in. Sweet, innocent and funny little Ivy would be better off with her family pieced back together. I knew that now. And even though saying goodbye to her hurt more than I ever thought it could, it was for the best.

Bridget's eyes filled with tears when I looked up. I gathered Ellie into a hug first.

'Good luck with everything over the next few days. Keep in touch and tell me everything. I want pictures and stories and videos every day,' I said, wagging my finger at Ellie.

'We will,' Ellie promised.

Bridget nodded and tears spilled onto her cheeks. Ellie took Ivy by the hand and led her back to the car.

'Are you sure you have to go?' Bridget whispered in my ear as we cuddled. 'Ivy will miss you so much. We all will.'

'I'm sure,' I replied, firmly.

I tried not to look back when I drove away.

I kept the music blasting the whole way along the motorway, reminding myself of everything I had to sort out when I got home.

The list consisted of:

Washing
Career
Head
Possible abnormal cells.

Drew was at the ferry port. He stood against the car looking into the distance as I approached and waved when he caught sight of me. I checked my reflection in the mirror; why did I still care whether my hair looked OK around him?

He wasn't Mr Whippy any more. He wasn't Mr Suave Boss Man either. He was broken. Missing Rae just as much as I was.

I got out of the car and walked to join him.

'It feels like a million years ago since I arrived here,' I said. 'I can't believe I'm going home.'

I stared at the seagulls dancing above the Irish Sea in the distance.

'Are you going to tell me the story of the guy then? The one you left behind?'

'Riley,' I said.

'Isn't that a girl's name?' he asked.

I smiled, wistfully.

'Nope, it's a man's name, too. And clearly is, in his case.'

'Right. Well, are you guys together or what?'

'What,' I replied. 'His ex turned up out of the blue. A bit like someone else I know.'

'Bloody exes always getting in the way.'

'You're telling me.'

'Why are you going home then? Is it because of his ex? You don't want to stay and fight her for him?'

I shook my head as an announcement told us it was time to board the boat.

I wondered what kind of romance trope my relationship with Riley had been. My kind, I guessed, without the happily ever after.

45

'Follow me,' Drew said.

The summer sun was setting in the sky ahead of us as Drew heaved open the heavy iron gate. As we stepped into the grounds, I swallowed my fear and wrapped my coat closer around my body.

I could do this.

Rows and rows of headstones stretched ahead of us. Their names passed in a blink of an eye as I followed Drew along the path. So many people. Gone.

I wondered how many of them had abnormal cells. Or growths. We were surrounded by statistics. Cancer. Heart disease. Liver failure.

Car crash victims. I shivered.

I caught sight of a small collection of teddy bears and flowers beside a small heart-shaped headstone for 'mummy and daddy's little angel'. Gulping, I put my head down.

Drew stopped at the side of a grave and knelt down. He gestured for me to do the same.

'Here,' he said.

I stood behind him.

Rae. It said so on the headstone, alongside the names of her gran and grandpa. She'd been so fond of them, so I knew she'd at least be content with where she was laid to rest. But still. This was so wrong. So not where she was meant to be.

'I can't believe she's . . . here,' I said, my eyes filling with tears.

Drew nodded wordlessly in agreement and closed his eyes. Was he going to pray?

'Can I ask something?' I blurted out.

'Sure.'

'Were you going to get married in a church? Or the Bahamas?'

He opened his eyes and smiled.

'Church, huge reception at my hotel then an epic honeymoon.'

'And she definitely still wanted me to be a bridesmaid?' I whispered.

He stood up and put his arm around me, pulling me closer into him. Drew smelled like he always had. Strong and secure. But I knew he was broken inside, just like me.

'She practically wanted you on the honeymoon, Becca,' Drew laughed. 'She wouldn't have married me unless you'd given us your blessing. You meant the world to her.'

'The feeling was entirely mutual,' I mumbled.

'I guess that's why I wanted to bring you here. So she can see that we made up. Does that sound stupid?'

'No,' I whispered, putting my head on his shoulder as we stood, staring at her grave. 'It sounds just right.'

The lump in my throat was growing larger by the second. I swallowed it down, determined to get through this. For Drew, for me, but mostly for Rae.

'I would have come around, you know,' I said. 'Of course I would have. After I'd read the letter and huffed a bit, I'd have agreed to support her. And you. And be your bridesmaid. I could never stay mad at her for long.'

He rubbed my shoulder. 'That would have meant so much to her.'

'I wish I'd been able to tell her. And stand beside you both on your wedding day. I wish she'd had all that. Death is so hard. So fucking final.'

'It is,' he agreed.

'I have an appointment on Wednesday,' I blurted out. 'They're checking for cervical cancer after abnormal cells were found during my smear test.'

He paused.

'God, Becca,' he said, eventually. 'That's . . .'

'I don't want you to say anything about it. I don't want sympathy or anything. I just wanted to say it out loud just now because I'm shitting myself about it.'

He turned me around and, instead of saying anything, pulled me into a huge hug. His familiar scent brought me back to my early twenties, with all the possibilities that lay before me.

'You'll be fine, Becca,' he said. 'Of course you will. I'll come with you to the appointment. Whatever you need.'

'No, Dad's coming,' I lied. 'And to be frank, he thinks you're an arsehole. But thanks for offering.'

Dad wasn't coming. He couldn't face hospitals since Mum died, but it was easier to lie. I didn't want Drew with me. I could face it on my own.

Drew pulled away from the hug and arched an eyebrow.

'Would you mind clarifying with your dad that I'm not actually an arsehole?'

'He thinks you cheated on me and then stole my best friend.' I shrugged. 'Not sure I can change his mind. But I'll see what I can do.'

Outside the cemetery gates, two girls wandered along with their arms linked. Heads bent, they were in deep discussion about something, and at exactly the same time they threw their heads back and cackled. Across the road, a couple strolled along holding hands.

Turning back to face Rae's grave, I asked Drew to give us a minute. He obliged and walked away, waiting for me by the gates.

I knelt down.

'Hey, you,' I said. 'Thanks for your letter. It was a total shock, by the way. You and Mr Whippy, who would have thought it, eh? But I'm not angry with you, Rae. It wouldn't have been my place to be angry with you. I didn't know that at first but I do now. I'm sorry that you thought I would be. But you know you and me falling out never lasted. Even when you made me talk to random guys in bars or made me do karaoke when I didn't want to. We'd always end up laughing about it, wouldn't we? We always came out the other side.

'And once we did, I would have organised the most epic hen do for you, Rae. We'd have made Linda do shots. Hired those butlers in the buff. We'd have danced into the early hours. We would have had the absolute best time of our lives, seen you out of your single life in style.

'And then you'd have married Drew. He's besotted with you, Rae. I mean, he's a total mess right now but I know why. I understand. We're friends again, though. I know you'd have liked to hear that. I'm actually glad you got together with him.

'I'm still a mess about it all. I've quit my job. My boss pushed me too far, Rae, and I just told her to shove it. And I went to meet Riley, you know, the book lady? Well, turns out she's not actually a lady. Oh gawd, you'd have laughed so much when I told you. I packed up all my stuff to stay with her and it turns out she's actually a GUY. And a gorgeous one at that. I kind of fell for him, too. But, oh, it's so complicated. He has a past, I'm a mess. Did I mention I'm a mess?'

I closed my eyes, tears falling onto my cheeks, and whispered.

'On the day . . . you know, you died, I went for a smear test. You know how much we always hated them, right? That was a real shock of adult life when we had to go for our first one.

'Anyway, turns out I have abnormal cells. It could be nothing but you know, a part of me keeps thinking about you . . . You never expected to die, did you? Yet here we are . . .'

A huge sob escaped my mouth and I buried my head into my knees. The cold air whipped around my head and I shivered, pulling my knees in tighter towards me. Next thing I knew, Drew was at my side again.

'I think we should get you home,' he said.

'Yes.' I nodded, in agreement.

'Bye, Rae,' I said, tears streaming down my face. 'I love you.'
Drew hung his head.

We walked along the path, our feet crunching in sync on the stones beneath our feet. Stars were starting to pop up in the sky. I wiped away my tears and gulped in a deep breath of evening air.

'Do you talk to her when you go?' I asked.

'Nope,' Drew said. 'I talk to her in my head.'

'You should try talking out loud.'

'Maybe.'

We reached the end of the path and our two cars parked directly under the same streetlight.

'Do you want me to come back to your flat?'

'Not a chance,' I replied. 'I'm fine on my own.'

He exhaled.

'It's a no, isn't it?' he asked, staring at me with his sad brown eyes.

I took his hand. 'I'm sorry, Drew. We can be friends, but it can't be more than that. Not after everything that's happened. I don't think it's what you really want either, not really. I don't want either of us to do something I know we'd regret.'

He sighed and nodded. 'I get it. In a weird way, I think I even agree. I'm glad we're friends again, Becca. I need you. You're the only one who really gets it.'

In a weird way, I needed Drew, too. But not in that way. Not any more.

'Me too.'

'Let me know how Wednesday goes,' Drew said. 'I can come with you, you know, if you change your mind. Whatever you need.'

'Thanks,' I replied. 'I'll be fine though.'

'I'll see you at the memorial.'

He kissed me swiftly on my forehead and walked away without looking back.

We got into our cars and I watched as he pulled away. I switched on the engine. The car radio blasted a Beyoncé song. I closed my eyes and pictured Rae and me dancing together, full swing, in the middle of the dance floor. I hummed the song and drank in the memory the whole way home.

My flat was exactly as I'd left it, but somehow the space felt much emptier.

I exhaled as I picked up the takeaway menus that had been posted through the door and scattered all over the hallway before hanging up my coat. It perched alone beside two empty pegs. I thought of Ivy's tiny nursery bag, jacket and welly boots cluttering up the entrance way at Bellinder Cottage, alongside Riley's coats and shoes.

I shook my head. I was back to real life now. Home.

The cushions slumped in defeat on my sofa, which sagged in the one place I always sat on. I looked out of my large tenement windows into the dark night and watched the streetlight outside my flat flicker, as it always did. I flicked the lamp switch in the corner and the whole room filled with a soft amber glow as I closed the curtains.

The pictures on my wall made me smile. Rae was still up there, grinning down on me. I hummed the Beyoncé song I'd heard in the car.

I squeezed my eyes closed and stood for a minute, breathing in and out.

I ignored the giant pile of washing in my suitcase and instead, pulled out my laptop.

I had to finish *Queen Bee*. Anna and Rosie were on the road to fixing their friendship and I was finally willing to let them.

46

The bus driver barely glanced at me as I beeped my card under the reader and squeezed past a buggy, sliding into an empty seat up the back. I put my earphones in and watched all the familiar sights of Glasgow flash past in a blur of memories.

Rae and I walking to high school together so we could save our bus fares for cigarettes. Rae puking at the side of the road into a bush after drinking too many cocktails (which was a general theme of our almost adulthood, not a one-off event). Drew and I going out for leisurely walks, with him bending my ear about possible career paths while I thought of the lesson plans I should be working on at home.

I glimpsed, in the distance, the derelict school building that once hosted my swimming lessons. I remembered struggling for breath as I dove deeper under the water to retrieve a small brick placed at the bottom of the pool. I couldn't progress to the next level in my lessons until I retrieved the brick, but I couldn't hold my breath for long enough without feeling I was about to pass out either. So I never progressed. Dad just said I could swim well enough without it.

As the bus pulled up to the hospital, I pushed on the button to indicate I was getting off. I'd get a taxi back, once it was all over.

Sliding my earphones back in, I checked my watch. I picked up my pace and watched my trainers pound on the pavement, taking me one step closer all the time towards my destination. Glancing up at the huge hospital towering above me, I wondered how many people were staying in there, feeling much worse than me. People with actual real-life cancer, patients in comas, women having babies and adoring them, women having babies and abandoning them. There was always such a mix of stories at hospitals, hidden behind the dull grey buildings and sickly-sweet scent that carried the whole way through the wards.

I flicked to the next song on my phone and navigated my way to the entrance, clutching my letter in my hand in case anyone asked for proof that I was, indeed, the one with the abnormal cells.

My breath caught in the wind as I glanced up, thinking I saw him. I shook my head. It couldn't be. I looked closer. He stood tall with one foot resting on the wall and his arms folded in front of him, looking from left to right as if he was crossing a busy road.

His gaze finally stopped as his eyes fell on me. I hadn't imagined it; he was here.

'What are you doing here?' I frowned. 'How did you—'

Riley's mouth formed a small, gentle smile as he took his foot off the wall and walked towards me. He had taken a smart but casual approach, sporting a light blue jumper and jeans. I looked down at my leggings and long T-shirt and grimaced. I hadn't exactly expected to see anyone I knew today, never mind Riley. I smoothed my hair back and stopped dead, to allow him to come to me. I tried to figure out how I felt about his sudden appearance at a hospital in Glasgow to accompany me to an appointment I didn't want him to know about. I suppressed the giddy feeling that paraded around inside me and reminded myself why I was here. The parading could be around some abnormal cells; this wasn't a celebratory reunion, after all.

'Your dad posted the letter to Bellinder Cottage,' Riley explained. 'You told me that he doesn't do hospitals and I knew you'd really wish Rae was here to come with you. I had to take a chance, in case you were going to be on your own.'

It was like he had read my mind.

'You're giving me a pity smile.' I looked up into his green eyes and arched my eyebrow.

'I am not,' he replied, indignantly. 'I'm actually just relieved I saw you. I had visions of standing around for hours looking from side to side like a confused puppy. At least you're here.'

'I can't actually believe *you're* standing here.' I blinked up at him. 'Where's Ivy?'

'I've agreed to leave her with Jackie. Just for one day and night,' Riley said. 'It's all part of rebuilding trust.'

Oh. He was 'rebuilding' with Jackie – what did that mean? Was he only here to give me moral support? I supposed that was lovely too. Amazing, actually. He'd come all the way here, after all, and he wasn't even looking for anything in return. A grand gesture, for a friend. Perhaps that was the way it should be.

I smiled up at him. 'Thanks for coming.'

'I did think I might have to dive into a bush if you'd turned up with that suave fella, Drew.'

'He wasn't invited,' I said. 'Anyway, what are you waiting for, Riley O'Connell? Let's get this show on the road. Some of us have abnormal cells to investigate.'

As we turned to walk through the main entrance, Riley's hand felt for mine and squeezed it tightly in his. He pulled my arm under his and we walked, arm in arm, through the main door. I squeezed his hand back without looking at him.

'You glad I'm here?' he asked.

'Stop fishing for compliments,' I replied, with a wry smile. 'Although yes, I'm glad.'

'Good.' He smiled.

It was over. The relief washed over me as I lay on my couch. Riley presented me with a gift-wrapped box.

I unravelled the ribbon tied around it and opened the box, peering inside.

Facemask, a candle, bath salts, an eye mask, a brand-new black notebook with the words 'Let's Do This Shit' emblazoned on the cover, Jaffa Cakes, a game of Scrabble, and *My Best Friend's Wedding* on DVD.

I looked up at him, my eyes shining. 'You didn't need to

bring me anything. Coming here and being with me was more than enough.'

Riley grinned in reply and shrugged. 'Do you know how much pressure it is for a romance writer to come up with a gesture? I was in a complete flap about what to do. It's hardly grand but, you know, I just wanted to do a little something to make you feel better.'

'Remember I told you I'd never had anyone do anything like that for me before?' I asked, smelling the salts in the small glass bottles. 'Now I have. This is the best thing. You being here with me. I am aware how cheesy it sounds and I don't even care.'

He reached over and placed his warm hand on top of mine.

'I think I'm starting to rub off a bit on you.' Riley grinned.

I looked down at his hand on top of mine and back up into his eyes. The feelings for Riley that I'd suppressed came tumbling back all at once. He had been there for it all, inviting me into his home when I was at my lowest point, reassuring me everything would be all right when I quit my job, supporting me with my writing dreams and goals, and waiting for me as I tackled one of the hardest moments of my life. Without even asking. I blinked.

'I think you might be,' I replied before following with a whisper. 'Jackie and Ivy are lucky to have you.'

I hated uttering her name, but I couldn't leave it hanging there between us. The reason why Riley and I couldn't be together. He was taken, after all. He wanted the happily ever after with his family, not with me.

He sat up a little straighter. 'Becca, Jackie and I aren't back together. She wanted us to be, but I drew a line under our relationship when she left. I have agreed to let her be part of our life now, as Ivy's mum. Nothing more.'

My heart jumped in my chest and I blinked again, looking up into his green, earnest eyes.

'Does she know all this?' I asked. 'She seemed pretty adamant that you guys were going to work it all out and live happily ever after. She pretty much packed my bags and told me to leave.'

Riley sighed.

'Yeah, I had a feeling she might have done something like that. I'm sorry. She's sorry, too. She asked me to tell you that, by the way. She's still working through a lot of things,' he sighed. 'I came to explain everything the night of the opening party. Then I saw you with that Drew fella and thought there was no point. It looked like you had worked things out with him in the meantime, so . . .'

'Drew wanted to give things another try, too,' I admitted. 'He asked me to think about it. We had a long talk that night, but I knew I wasn't going back there. I couldn't.'

'So,' he said, raising an eyebrow. 'We're back at square one.'

'Not quite square one,' I replied. 'Pretty sure we raced past first, second and third base at the cottage. All of the bases, in fact.'

'True.' He smirked, taking hold of my hand. 'It was just a shame it was cut short.'

I nodded and gently nudged Riley's hand. He looked up into my eyes and I leaned towards him, my hand caressing his knee, and our lips met in a slow kiss. The passion that we'd had at the cottage was still there, but this time it felt like there was more. It wasn't just lust, this kiss was offering the promise of more. A foundation for love and a future together, even. It lasted for a long time, like we were teenagers again and all we had was time to kiss and stare into each other's eyes.

I pulled back at one point and looked at my hands.

'We can't . . . you know,' I said. 'After the procedure.'

'Oh, no, I wasn't expecting that, Becca,' he said. 'I just . . . it felt good to kiss. Just kiss.'

'Well, don't get any big ideas, Mr Romance Writer,' I replied, snuggling into his blue jumper. He kissed me gently on the side of my head.

'When do you get the results back?' he asked, his voice sounding tense as though he was holding his breath.

'A couple of weeks,' I replied with a yawn, trying to shrug it off. I didn't want to think about this, not now. Riley and I were in a bubble of bliss. The last thing I wanted was to think about the colposcopy. It was over and done with.

'Why don't you try and go to sleep?' he whispered.

With Riley at the end of my sofa, a pile of thoughtful gifts, and zero expectations or anywhere to be, I closed my eyes and murmured that I would try.

There was a dull pain in my abdomen as I tentatively opened one eye and glanced around. Shadows bounced around the living room as a car splashed past in the puddles outside. I realised the dark blue curtains in my bay window remained fixed firmly against the wall. I felt around, expecting Riley to be curled up at the bottom of the sofa, but he wasn't. I stood up and wandered around my flat, but couldn't find him in any of the rooms. I lifted my phone to check the time and there it was, a message from him.

R: *I don't think I can do this. I want to be with you but you were right, it's all too hard. I need to get back to Ivy. I'm sorry, Becca.*

I threw my phone down on the couch in disbelief, staring as it lay there in front of me on the couch. Tears stung in my eyes as the realisation began to sink in.

Riley was gone.

47

'Ding-dong, the witch is dead!'

Joanna's voice was triumphant as she sang down the phone. I'd finally got round to calling her back, after many, many missed calls and messages.

I had dozed in and out of life in the days following the colposcopy. I tried not to think about Riley, but it wasn't easy. The whole day felt like a fuzzy dream that I kept playing over and over again in my mind, from his sudden appearance at the hospital, to the kiss and then his sudden, heart-wrenching exit, with nothing more than a text to explain. I hadn't written back to him.

I felt lost. No messages, no memes, no encouraging comments on my manuscript. Nothing. I shouldn't have let myself grow so close to someone again so quickly. I'd jumped too quickly into our writers' retreat, friendship and possible romance because I was still reeling from Rae's death. I ached for closeness with someone and Riley had been there though it all. But then he'd left.

I almost wished he hadn't come at all.

'What happened?'

'She's not coming back under "mutual agreement" with the council, apparently. Allegations of bullying from our school and from her previous one. Once the floodgates opened, everyone just started pouring in. Did you submit a complaint?'

'Nope,' I replied, stretching my arms above my head, keeping my phone glued to my ear with my shoulder. 'I didn't think they'd take it seriously.'

'You can come back now, Becca! She never put anything through HR when you quit, or she fired you, or whatever. I checked with the office manager. They're expecting you, as normal.'

'Susie in the office told you?' I laughed lightly. 'Surely that breaches all sorts of GDPR laws.'

'Oh yeah, maybe,' she replied. 'Don't say anything.'

'Course I won't.'

I didn't care. It meant I had a job to go back to. If I wanted to. Maybe I could go back to teaching with the Demon Head-mistress no longer around. I hadn't even thought it would be a possibility.

We hung up and I stared again at my screen. I'd been hovering around the 'send' button for what seemed like hours.

After I'd slept, I'd written. And written. And written some more. The words just kept pouring out and I couldn't stop. I had time, of course. I had nothing but time.

And now *Queen Bee* was finally finished. I pressed 'send' and held my breath. Within seconds, my phone buzzed with a call.

'Argh, you finished it!' the voice said as soon as I answered.
'I did.' I smiled at the excited voice.

I'd thought long and hard about who could provide feedback for *Queen Bee*, now that my relationship with Riley was up in the air. Or whatever it was. I'd considered Drew, but it wasn't really his thing. I'd even looked up Zander, thinking he might be able to spare some time, but decided against it. It wasn't exactly the same genre as he wrote, plus he was probably too busy plotting his own fictional murders to review my work.

That's when I thought of Eimear. She was like a living, breathing cheerleader for Riley's career and said she would be happy to critique for him. I wasn't sure if the offer extended to me, but I'd dropped her a message via her yoga page to ask. She'd called me straight away and said she'd LOVE to read it. When I sent her the first few chapters, she devoured it and said it took her straight back to her own childhood. I danced a little when she said that. She texted me every day, asking how it was going, and even helped me with a couple of plot issues that had cropped up. I'd also offered to help her with her yoga book, if she was still interested in writing one, in return, but she didn't take me up on the offer.

'I can't wait to finish it, Becca. I'll read it as soon as I get home. This is so exciting!'

You couldn't fault her enthusiasm. In amongst all our conversations, she mentioned seeing Riley, but I never asked anything or took the bait. It was hard thinking of him getting on with his life, but I had to move on. My heart hurt when I thought of him.

PLOT TWIST

'Thanks, Eimear. I think your suggestion about the final scene in the show worked out well. I love the fact that Rosie takes over from Anna and then they both say the last line together,' I said.

'Eeek, I can't believe you took one of my ideas on board. OK, I'll message you later. Well done, Becca, this is going to be amazing. I'm sure it'll be on the shelves in no time. Byeeee!'

I couldn't help but smile as I hung up.

A new blossoming friendship was one of the unexpected outcomes of my trip to Rathcliffe, but I was very grateful for it.

48

Adam took a seat on my sofa. I offered him tea, but he shook his head and clasped his hands in front of him in prime prayer position. Linda would be proud.

He cleared his throat and opened his mouth to speak, just as I felt my mobile vibrating in my pocket.

'One second, sorry, Adam.' I hit the answer button.

It was an unknown number. My heart started beating faster.

'Hello, Becca speaking,' I said, my voice cracking.

'Becca, it's Doctor Peters. We met at your colposcopy appointment. How are you doing?'

Christ, I wasn't ready for this. Not today. It was Rae's birthday. Her memorial. I couldn't deal with any more than that. I wasn't ready. The blood rushed to my head and I looked across at Adam, who was completely oblivious, gazing around my living room. I contemplated yelling down the phone that she had the wrong number, but I'd given it away at the start of the phone call. She'd reached Becca, with the possible abnormal cells. She'd caught me.

'Hello, Doctor Peters. I'm fine thanks, how are you?'

The pleasantries were completely ridiculous. We had to cut to the chase here, get it over with. Rip it off like a plaster. I closed my eyes. Breathe, Becca. While you still can.

'Fine, thank you. I just got the results of your colposcopy through, Becca, and wanted to call you straight away. I know how worrying it all is.'

Spit it out, Doctor Peters.

'And?' My voice sounded small. Pathetic, almost.

'It's good news, Becca. Your biopsy didn't detect any abnormal cells. It's known as a "normal" result,' she said.

Normal. No abnormal cells. No cancer. No death. I squeezed my eyes closed even more tightly as relief flooded my body. I steadied my shaking hand that was holding the phone.

'Oh, thank you,' I whispered. It was all I could manage.

I opened my eyes. Adam stared at me, a curious expression etched on his face.

'You'll get a letter to confirm it, but I wanted to let you know as soon as possible. You said you'd been through a difficult time lately.'

I exhaled.

'Are you sure? It's all fine? What about follow-up, do I need to do anything?' I asked, applauding myself for the sensible questions.

'No follow-up, you should just attend your smear as normal when you're next invited to.'

Normal. Everything was normal. I exhaled and thanked her

again, the words tumbling out of my mouth. I could feel her smiling on the other end of the phone as she said goodbye.

I wondered how many other phone calls she had to make that day; how many people got the good news. How many others wouldn't be so lucky.

But I was fine. All the worry was over. As I hung up the phone, I let out a small squeal and threw myself at Adam, enveloping him in a bear hug. He gasped in surprise and patted my back awkwardly.

'Good news, I take it?' He lifted an eyebrow.

'Great news,' I replied, moving back to my position on the couch, and grinned at him. 'My colposcopy results were clear. Fine. Normal. She said I'm normal.'

'I'm not sure I would go that far.' Adam grinned, and I punched him lightly on the arm. 'But I'm glad to hear it, Becca. I'm really happy to hear it.'

I sat back against the couch, closed my eyes and exhaled.

I thought of Rae. I always thought of Rae. I couldn't help but feel like this was her present to me on her birthday. And it was the best present she could have given me.

I had to tell Dad, of course. He kept calling to check in on me. I'd assured him I'd let him know as soon as I did, but he still asked me every day.

'Anyway, Adam,' I said, still smiling. 'What was so important it couldn't wait a few hours 'til the memorial?'

Adam shifted in his seat and looked down at the floor before pulling his eyes up to meet my gaze.

'I'm so glad that we've been able to stay in touch. It's really helped having someone to talk to,' Adam started. 'After Rae died, I felt so guilty.'

'*You* felt guilty? Why would you feel guilty, when it was my fault?'

He turned to look at me, frowning. 'Your fault? What do you mean?'

I let out a long sigh. 'Rae wasn't meant to come through that weekend. I was the one that persuaded her to come through earlier. I hadn't seen her in ages, and I really wanted to spend some time with her.'

My voice wobbled as my eyes filled with tears. It was a relief to confess it, finally, out loud to someone, the guilt that haunted me through the day and into the depths of night.

'Becca,' he said quietly, rubbing my shoulder. 'It wasn't your fault. My mum asked her to come through that weekend too. Rae drove up early so they could go and see my cousin's new house.'

I looked at Adam, to check he was definitely telling the truth and wasn't throwing me some sort of pity story, but his eyes shone back earnestly. I gulped.

'It wasn't my fault,' I repeated.

'It wasn't anyone's,' he said. 'Just an awful, horrible accident.'

I felt my whole body relax, as I sat back on the couch.

'It's such a relief to hear that,' I confessed. 'I know it doesn't change anything. It's not like it brings her back but I blamed myself. I'd been complaining that we never saw each other any more. I just wanted her here.'

'Everyone wanted her home, Becca. I'm sorry you've been carrying that burden around with you. I wish you'd said earlier.'

I wished I had, too.

'I know what it's like,' he continued. 'To carry that kind of guilt with you. I feel like I've been weighed down with it since Rae died, too. It's what I wanted to talk to you about.'

I frowned. 'You have? Why do you feel guilty?'

He shifted uncomfortably on the couch.

'There was something that Rae didn't know about me,' Adam explained. 'And I guess I wish she did. She died without really knowing me.'

He looked down at his shoes.

I moved closer towards him and gripped his shaking hand.

'You can tell me, Adam,' I promised.

'I wish I'd told her,' he whispered, his eyes squeezed closed. 'That . . . I'm gay.'

As I wrapped my arms around him, I felt his heart beating in his chest. I held him close against me, wondering whether it was right for me to tell him the truth.

'She knew, Adam,' I whispered, eventually.

He pulled away from me, eyes wide with shock.

'What do you mean?' he frowned. 'She couldn't have known. She would've said something. Wound me up about it, probably.'

I shook my head.

'We saw you with someone while we were in a bar in Glasgow one night. About five years ago. She thought about coming over to talk to you, but we left instead. She wanted to wait for you to be ready.'

He sat back against the sofa and exhaled.

'I can't believe it . . . I can't believe she knew.'

'She would never have wound you up about it, Adam. She just didn't want to put pressure on you when you weren't ready to come out.'

'My mum doesn't know though, does she?' he asked, his face etched with anxiety.

I shook my head. 'Rae never said a word.'

'Linda's as holy as they come, Becca. But I'd like to tell her, and dad too. Especially now. But it's scary, you know?'

I nodded. 'It is. I know I'm not Rae, but I'm here for you. We can talk any time. And if you do decide to tell Linda and Jim, I can be right there with you, if you want. Whatever you need.'

'Thank you,' he smiled, his face flushed. 'I think I'll talk to them on my own, though. I've got someone I'd like to introduce to them. I'd like you to meet him, too. I think it's time. Life is too short, you know?'

'I'd love to meet him,' I smiled.

'I'm glad Rae knew,' he said. 'I wish I'd been the one to tell her, but I'm happy she knew who I really was. That helps.'

As I squeezed Adam the Absolute Worst into a tighter cuddle, relief flooded through me. In the space of one short conversation, the guilt that had plagued me had been lifted, plus I'd managed to ease Adam's guilt too.

'Right,' he said, standing up. 'Enough of this drama. Let's get to the memorial. Linda will go mad if we're late.'

I checked my phone. 'Drew's on his way to pick us up. He says he'll be outside in five minutes.'

Drew was in the driver's seat, sporting his kilt. Adam and I climbed into the back seat of his car.

'Thanks for the lift,' I said.

'Aw, look at you two being all civil to each other.' Adam smiled. 'Rae would be so pleased.'

Drew offered me a small smile in the rear-view mirror.

'She would.'

'Fuck's sake, bagpipes?' I murmured.

The tune was so hauntingly beautiful that tears sprang in my eyes almost immediately.

'Linda loves a good bagpipe,' Adam replied. 'And Rae would love it. The drama of it all.'

The wail of the music floated across the Ayrshire countryside as we drove into the small estate where Rae's extended family owned a holiday home.

Breathe, Becca.

I sniffed and moved my sunglasses over my face. I closed my eyes and thought of the doctor's phone call earlier. Rae's birthday gift. I never used to believe all that stuff about people watching over you when they died, even though I'd have liked to think of Mum having a good old nosey down at what I was up to. With Rae, somehow, it felt different. I could still feel her energy, as though it was part of me. It was hard to explain.

I held Adam's hand for a moment in the back seat. I knew Rae would be pleased that we'd become firm friends, even if she'd never have admitted it.

'We can do this,' he whispered, squeezing it tightly.

'We sure can, Big Bird,' I replied as we took a moment, before climbing out of the car.

My whole world collapsed at the start of the summer. I couldn't believe how alone I'd felt. I'd lost my best friend and felt like there was no one else in the whole world who would ever be able to fill that gap. And no one ever would. Nothing was the same without Rae. But friendship had blossomed in a series of unexpected places, from Adam and Drew to Bridget and Ellie, Eimear, and, of course, Riley.

Riley was always there, somewhere, in the back of my mind.

We were ready to face the music. The bagpipes. The drama. Adam was right, Rae would have loved this. I walked in the middle of the two of them, Drew and Adam, as we approached Linda and Jim. Some of the family had already arrived and were sitting outside, enjoying the August sunshine.

All her family and friends gathered in one place to celebrate her thirty-second birthday. If only she could be here to enjoy it. The fluttering panic in my chest had subsided somewhat over the summer. The gut-wrenching pain was still there, though. I wasn't sure it would ever go. In a way, I could handle that. It showed how much I'd cared for Rae and how loved she really was.

'Becca,' Linda said. 'There's someone here to see you. A gentleman.'

'Oooh,' Adam teased. 'A gentleman.'

And there he was, resting his foot against a tree at the side of the house. Riley. My heart thudded in my chest as I surveyed his familiar side profile.

'He contacted me to ask for the memorial details,' Drew explained in a low voice. 'Hear him out, Becca.'

Adam squeezed my arm, while Drew walked towards Rae's family. As I approached Riley, the sound of the bagpipes came to a halt.

'He's just warming up,' Riley explained, giving me a small smile. 'The bagpiper fella.'

I gazed up at all six foot something of him. Yup, still as handsome as ever. Still Riley.

'I've had more of these grand gestures in one summer than I've had in a lifetime,' I said wryly, as he stepped into a walk beside me. 'Between you and Drew, I don't know whether I'm coming or going.'

'I'm so sorry, Becca,' he said as we walked towards the grass area nearby, out of sight of the rest of the gathering. 'I shouldn't have left your flat like that. It just all got a bit much. I couldn't stop thinking about Ivy. I wasn't sure if I was ready to let someone into my life again.'

There was a small pause before I responded.

'Someone who might leave,' I said, eventually.

I had to say it out loud. I knew when Riley left he was worried about the possibility of cancer. The cells. The impact that an illness would have on Ivy. I'd worried about that too, of course I had.

We followed a path that led to a small, sandy beach, with rocks to one side stretching out to the sea. I gazed out into the distance, watching two seagulls glide above the water. Riley. I wondered if my expression portrayed the excitement I felt fizzing in my stomach when I looked at him. I'd managed to get pretty good at hiding it over the time we'd spent together but I had to be more guarded now than ever. What I felt towards Riley had taken a complex twist when he'd left.

He nodded and let out a long sigh. 'I can't believe I let you down like that. When I got home, I realised I'd made a huge mistake but I didn't think you'd want to talk to me, not after I just buggered off and left. I'm so sorry.'

In a weird way, I understood. I'd told him my mum had passed away after a cancer battle when I was four. It was perfectly logical to think that the same could happen to me, with Ivy the same age. It was also reasonable to want to steer clear of that possible heartbreak on his daughter's behalf, as well as his own. It stung, but I understood.

'I guess I get it.' I shrugged. 'So, what are you here for now?'

Trying to appear casual, like my whole everything wasn't completely invested in waiting for his answer, I picked up a stone and tried to skim it in the water. Instead it plonked near the water's edge. I looked up at him tentatively and he smiled.

'To make it up to you, if you'll let me. I thought coming to support you at Rae's memorial would be a good first step,' he explained. 'And then, maybe we could see where it goes with us? Give us a try? If you want. No pressure or anything.'

It reminded me of arriving in Bellinder Cottage at the start of the summer and Riley persuading me to stay. No pressure. He edged closer to me, his fingers touching mine as the familiar bolt of energy fizzled through my body.

'Wait,' I said, arching an eyebrow. 'Is this because you can't write without me? Did you discover that I was actually your muse all along?'

He laughed.

'Not quite. Actually, I've been in the zone since you left. I think the whole heartbreak thing helped. But before you say anything, it's not something I want to keep exploring.' He turned to face me. 'I want to be with you, Becca, no matter what your results are. I know that now. I really do.'

I exhaled. It was exactly what I wanted to hear. What I needed to hear.

'I got the all clear. Just before I came here,' I said eventually, smiling up at him.

He turned around and paused for a second, a grin slowly spreading across his face, before he threw his arms around me, lifting me from the ground.

'That's brilliant news, Becca,' he whispered in my ear, holding me tight against him. I breathed in his familiar scent.

'It is,' I replied. 'I think it was Rae's birthday gift to me.'

'I think it was,' he agreed, placing me back on the ground.

I moved back slightly, but Riley pulled me back into a tight hug.

'Not yet,' he murmured.

We stayed still, huddled together on the beach, without saying a word. The wind whipped my hair and I shivered, so Riley pulled me closer into his dark blue jacket. It felt cosy. Like home.

'But what about Ivy?' I asked, eventually. 'She's just getting used to having her mum back, Riley. I shouldn't get in the middle of all that.'

He pulled back and held my arms at either side, gazing intensely into my eyes.

'Ivy was the one who told me to come for you. She told me to stop moping around.' Riley gave a lopsided grin. 'I've been miserable since you left, Becca. I explained to Ivy that Jackie and I aren't getting back together. She's happy to have her mum back in her life, but she misses you, too. We both do.'

'And Jackie?'

'She's sorting herself out,' Riley said, as we started walking along the beach. 'Going to narcotics meetings, so I guess it's one day at a time. She's living in one of the cottages Bridget and Ellie rent out, for now. I guess she'll get her own place at some point . . . She actually asked me to apologise to you. I think she'll be sticking around this time. Will that be a problem, do you think?'

He stopped in front of me and took one of my hands in his. I blinked.

'For me?'

'Yes, for you. I'm in this, Becca,' he said, staring me out with his green eyes. 'For the long haul. I came to the hospital that day and now the memorial because I want to be here for it all with you. I'll keep turning up for the big events and small stuff, too. If you'll have me.'

I was under no illusions that what I was contemplating agreeing to was a lot. If Jackie stuck around, if Riley and I got together, if I moved to Ireland at some stage, I would be right in the middle of it all. The problem was, I couldn't *not*. It seemed that, somewhere along the way, I'd fallen for Riley head over heels. Maybe quite literally the evening I'd decked it outside the pub, or perhaps it was before that. As soon as I laid eyes on him and put his face to the person I'd been conversing with for months, I knew Riley was someone pretty special. Despite all the baggage, obstacles and plot twists we'd faced along the way, I had to give us a try. It was our own chance at a happily ever after.

'I will have you, Riley O'Connell,' I replied, with a nod. 'How could I not?'

He leaned down and pulled me into a long, lingering kiss. I held onto him tightly, losing myself in the moment.

Somewhere in the distance, I heard a loud wolf whistle.

'Oi, put her down!' Adam's voice called from across the grass down towards the beach. I grinned and clutched onto Riley's hand.

'Almost forgot where we were for a second,' I called to Adam.

'Hurry up, Becca, we're about to get started.'

I sighed. My stomach had gone from backflips of happiness to dread, twisting at the thought of saying goodbye to Rae all over again as reality came back to bite.

Breathe, Becca.

'I'm here, Becca. We'll do it together. All of it. I'll be here for everything, if you'll let me.'

'Only if you'll let me, too.' I smiled up at him.

'You'd better believe it.' He grinned.

I nodded and squeezed his hand. I could do this.

We could do this.

EPILOGUE

TWO YEARS LATER

The jewellery store was about to close when I arrived. Despite carrying an umbrella, my hair was soaked from the torrential downpour. The wind had blown me halfway across Dublin as I attempted to make it on time.

Sorry,' I apologised, shaking the stray drops from my coat. 'It's me, the one that asked for the man-gagement ring.'

'Ah, yes.' The assistant offered me a wide smile. 'Thanks for coming in. I'll just nip through the back and get it.'

I didn't even really need it today. The traffic was backed up because of the storm, everyone was beeping their horns and swearing at one another, trains were cancelled and delayed. The streets were full of grumpy people trying to navigate their way home.

It was hardly a 'proposal' sort of day.

But I just had to make the journey through, so I could see it.

When I'd shared my secret plans with Bridget, she insisted that I couldn't possibly propose to Riley.

She balked at the very idea of it, insisting it was Riley's place, as the romance-writing man who would want to plan the most over the top proposal the world had ever seen.

Therein lay the problem.

The more I thought about it, the more I realised that it was what I wanted to do. Riley had never experienced the grand gesture that he always talked about. He had dished them out, talked about them, penned a good few, but never been on the receiving end of one. Coming to Rae's memorial to insist he would continue turning up time and time again for the rest of the big and small events in my life had been a firm favourite of mine. Somehow, along the two years we'd been officially dating, I'd never returned the favour.

And now he was feeling the pressure to propose. I could practically feel the tension, on par with the time he'd been working on his second novel when I'd first arrived at Bellinder Cottage. As it turned out, *Too Far Gone* finally hit the shelves last year and topped the charts as another bestseller. Not that I'd had any doubts. But the pressure to propose was becoming a whole new weight on his shoulders.

Last week, during an interview with an Irish newspaper, he'd been asked when he planned to propose to his 'children's author and teacher girlfriend'. It still made me want to do a little dance when I saw that in print. I was a real-life children's author. *Queen Bee* had even been nominated for an actual children's book award, thank you very much. It didn't win, but I was still riding high on the very idea of it all. Being an award-nominated author also helped when it came to my creative writing school for children, which had become very popular over the last year, with kids from far and wide attending my after-school classes and summer workshops, based at Ellie and Bridget's cottages.

Their business had been slow, at first. We'd all mused over various ideas to help with promotion, before coming up with a concept that might just hit the mark to set it apart from all the other holiday lets on the market.

And so, The Writers' Retreat was born. We'd created a space for my children's classes and group discussions, and it had quickly become a hub of creative activity. Riley launched his second book there, which attracted several authors to do the same. He'd even started his own creative writing classes for aspiring romance writers, which were always fully booked, with waiting lists. Somehow, what seemed like overnight, writers from all over the world were booking up to follow in our footsteps to come along and soak up the inspirational setting of Rathcliffe for their very own writers' retreats.

We managed to keep Bellinder Cottage, thanks to the various new ventures, and our happy bubbles just seemed to keep expanding.

It all made for a very interesting newspaper article and Riley had been delighted to talk about it all, until he was asked whether there were any marriage plans on the horizon. He'd tried to laugh the interviewer's question off and said something about certainly feeling the pressure. Of course, the editor had used it as the headline for the piece, Riley O'Connell: Under

Pressure. Katrine insisted that all publicity was good publicity, but Riley was mortified. And it wasn't that easy to embarrass a romance-writing man.

So, I'd decided to take it out of his hands. I'd even had a ring made. And not just any old ring. It was an exact replica of the wedding ring belonging to Riley's dad, the one that had been stolen from Bellinder Cottage all those years ago.

Yes, I felt a little smug about that.

I'd found a picture of the ring in one of the family photo albums in the eaves of Bellinder Cottage and took it to the jeweller to see what they could do.

The shop assistant presented me with the box and smiled, with a hint of pity, as though I was a tiny bit mad. They had made a big deal about the man-gagement ring when I'd asked them. I wondered what century everyone was living in, when a jewellery store thought proposing to a man was such an obscure concept.

But the ring was just perfect, exactly how I'd envisaged and precisely like the picture.

I ignored the shop assistant's pity smile, thanked her and placed the box firmly in my handbag, setting out to dodge the rain again on my way home.

I knew Riley was going to love it.

Now, I just had to organise the rest.

Bellinder Cottage was in darkness when I got back after my secret trip. My hair hung around my face like a wet dog's, and

I rather suspected I smelled like one too. My umbrella was completely mangled after trying to compete with the force of the wind, while my shoes held puddles of water.

It had been one of those days.

All I wanted was a bath, a takeaway and an early night.

I peeled my shoes off at the front door, as puddles appeared at my feet. Ivy was staying with Bridget, Ellie and the twins tonight. It was Thursday, after all. But Riley was meant to be home. He'd had a meeting earlier with his publishers to discuss the approach to his third novel, but that had been hours ago. I hadn't heard from him since. I unlocked the door and there he stood, in the dark hallway, dressed in what looked like a suit.

'What the fuck are you doing standing in the dark?' I frowned, hanging my coat up. 'And why are you all dressed up? I thought we were ordering pizza tonight? I need a warm bath, that weather is crazy out there.'

Riley said nothing but smiled and took my soggy hand, gesturing for me to follow him. We walked along the hallway towards the low, hazy glow of the living room. I gasped as I opened the door. The whole room was filled with flickering candles. He'd lined a series of black-and-white polaroid pictures of us up around the room, too, on little tiny pegs. There was one of us at *Queen Bee*'s launch. It was my favourite picture of, well, myself. I'd been grinning up at Riley before whispering 'I really did it' when Bridget snapped the shot. There was another of the two of us outside Bellinder Cottage, with Ivy giving the peace sign in the middle. Another black-and-white picture hung near the fireplace of us at The Writers' Retreat, where Riley grinned at the camera while I pulled a funny face. The sight of all the pictures reminded me of Rae's memorial. I'd told Riley it had been my favourite part. Of course, he'd remembered.

He looked up at me, his green eyes sparkling.

'No . . .' I stammered, realising what was about to happen. 'You can't.'

'Becca, I thought of all the magical places I could do this and all the grand gestures I could pull out of the bag, but nothing felt quite right. Except here at Bellinder Cottage. Home,' he said, clasping my hand. 'I fell in love with you before I even met you and—'

'Stop,' I insisted, rolling up my soggy sleeves and scraping my wet hair back from my face.

'Why?' He looked at me, confused. 'I've written something, too . . .'

'So have I,' I retorted. 'But it's not finished.'

'Ah, the old writer's dysfunction.' He winked. 'Happens to the best of us.'

'Noo, Riley.' I pouted. 'This isn't how it's meant to happen.'

'Did you make another timetable for it? Sorry, I must have missed the memo.' He grinned.

I couldn't help but smile, before sighing.

I wasn't letting him do this on his terms. I had the ring in my bag.

I could still do this.

'OK, well, fuck it then.' I shrugged. 'I'll just . . .'

PLOT TWIST

I knelt down in front of him as Riley stood back, his mouth hanging open. His lips broke into his wide, easy grin.

Breathe, Becca. I cleared my throat as I gazed up into his eyes.

'Riley, I don't have the words prepared to say what I want to say. The romantic stuff is definitely more your domain. So instead, I'm going to borrow a quote from my favourite author.'

I paused and he smiled, as I continued. 'To quote Alice in *The Fall Out*: "I waited for you without even knowing what the wait was for. Before you, each morning was bleak and every evening was empty. I know now. I almost lost you once and I won't do it again. You are my soul and I am yours."'

Riley grinned as he bent down on one knee in front of me. He clasped my shaking hands in his. I looked into his eyes and felt tears rising in my own.

'Becca, I've also chosen to read a line from my favourite author. To quote Anna in *Queen Bee*: "No matter what I do, I look round and you're cheering me on with everything you have. I didn't know how much I needed that. A best friend for life." Becca, you are my best friend. I love you with everything I have, and I want you by my side for everything that's to come.'

I gulped as he reached into his pocket and produced a black box. I narrowed my eyes and fished in my handbag too, presenting the ring box. Riley threw his head back and his loud laugh vibrated around the room. I grinned through my tears.

We opened the boxes at the same time. I gazed down at the ring he'd selected for me. A large diamond flanked by a series of smaller stones. It was beautiful. Perfect.

'I love it!' I exclaimed.

Riley audibly gasped as he examined the ring I held in front of him.

'That ring,' he said, taking it carefully out of the navy-blue box. His mouth formed a perfect circle. 'It's exactly like—'

'I know,' I nodded, my smile wide. 'It's exactly like your dad's wedding ring. The one that was stolen from Bellinder Cottage. I contacted antique stores and jewellery stores across the country hoping I could find the actual ring, but no one had it. So I went through old photos and contacted a jeweller in Dublin to make it for you.'

Riley traced his finger along the platinum band. 'I . . . I can't believe you did that.'

I grinned. 'Now, who's the best at grand gestures? In your face, Riley O'Connell.'

'That's going to be a tough one to beat, for sure. But I'll spend my life trying, if you'll let me.'

I offered a wobbly smile as he cleared his throat.

'Becca Taylor, will you marry me?'

I placed the ring on his finger, in return.

'Only if you'll marry me first.'

Acknowledgements

I started writing *Plot Twist* at a time when the world stood still, during the Covid pandemic. Balancing work and home schooling, writing fiction gave me focus and much-needed distraction.

With the novel underway, I participated in a social media 'pitch' event and the premise caught the attention of Julie Fergusson from The North Literary Agency. I'm not sure I'd have completed *Plot Twist* without Julie's unwavering encouragement, support and direction as my literary agent. A huge thank you to Julie and the team at The North.

Priyal Agrawal from Headline Publishing has been an endlessly enthusiastic editor, from first read through to finalising the manuscript. Thank you, Priyal, and everyone at Headline for believing in the book and helping me to shape it for publication.

I am lucky enough to be surrounded by the most supportive family and friends. A big shout out to my friends, many of whom I've known since school, for all the laughs and life lessons we've learned along the way.

Rathcliffe is a fictional town, but its beauty and warmth has been drawn from my experiences visiting family in Ireland, having spent summers there since I was a child. I want to say a very special thank you to my mum, Máire, and dad, Paddy, for everything you do.

Finally, I want to thank my husband and best friend, Chris, and my three children, Orla, Leah and Calum, for being everything I ever wanted and more.

I hope you have enjoyed reading *Plot Twist* as much as I enjoyed writing it.

Breea